ROMANTIC TIMES RAVES ABOUT AMANDA ASHLEY:

EMBRACE THE NIGHT
"Sensuous! Mesmerizing! Electrifying! A must read for all vampire romance fans!"

DEEPER THAN THE NIGHT
"The very versatile Amanda Ashley does a wonderful job . . . a fast-paced and fun-filled read!"

SUNLIGHT, MOONLIGHT
"Two highly entertaining fantasy tales for the price of one!"

SHADES OF GRAY
"Amanda Ashley enriched the vampire genre with this breathtaking and timeless story of star-crossed lovers."

JUST ONE MORE KISS . . .

Falkon drew Ashlynne closer. Just one more kiss, he told himself, and then he would let her go. But one kiss became two, and then three. She was fire and honey in his arms, warm and sweet, so damn sweet. Her skin was soft and smooth beneath his hands. She moaned softly as his thumb inadvertently stroked the curve of her breast. It had been months since he had lain with a woman, tasted one, caressed one. Need and desire swelled within him, urging him to take what she was offering. Except she didn't really know what she was offering. She was pure and untouched, a virgin in every sense of the word, and he had no right to defile her.

The Captive

Amanda Ashley

LOVE SPELL BOOKS ◆ NEW YORK CITY

LOVE SPELL®

February 2000

Published by

Dorchester Publishing Co., Inc.
276 Fifth Avenue
New York, NY 10001

ISBN 0-505-52362-0

To Mitch
for sharing his poetry with me
yet again

To Rick Thomason
for helping me over the rough spots,

and

To Flo Robison
who came up with
most of the other-worldly
names

Thanks muchly, guys and gal
I couldn't have done it without you

If I looked into a star . . .
would I see your soul
so bright upon my heart
so soft upon my lips

it moves across time
filling me. . . .

wrap the stars up tonight
and carry them closely
for my love will soon
inhale the universe . . .
pulling all inside
to give
to
you

—Mitch Dearmond

The CAPTIVE

Chapter One

The first time Lady Ashlynne Myrafloures saw the prisoner who would be known as Number Four, he was nearly naked, lying facedown in an ever-widening pool of his own blood. She could not see his face, covered as it was by a tangled mat of long black hair. His back was a broad expanse of bronzed flesh, most of it laid open by the lash. A dirty bandage, stiff with dried blood, was knotted around his right thigh.

She watched in horrified fascination as three of the mine's biggest guards fought to hold the prisoner down while a fourth guard attempted to collar him.

Stubbornly, and surely knowing he could not win, the prisoner struggled to fight them off, his fingers digging into the hard ground for purchase, his whole body trembling violently with the effort it cost him to resist.

Stay down. The plea was a silent cry in Ashlynne's throat. *Please, just stay down.*

But he didn't stay down. He went still for a brief moment and she could almost see him gathering his strength; then, with a feral scream of pain and rage, the prisoner surged to his feet, every muscle taut and quivering with the effort, his eyes blazing with defiance as he made a last desperate attempt for freedom.

She cringed as Dain plied the whip with stunning, terrifying accuracy.

The sinuous strip of thick black Parthian leather whistled through the air, tearing open the skin on the prisoner's left cheek. It was a cruel weapon, that lash. Her father had often spoken of Dain's skill. Dain wielded it with an expert hand, her father boasted; he was able to flay a man's back to the bone or flick a fly from a karu-atar's ear with equal skill. She had always thought her father was exaggerating, but no more.

As many times as she had heard of Dain's whip, this was the first time she had seen it in action. There were other, less barbaric, more refined methods of inflicting punishment, but her father had always maintained that there was nothing quite so painful, or so devastating to a man's pride, as an old-fashioned flogging carried out in public. It was also, he had once asserted, a remarkably effective deterrent to those who were made to watch.

To her horror, she knew her father was right.

"Dain! Enough!" Parah, chief overseer of the mine, strode into view.

Looking disappointed, Dain let the whip fall to his side.

In the end, as she had known he would, the prisoner lost the battle. She couldn't help but admire his courage even as she wondered at his wisdom. Certainly he had known he could not win; certainly it would have been far less painful simply to submit to the inevitable.

Humbled and bloody, he fought until they forced him to the ground, where they held him down spread-eagled on his stomach. A hoarse scream of outrage erupted from his throat as a heavy lynaziam collar as wide as the span of her hand was locked around his neck; lynaziam manacles were also fitted to his wrists and ankles.

He would soon learn the folly of further resistance, she thought sadly. Dain had only to activate the controller in his hand to bring Number Four to heel. Pressure applied to the top of the control panel would send blinding pain searing through every nerve and sinew of the prisoner's body; if depressed three times in rapid succession, the result was a slow, agonizing death. Pressure applied to the sides of the controller activated the magnets located within the manacles on the captive's wrists and ankles. Pressure to the left side would cause the thick bands on his wrists to snap together, turning them into unbreakable handcuffs; pressure applied to the right side of the controller brought the shackles around his ankles together, effectively hobbling his feet so that he could neither walk nor run. No man alive possessed the strength to force the manacles apart once they had been activated.

She had been told the cruel restraints quickly subdued even the most recalcitrant of prisoners.

There was one more indignity for him to endure. She heard Parah shout, "Number Four," and Dain came forward carrying a glowing brand.

A hoarse cry of pain emerged from the prisoner's throat as a large number four was seared into the flesh of his left arm, high up, near his shoulder. Then he was jerked to his feet.

Sickened by what she had seen, Ashlynne was about to turn away, intent on hurrying back to the peace and safety of the jinan, when the prisoner looked up. She drew back, her heart pounding. She was not supposed to be down here, would surely be punished if her presence were made known. Had he seen her?

She peered around the tree she was hiding behind, and his gaze locked on hers. The power of that look, the sheer fury of it, held her spellbound, like a rabbit caught in a snare. She could not determine the color of his eyes, but she could feel them boring into her, as hard as the rocks scattered upon the seashore. Tortured eyes that burned into her and through her, making her suddenly ashamed of the soft blue velvet of her dress, the white ribbon in her hair, the unblemished gloves upon her unblemished hands. Ashamed because it was the endless toil of men like this one who provided the funds for the outrageously expensive clothing she wore, the fine house in which she had lived her whole life, the very food she ate.

Why had she come here?

She wanted to turn away, to run away, but his gaze held her fast. Never, in all her life, had anyone looked at her as this man was looking at her. Never! She was Ashlynne, daughter of Lady Jadeleine and Lord Marcus Myrafloures. She was accustomed to being treated with deference and respect. But this man, this dirty, bleeding criminal, looked at her with open contempt, as if she were some form of dirt to be shaken from the soles of his feet.

With a soft cry of dismay, Ashlynne lifted her skirts and ran up the path toward home.

"It's very quiet you are this evening," Jadeleine remarked at dinner that night. "Is something amiss, my daughter?"

Ashlynne had been toying with the food on her plate. She looked up at the sound of her mother's voice. Jadeleine wore a gown of emerald green that matched her eyes and complemented her complexion. Her hair, a shade darker than Ashlynne's, was short and curly. As always, she looked beautiful, calm, serene.

Ashlynne shook her head. "No, nothing's wrong," she replied politely.

"You look quite pale," her father said. "Are you ill?"

"I'm fine, Father. Truly." Ashlynne pursed her lips and then said, in a rush, "Magny mentioned that some new rebel slaves were transported from Romariz today. She said they were rebels from Daccar and Riga Twelve, and quite fierce."

Jadeleine and Marcus exchanged troubled glances.

"Indeed?" Marcus lifted one brow, his displeasure at learning that Ashlynne had been gossiping with the overseer's daughter clearly reflected in that simple gesture.

Ashlynne nodded. Magny was Parah's only child. It was from Magny that Ashlynne learned all the latest gossip from the mine and the city. She was a year and a half older than Ashlynne. Her parents considered Magny wild and willful and a bad influence, but she was the only other girl in the area close to Ashlynne's age.

"I had no idea you were interested in what went on at the mine," her father said, looking somewhat amused. "But if you must know, several slaves did arrive this morning."

"In good health?" Ashlynne asked, and then wished she had not. In all the years they had lived here, she had never before shown any interest in the captured rebel prisoners who were sent to toil in the mines.

She could see by the expression in her father's eyes that he was thinking the same thing. "Those who survived the journey are well enough," he replied.

Well enough, Ashlynne mused, remembering the bloody bandage on Number Four's leg.

"How many did we lose?" Jadeleine asked. Business was rarely discussed at mealtime, but tonight seemed to be an exception.

"Only three. Two died of a fever while

onboard ship. One attacked an officer and was terminated. The remaining six will be put to work after they've been quarantined."

Despite all of the modern technology at their command, ore from the mine was still dug out of the ground using human labor. Ashlynne had never wondered why until now. Surely robots could do the work faster and more efficiently. There had been a time when robots and androids had been used for practically everything. Ashlynne had been glad when their popularity waned. She had never liked them. Soulless creatures, they had made her feel uncomfortable.

She looked up, about to question her father, when she realized he was studying her intently. He was a tall, handsome man. His dark brown hair was sprinkled with gray; his eyes were blue. Some claimed he was austere and unforgiving, but she had never known him to be so. True, he was strict at times, but never cruel. In addition to his responsibilities as owner of the mine, he held the highest seat of power in the Tierdian government, and as such, he and his family were regarded as royalty. Because of her father's wisdom and diplomatic skills, Tierde had been at peace for the past twelve years.

She smiled at him. It wouldn't do to ask any more questions about the prisoners, she thought, not now. He must never know she had gone riding outside the compound, snooping in places she was forbidden to go.

Ashlynne turned her attention to her dinner while her parents resumed their conversation. She stared at her plate, made of fine china, at

the heavy silver flatware, the elegant candle-
sticks in the center of the table, the fragile crystal glassware that glistened in the candlelight.
Her plate was filled with a variety of steamed
vegetables, fluffy brown rice and fresh fruit,
and she wondered, for the first time, what type
of fare the mine slaves received. Funny, she
had never wondered about that before. Never
wondered, or cared, until now.

Magny had told her the most recent batch of
prisoners were mercenaries who had been captured fighting against the Romarian cause, and
that most of the captives were from Daccar.
The inhabitants of that distant planet were a
dark-haired, bronze-skinned race, rumored to
be barbaric in the extreme, and said to be enemies to all but their own kind.

After dinner, Ashlynne followed her parents
into the back parlor. She sat down at the piano,
playing softly, while her mother and father discussed mine business. Tierde was the last free
planet in the quadrant that produced baneite,
the rare black crystals that were a primary
source of power for the star ships of Romariz
and Trellis, as well as several of the other planets in the quadrant.

Her fingers moved over the keyboard effortlessly, hardly aware of the tune she played, her
thoughts focusing on Number Four, as they
had ever since the moment she had first seen
him. She had rarely seen any of the slaves close
up, save for the ones who occasionally worked
inside the compound. If Magny had not dared
her, Ashlynne knew she would never have
found the courage to venture down to the land-

ing bay. Her father had forbidden her to go anywhere near the place, and now she knew why. She wished, suddenly, that she had listened.

Leaving the piano, she went outside. The twin moons of Tierde lit her way as she walked along the narrow footpath that led to the far side of the yard.

She stared up at the moons. It was the Term of Tranquils. Riasna shone a pale, pale blue at this time of year. Brell was a golden amber. Legend had it that Brell and Riasna had been lovers. When Riasna died, her soul had gone to live in the sky. Unable to live without her, Brell had hurled himself from a cliff. In taking his own life, he had angered one of the ancient gods, who had decreed that, because Brell had done that which was forbidden, he would be cursed to spend all of eternity pursuing his love, able to catch her only four times each year at the beginning of each new term.

When she reached the back wall, she climbed up on a large flat rock. Standing on tiptoe, she peered over the top of the wall. Far below, she could see the ocean, the light of the twin moons shining on the water, playing in the waves that tumbled over the shore. And near the ocean, the mine, and the squat shapes that were the mine's outbuildings, were visible. Number Four. She pressed her hand to her left arm, trying to imagine the pain he had endured as they burned his flesh. He was down there somewhere, huddled in one of the small stone cells that housed the slaves.

What was he thinking? Was he one of the rebels? Had he left a family behind? Magny had told her that some of the prisoners refused to adapt, refused to obey. Rebellious and unmanageable, they were terminated, their bodies tossed into the endless depths of the sea. Would Number Four be one of those, an intractable creature who would choose death over servitude?

Jumping lightly from the rock, she wandered through the gardens, pausing to admire the way the moons' light shimmered on the water in the small pool at the base of the waterfall. The garden was like a faerie land, with its tall gray-green ferns and the profusion of colorful flowers.

With a sigh, she returned to the house. Her parents were in the main room, reading to each other as they often did in the evening. They shared everything . . . the running of the mine, a love of books and birds and science.

She watched them for a moment, and then, feeling as though she were intruding, Ashlynne bid them goodnight and went upstairs to her room.

Later, as she lay there in the dark, warm and safe in her own bed, Number Four's image rose up to haunt her. Dark bronze flesh streaked with blood. Eyes filled with hatred. What color eyes? she wondered. Long black hair, matted with dirt and sweat. Wide shoulders. Legs as solid as tree trunks. Arms corded with muscle. A jaw roughened by a coarse black beard.

Number Four, so-called because that was the number of the dead slave he was replacing. Number Four . . .

She fell asleep still thinking of him.

Chapter Two

Falkon stared at the bloody bandage wrapped around his thigh, wishing the laser wound had pierced his heart instead of his leg. Wishing he was dead.

A prisoner on the mining planet of Tierde. It was a fate worse than death. He came from a wild and untamed people. Never, in all his life, had he been forced to submit, to bend his will to the will of others. Never had he been confined in such small quarters; never had his freedom, more prized than life itself, been taken from him.

Lifting his shackled hands, he fingered the heavy collar that circled his neck, wondering what depraved monster had devised such a cruel instrument of torture. He could barely breathe, scarcely swallow.

He stared at the lynaziam cuffs on his wrists. He had spent an hour trying to pull the metal apart, but to no avail. The thick bands, held together by a powerful magnet inherent deep within the metal itself, held fast. His hands would remain locked together until the overseer decided to release him. Falkon cursed under his breath. His shoulders ached. His back ached. The brand on his arm ached. His thigh throbbed dully, monotonously. He had spent hours, days, pacing the cold stone floor, wishing he could stretch his arms.

Lying on the thin straw pallet that served as his bed, he stared at the small square opening cut into the thick wooden door. Through it, he could see a slender ribbon of midnight sky. And a single shining star, twinkling like an ice-blue crystal suspended high in the heavens.

He had been imprisoned in this accursed place for ten days. It seemed an eternity. Onboard ship, the prisoners had been bathed with a strong-smelling disinfectant. He had been examined by a heavy-handed physician, who had poked and prodded every inch of his bruised flesh until he had wanted to scream. The laser gash in his thigh had been examined, and he had been pronounced in good health.

He had a vague recollection of being examined again after the beating he had endured while being collared. The mine doctor had rebandaged his thigh and looked after the cut in his cheek, saying he would be back to check on his wounds within the week. That had been ten days ago, and he had seen no one since then save for the scrawny, one-eyed man who brought him his meals twice each day.

He blew out a heavy sigh of resignation. He had known it was futile to resist, known he couldn't win, and yet the thought of submitting without protest had never occurred to him.

Ten days of isolation in a room no bigger than the storage locker on his ship. The closeness, the lack of sunlight, was driving him slowly insane. Never, in all his life, had he been imprisoned. Rarely had he spent more than a few hours at a time within the confines of four walls. He was a fighter, a rebel, a mercenary. He had spent most of his adult life at war. Away from home, his bed had been the ground, his blanket the sky.

He stared at the four cold walls of his prison, and prayed for death. Night and day, hour after hour, the same hopeless prayer.

With a sigh, he closed his eyes. The gash in his thigh ached anew with each breath. The wound, sustained in the heat of battle before he had been captured, was festering. He smiled into the darkness. With luck, it would kill him. Better he should die than spend the rest of his life, short as that was likely to be, imprisoned on Tierde. It was not in him to be a slave. He would fight to be free with every breath in his body, even though he knew he could not win. But he could not submit. To do so would be like turning his back on everything he had fought for, everything he had once loved. . . .

An anguished cry rose in his throat as he thought of his wife and infant daughter lying in a pool of blood in the wreckage that had once been their home, killed by Romarian sky cannon. Killed because he had gone to fight against the Romarian hordes invading Riga Twelve. It had not been his fight, but he was a warrior, the highest paid mercenary in the galaxy, and fighting was in his blood. He would have fought the Romarians for nothing. He had hated them all his life. They were a cruel, heartless people, determined to enslave every planet in the galaxy.

Their attack on Riga Twelve had been proof of that. Riga Twelve was a small farming planet, one that had been neutral for centuries. Its people had never posed a threat to any one. The ruling Jigahn of Riga Twelve had sent him an urgent message, begging him to come to their aid, promising to pay Falcon any price he asked if he would teach their people to fight. He had accepted the call even though he knew that, in the end, the people of Riga Twelve were sure to go down in defeat. The Rigan army had fought valiantly, bravely, and he had been proud to fight at their side.

The fight had been in vain; the end, when it came, came quickly. The ruling family and all those who refused to lay down their arms and acknowledge the new regime were executed, the Romarian army took over the capital city, and the fighting was over. The people of Riga Twelve, once a free and peace-loving people, now lived in bondage, slaves of the Romarian Republic.

Falkon had managed to escape from Riga Twelve. He had known he would be executed if the Romarians captured him; he had not expected them to take revenge on his family.

When they caught him, he had been prepared to die. Had wanted to die. He had attacked the Romarian soldiers without mercy, boldly inviting death, and it had been denied him. Instead of executing him, they had taken him to see what was left of his home, his family, and then they had taken him to see Jayson Drade.

"Drade." The name tasted like bile in his mouth.

Drade, who had shared a room with him at the Training Academy, who had once been his friend. Drade, who had fought at Falkon's side until General Ralf lured him away to the Romarians with the promise of wealth and power.

Drade, who had ordered the attack on his family. Drade, who could have had him executed quickly and cleanly, but who had sentenced Falkon to life in prison instead, knowing he would find confinement worse than death.

Falkon swore as the memories unfolded. He had managed to escape his guards the night before he was to be transferred to the prison, had managed to elude those who hunted him for five years. Five years of fighting against the Romarians, of trying to get close to Drade. Five years of seeking vengeance. And then he had lost his freedom for the second time. He had been wounded in a battle and taken prisoner by the enemy. Just his luck that one of them had recognized him. They had contacted Drade, who had instructed that Falkon was to be sent to the mines of Tierde. He could still hear Drade's laugh over the comport as he said, "Let's see if he can escape from there."

Sitting up, he ripped the bandage from his thigh and dug his fingers into the wound. Pain screamed through his leg. Stifling a groan, he dug deeper, relishing the agony that ripped through him, the sticky warmth of his own blood as it flowed over his hands and down his leg into the dirt beneath him.

Blackness swirled around him, beckoning him, and in the center of that endless void he saw a young woman dressed in blue.

A strange restlessness possessed Ashlynne during the next two weeks. None of her former occupations brought her pleasure. Reading bored her. Playing the piano had lost its appeal. Needlepoint seemed an enormous waste of time. She lost interest in sculpting. Her poetry, once light and brimming with the joy of life, was now filled with pathos and despair. She picked up her brushes and tried to paint, but instead of turning out sunrises, tranquil seas, or brightly colored birds, as had once been her wont, her canvases now depicted bleak landscapes and turbulent oceans beneath dark and stormy skies.

Only horseback riding held her interest. One afternoon, tired of riding in the corral, she snuck out of the jinan and roamed the island, carefully avoiding any path that led in the direction of the mine. He was there. Number Four. The nameless man who now plagued her days and haunted her every dream.

She was almost caught returning to the jinan. Heart pounding, she put her hand over Artemis's nose to keep the mare from whinnying, praying her father wouldn't see her standing just inside the gate. If there was one thing her father was adamant about, it was his insistence that she not leave the compound unchaperoned. She blew out a sigh of relief when he turned and went in the other direction. Never again, she thought. Never again.

Two weeks to the day after she had seen the prisoner, her parents left for Partha. Her father had business in the city; her mother wanted to visit friends. Ashlynne pleaded the onslaught of her monthly flow and begged to stay home.

Her mother frowned and looked doubtful. Her father gave his permission.

"We will return day after tomorrow," Jadeleine said. "Be sure to stay inside the compound while we are gone. Carday will be here to look after you."

"I want you inside the house by dark," her father said. He gave her a perfunctory hug. "I had a letter from Niklaus today. He wants you to come for a visit this summer."

Niklaus Hassrick. Her husband-to-be. A man almost fifteen years her senior. A man she had never met. "Do I have to go?"

Marcus nodded. "It will be good for you to meet him and his family before the wedding, don't you think?"

"I guess so. But why can't he come here?"

"He's a busy man, Ashlynne. He can't afford the time away."

Ashlynne forced a smile. "Have a good trip, Father. Mother."

She waved goodbye to her parents, sighed with relief as she watched them climb into the shuttle craft. For the first time in her life, she was alone. Well, she amended, almost alone, with only old Carday in the house to look after her.

What to do first? With carefree abandon, she kicked off her shoes, peeled off her stockings, unbraided her hair and let it fall in wild disarray down her back.

Running upstairs to her room, she took off her dress and petticoats, then pulled on a pair of soft leather breeches and a loose-fitting cotton shirt that she had bought from a wandering band of gypsy travelers but had never had the occasion, or the courage, to wear.

Sitting on the edge of the bed, she pulled on a pair of thick wool stockings and her riding boots, and then she ran down the stairs and out to the stables located behind the house.

She waved away Otry's offer of help, preferring to saddle Artemis herself. For these two days, she would do as she pleased. She would wear pants and ride astride. She would let her hair fly free in the wind. She would go to bed late and sleep late, eat what she wanted when she wanted. And pray that Carday and Otry would hold silent and not betray her.

Swinging into the saddle, she opened the side gate and raced out of the yard and down the narrow, tree-lined path that led to the beach. When they reached the shore, she gave Artemis her head, and the fleet little mare lined out in a dead run, her dainty hooves flying across the sparkling golden sand, eating up the miles until Ashlynne reined her to a halt.

Ashlynne lifted her face to the sun and smiled. It was a beautiful day. The water was as clear and as blue as the sky. Tall trees grew along the shore, their leaves a bright emerald green. Tiny wildflowers bloomed on the hillsides. Beyond the tree line, she could see the high red sandstone walls that enclosed the compound where she had lived her whole life.

She let the mare rest for a quarter of an hour, then turned her toward home. Cresting a ridge covered with short yellow grass and white star daisies, she stared down at the mine spread below. She had not intended to come this way, but something—someone—she thought ruefully, had drawn her in this direction.

She looked at the dark cavern that led down into the bowels of the crystal mine. Was Number Four down there, laboring in the heat and the gloom? Had the wound in his thigh healed? Did he have a limp? Was his back scarred from the cruel beating he had received? Had he learned to submit, to bend his will to the will of Parah and the other overseers, or had he been terminated, his body unceremoniously tossed into the depths of the sea?

Ashlynne shuddered as she remembered the way he had looked at her, his eyes filled with loathing and rage. She had an overpowering desire to know the color of those eyes.

She studied the mine. It was late afternoon, and there was no one in sight. At this time of day, all the overseers and the prisoners were likely deep within the cavern. Magny had told her that the slaves were driven into the mine shortly after dawn, where they toiled until midday, at which time they were given three-quarters of an hour to eat and relieve themselves.

They never left the mine during the day; at nightfall, they were herded into their cells.

She could hardly imagine such a life, a life of constant hardship and misery, a life spent in the bowels of the earth, never seeing the sun, forced to submit to the will of another . . .

Ashlynne frowned. Wasn't she being forced to submit? Forced to wear dresses and shoes when she preferred breeches and boots, forced to walk when she wanted to run, to be docile when she wanted to be rebellious? Forced to marry a man she had never met? Funny, she had never thought of it quite like that before.

Feeling reckless and defiant, she reined Artemis down the hill and across the wide wooden bridge that led to the mine.

Ignoring every dire warning she had ever heard, she dismounted near the long row of small stone cells that housed the prisoners. She had never seen the prison cells close-up. She had never been allowed to come here to visit Magny; Magny always came to her.

Dismounting, she walked toward the overseer's residence. It was not nearly so large or so fine as her own. Only when she knocked on the door did she remember that Magny had gone to Partha the day before and wouldn't be back until the following night.

She was about to climb back into the saddle when she saw the row of cells on the far side of the compound. Looking quickly around to make sure no one was watching, she tethered Artemis to a post and went to get a closer look. The cells, each one fashioned from dark gray stone, reminded her of play houses for children. Surely a tall man could not stand erect in one of those squat, flat-roofed dwellings.

There were thirteen cells. Thirteen heavy wooden doors reinforced with thick iron straps. Thirteen, she mused. Bad luck. All the doors, save one, were open; the cells empty. Each cell was numbered in bold black numerals.

Curious, she stepped into the nearest cell. It was dark inside, rank with the odor of old sweat and excrement. Grimacing, she covered her nose with her hand and looked around. The roof was only inches from the top of her head. There was a pile of dingy gray blankets in one corner, a covered chamber pot in another, and that was all. No table. No chair. No light of any kind, not even a candle.

Shuddering with revulsion, she backed out of the cell. Why did her father permit the slaves to live in such squalid conditions? Even though the prisoners were, for the most part, criminals condemned to life in the mines, sure-ly they deserved at least a modicum of com-fort. At the very least, they deserved a candle to turn away the darkness of a long night, a fire to turn away the cold. There wasn't even a win-dow, only a narrow slit near the top of the door. She knew somehow that the opening was so the guards could look in, not so the prisoners could look out.

With some trepidation, she walked down the row, coming to a halt in front of the door marked number 4. It was closed, and locked.

She took a deep breath and then, standing on tiptoe, her hands braced against the rough wood, she peered through the narrow opening at the top of the door.

He was there. She felt his presence before she saw him. He was lying amid a pile of ragged blankets. Even in the dim light, she could see he was shivering, his body racked by chills. A low groan reached her ears, a sound of such pain, such exquisite anguish, it made her heart ache.

Turning on her heel, she marched toward the overseer's office. She could see Dagan sitting inside. She had met him once, and thought him a nice young man. He was second in command to Parah.

Lifting her head and squaring her shoulders, Ashlynne marched into the office as if she had every right to be there.

Dagan glanced up, the color draining from his face when he saw her standing there.

"Lady Ashlynne," he gasped, obviously appalled by her presence. "What are you doing here?"

"There's a sick man in cell number four."

"Begging your pardon, Lady, but how would you be knowing such a thing?"

"I looked."

"You should not be here."

"I want you to look after Number Four."

Dagan shook his head. "That prisoner was a dangerous mercenary who escaped incarceration before. I have no authorization to change his treatment."

"I'm authorizing you."

"I mean no disrespect, Lady Ashlynne, but I don't take my orders from you."

34

"I should hate to have to tell my father that your negligence cost him a valuable worker."

Dagan scratched his cheek, obviously judging the weight of her threat. And then he sighed. "Very well, Lady Ashlynne."

Rising from his chair, Dagan picked up an emergency medical kit and followed her across the compound to Number Four's hut.

Withdrawing a flash key from his pocket, he unlocked the door. "I'm no doctor." He thrust the kit into her hands, then drew a controller from his pocket. "You do what needs to be done. I'll keep watch."

Ashlynne hesitated, but she had come too far to turn back now. Taking her courage in hand, she stepped into the cell.

With the door open, she could see the prisoner clearly. It was obvious, even to her untrained eye, that he was ill. His face and chest were sheened with perspiration, his dark eyes were glazed with pain. She wrinkled her nose against the abominable odor that emanated from within the cell.

Ashlynne glanced over her shoulder at Dagan. "Why hasn't anyone looked after this man?" she asked, her voice heavy with accusation.

"I don't know, Lady. The doctor said he wouldn't be fit to work for two weeks." Dagan shrugged. "I thought Parah was looking after him."

Ashlynne grunted softly. Crossing the room, she knelt beside Number Four. The coldness of the stone floor seeped through her breeches. "I've come to help you."

His eyelids fluttered open, and she saw that

his eyes were a dark blue-gray. He stared up at her, his eyes wild, like those of an animal caught in the jaws of a trap. An apt comparison, she mused, for he looked more beast than man. Thick black bristles roughened his jaw. His long black hair was disheveled and greasy. The gash in his cheek had scabbed over. When healed, it would no doubt leave a nasty scar. The number four branded on his arm was an angry ugly red, still black around the edges.

Ashlynne wrinkled her nose. Part of the stench emanated from the prisoner. "He needs a bath."

"Parah allows the prisoners to bathe once a month."

"I want a basin of hot water, a bar of soap, and a lamp." She paused. "I also need a cup of black bark tea laced with rum and honey, and some toweling."

"I don't think that's—."

"Do it!"

With a shake of his head, Dagan went off to do her bidding.

While she waited for Dagan to return, Ashlynne drew back the blankets, felt her cheeks grow hot when she saw that the prisoner was naked save for a scrap of burlaplike cloth that covered his loins.

Taking a deep breath, Ashlynne peeled the bandage from the prisoner's thigh. She pressed a hand to her mouth, her stomach churning, as she gazed at the wound. Thick yellow pus and black-red blood oozed from the center.

She stared at the wound, horrified by the

ugliness of it, the stink of it. She couldn't imagine the pain he must be feeling.

When Dagan returned, she swallowed the bile in her throat and began to wash the ugly wound.

Falkon stared at the girl kneeling beside him, wondering if he had died. Surely only angels had silver-blond hair and eyes the color of new grass. Surely only an angel had such gentle hands. She washed his face and chest, his arms and legs, his back and shoulders. The warm water felt cool against his burning flesh.

With quick efficiency, she applied a medicated pad to his thigh. It sucked out the poison, eased the pain, and disinfected the wound all at the same time. A second pad drew the edges of the wound together. After making sure the medi-pad was doing its work, she taped it in place. She worked quickly, efficiently, hardly looking at him.

He wished for the strength to refuse the medicine she offered him, to refuse the cup of strong black tea she held to his lips, but the instinct to survive was strong within him, stronger than his wish for death. He swallowed the small blue capsules she placed in his mouth, drained the cup. A part of him, a small part he refused to acknowledge, blessed her for her kindness even as the rest of him, the strong part that would not yield, hated her for it.

Hated her for the pity he read in her eyes.

Hated her because she was one of *them*.

Hated her because his wife and child were dead and she was alive . . . alive and beautiful, with her whole life ahead of her, while he had nothing to look forward to but endless days of slavery and long, lonely nights of darkness.

But he was too weak to maintain his anger, too weary to cling to his hatred. His eyelids were suddenly heavy, too heavy to keep open. Her face was the last thing he saw before sleep claimed him.

When he was resting comfortably, Ashlynne left the cell. Outside, she brushed a wisp of hair from her forehead, squinting against the glare of the sun.

"I beg you, Dagan, tell no one I was here."

He fidgeted under her gaze. "I should tell Parah."

"If you do, if anyone finds out I was here, I'll be punished."

"Lady Ashlynne—"

"I have one more favor, Dagan. I want you to tell Parah that the doctor isn't doing his job and should be severely reprimanded. Another day or two, and the prisoner would probably have died. Do you understand?"

"Yes, my lady. I'll take care of it. But . . . I really should tell Parah about your visit."

"You must do as you think best, Dagan." She offered him a dazzling smile. "Whatever you decide, you have my gratitude for what you've done."

Dagan released a heavy sigh. He knew what he ought to do. And he knew what he would do. And they had nothing in common.

Chapter Three

The strange restlessness that had plagued her since the day she had visited the mine continued to haunt Ashlynne. Days turned to weeks, the weeks to a month, and with every hour, her sense of unease grew stronger.

With her parents home, she dared not leave the compound to ride along the beach. It was strictly forbidden. There were dangers outside the compound's protective walls—a chance encounter, however unlikely, with an escaped prisoner; the lure of the jungle, wild and emerald green; the threat of attack by ferocious beasts; the churning riptides along the northern shore. She had always avoided the jungle, but the ocean, ever seething, ever changing, called to some primal sense deep within her and she answered whenever she had the chance.

Her days, once filled with pleasant diversions, now seemed boring. She was tired of reading, tired of playing games and watching vids on the tele-screen, tired of playing the piano. Tired of painting and sculpting.

Tired of living behind the compound's high walls. For the first time, it occurred to her that she was as much a prisoner as the slaves who labored in the mine. As much a prisoner as Number Four.

Number Four. She spent far too much time thinking about him, wondering about him, daydreaming about him. It had to stop.

She heaved a great sigh as she went to the window and watched the storm rage across the sky. Slender bolts of brilliant white lightning slashed through the roiling thick black clouds. Thunder rumbled in the heavens, vibrating through the earth. Rain pelted the window. The wind howled through the night like an angry, ravenous beast.

A streak of lightning stabbed through the clouds on the far side of the compound, and a tree burst into flame. It flared for a moment, burning like a giant candle in the darkness, and then the rain snuffed it out.

The elements were still raging when she climbed into bed. Drawing the covers up to her chin, she closed her eyes. She had always loved the savage unpredictability of the storms on Tierde. Lightning sizzled across the skies, casting eerie dancing shadows on the walls.

Gradually, the fierce rain lessened to a slow, steady rhythm, which soon lulled her to sleep.

By morning, the storm had passed, leaving behind a wide swath of destruction. Trees and plants had been uprooted; debris-floated on the surface of the pool. The tree that had been struck by lightning stood like a dark sentinel near the side wall.

Her parents conferred, then her father called the mine and told Parah to send one of the prisoners to the jinan to clean up the wreckage.

She wished, but didn't dare believe; prayed, but expected no answer. It was too much to hope that Parah would send him—Number Four, with his shaggy black hair and cool blue-gray eyes.

She stood at the back door, one finger tapping restlessly on the wall, her gaze fixed on the side gate. She felt her heart jump into her throat when she saw Number Four enter the yard, followed by Dain. Some prayers, it seemed, were answered after all.

She stood in the doorway, listening surreptitiously while her father issued his instructions. Number Four was to dig up what was left of the tree that had been struck by lightning and haul it away, and then he was to clean up any other debris left by the storm.

Excitement bubbled up inside Ashlynne's stomach as she found a book, grabbed a couple of big yellow apples and headed outside to sit in the sun and read.

She found a perfect place on a flat rock a few yards away from where Number Four was

41

working. Pretending to be engrossed in the old novel she had hastily pulled off one of the bookshelves in the library, she studied Number Four from beneath the veil of her lashes. She hadn't realized how tall and broad-shouldered he was. He wore a pair of loose-fitting tan leather breeches and black mud boots, nothing more. His skin was a deep golden brown; each muscle was clearly defined beneath his taut skin. The gash on his cheek had healed, leaving a thin white scar. Sunlight glinted off the thick lynaziam collar at his throat, off the heavy shackles on his wrists. His hair, as black as the baneite crystals he dug out of the mine, fell past his shoulders. She had never seen anyone quite like him before. He was beautiful, wild and untamed. Exciting. Forbidden. As dangerous as one of the big black mountain lions she had seen at the circus when she was a little girl. The cats had been prisoners, too, she thought, locked in cages at night, controlled by a collar and leash by day. . . .

Falkon listened to his instructions in silence, nodded that he understood. A muscle worked in his jaw as he began shoveling dirt from the base of the fire-ravaged tree. He sent furtive glances at the girl. There was no doubt in his mind that she was the one who had watched him from behind a tree that day at the dock, the same one who had come into his hut and tended his wounds. She was even more beautiful than he remembered. She wore her hair in queenly fashion in a thick coil atop her head. Her skin was the color of pale honey, her cheeks were dusted with a light sprinkling of golden freckles. Her eyes, those deep green eyes that had been haunting his dreams, seemed intent on the book in her lap. He recalled the way she had looked at him when she treated his wounds, her expression one of pity and revulsion. Much as a fine lady might look at a wounded cur.

Rage spiraled through him as he shoveled dirt from the tree's roots. He was a sky warrior, meant to fly, to fight, not to dig in the earth like a Hodorian slime-worm! Among his own people, he was a hero, treated with honor and respect. He had achieved scores of battle honors, saved dozens of lives at the risk of his own.

He felt the girl watching him. Did she take pleasure from his captivity, he wondered, in knowing that the fine clothes she wore, the food she ate, everything she possessed, came from the forced labor and misery of others? She was his enemy, as he was hers. No doubt it brought her an enormous sense of satisfaction to watch him toiling in the hot sun.

Boldly, he lifted his gaze to hers.

Ashlynne's senses reeled as Number Four's impertinent gaze met her own. The hatred in his eyes was almost palpable. She saw him glance at the guard, his thoughts as clear as the words on the book in her lap. Could he kill Dain before Dain activated the collar? And if he managed to kill the guard, how far would he get before they came after him? If he managed to put a good distance between himself and the mine, would the collar still be effective?

She held his gaze for a timeless moment, and

then she shook her head in silent warning. Though many had tried, no one had ever escaped from the mine. Those who were not caught were usually found dead in the dark green heart of the jungle, their bodies mauled and mangled almost beyond recognition. The ones who were caught were returned to the mine and placed in solitary confinement. One month for a first attempt; two months for the second, and so on. Magny said few men were foolish enough to try to escape a second time.

He moved so fast, she saw only a blur. Number Four lunged forward, his hands closing around Dain's throat, and the two men crashed to the ground. The controller, knocked from the overseer's grasp, flew through the air to land inches from where she sat.

Startled by the speed of Number Four's attack, Ashlynne jumped to her feet, her book and the remaining apple tumbling to the ground.

The two men scuffled for several moments, rolling over and over like playful puppies, only they weren't playing. Number Four drew back his arm and drove his fist into Dain's face and the guard went limp.

Breathing heavily, Number Four stood up. Fear washed through Ashlynne when his eyes met hers. Stark, unreasoning fear.

With a cry, she reached down, scooped up the controller and pointed it at Number Four, her thumb hovering over the activation panel on the top. His blue-gray eyes, as turbulent as a storm-tossed sea, raked over her from head to foot.

And then he took a step toward her.

Fear clogged Ashlynne's throat. Her heart was racing wildly, pounding as if she had been running for miles. He didn't look exciting and mysterious now, only savage and ferocious and completely untamed. The sun glistened on his sweat-sheened flesh, glinted on the thick collar at his throat.

"Lady Ashlynne!"

She glanced past Number Four to see Dain struggling to his feet. Number Four took another menacing step toward her and she tossed the controller to Dain, who caught it in mid-air and quickly applied pressure to the top of the control panel.

The effect was immediate.

A hoarse cry erupted from the prisoner's throat as the collar was activated, a harsh rasping cry that seemed torn from the very depths of his soul.

Caught in the inescapable grasp of the collar's power, Number Four dropped heavily to the ground, writhing in an agony she could not begin to imagine, his body twisting, thrashing helplessly in a vain attempt to escape the pain that engulfed him.

Ashlynne had been told the pain was akin to being severely shocked over and over again.

She watched in horror as Number Four's body convulsed, his muscles bunching, quivering. Sweat oozed from every pore. Once begun, there was no way to end the punishment until it had run its course. Moments passed, each one seeming an eternity as she watched. Spasms coursed through him, his face was contorted in a harsh mask of agony.

45

She bit down on her lower lip, wishing there was a way to end his suffering. She had never seen the effects of the collar before; she hoped never to see them again.

Gradually, the punishment diminished, then ceased. Number Four lay on the ground, gasping for breath, his knees drawn up to his chest, his body drenched with perspiration, his eyes tightly closed. His muscles continued to twitch convulsively.

She flinched as Dain kicked Number Four in the back.

"Get up!" the overseer ordered curtly. "You've still got work to do." A cruel grin twisted Dain's thick lips as he watched the prisoner struggle to his hands and knees. "A month in the hole should cool that temper of yours."

Falkon stood up, swaying unsteadily. He felt weak, drained. Every muscle in his body ached.

"Get back to work." Dain held the controller in his right hand. For all the pain it caused, the controller left no lasting ill effects. It was a remarkably effective instrument. He had worked in the mine for ten years and in all that time, he had never had to punish the same slave twice. It was a lesson learned once, but learned well.

Picking up the shovel Number Four had dropped, Dain thrust it into his hands. "Move it."

Jaw clenched in silent protest, Falkon took the shovel and turned back to the task at hand. He could feel the woman watching him, her eyes burning into his back. Damn her! Damn them all!

The earth was hard and unyielding. The punishment had left him feeling weak and a little light-headed. He cursed viciously under his breath, his pride in shreds. It was humiliating enough to be a slave without her standing there, watching him writhing in agony in the dirt, helpless as a worm squirming on a hot rock.

Why the hell didn't she go back into the house where she belonged? Time and again, he thrust the shovel into the earth, wishing the tool was a weapon, wishing that it was Drade at his feet. At last, he exposed the tree's roots. He was panting heavily now, plagued by a relentless thirst.

Dain picked up his communicator and called the mine office. "Dagan? I need a couple of men up here to haul this tree away." He paused a moment, his gaze never leaving the prisoner. "Right. We'll be there in a few minutes. Out."

With a mocking grin, Dain touched the left side of the controller, activating the magnets within the heavy lynaziam shackles on the prisoner's wrists. The bands snapped together with a sharp click.

"Let's go," Dain said, jerking his head toward the path. "The hole awaits."

Eyes forward, Falkon started down the path that led to the mine compound. He refused to look at the girl, but he could feel her gaze on his back, knew she was watching him with those enormous green eyes.

He cursed her all the way down the hill.

Solitary confinement. Falkon squatted in a corner of the hole, his head resting against the damp dirt wall at his back, his eyes closed. He had thought his cell the worst kind of prison, but he had been wrong. This was worse. Much worse.

It was a hole he had dug himself. A rough square, four feet wide, four feet deep. They had stripped him of his boots and breeches and ordered him inside, then covered the hole with a canopy made of thick ebonywood. A narrow slit in one corner allowed him just enough air to breathe. The earth beneath his feet was damp and cold.

It was like being buried alive.

They opened the hole once each day, just long enough to pass him a loaf of dark brown bread, a bowl of weak broth, and a cup of sour wine, and then he was left with his own company again, his own dismal thoughts.

By the end of the first week, he could scarcely tolerate his own stink. The air in the hole reeked of excrement and sweat. During the day, he spent hours staring at the narrow ribbon of light that filtered through the slit in the wood. The sun pounding down on the thick black wood turned the hole into an oven. Sweat dripped down his body to puddle at his feet. The collar and manacles chafed his skin. At night, he huddled into a corner, his body shivering convulsively in an effort to warm itself.

The close confines of the hole pressed in on him. He stared into the darkness that surrounded him, his hatred for the overseers, for the mine owners, for Drade, growing until he thought he might choke on it.

In his imagination, he killed them all over and over again, devising new methods of torture, of execution. His favorite was to put them in the hole he now occupied and leave them to rot. All of them. The overseers. The couple who owned the mine, who now owned him, body and soul. Their servants. Their daughter, with her long silver-blond hair and eyes as green as the oceans of Daccar. Ashlynne.

He muttered an oath, and then he swore aloud, unleashing a long string of the most foul profanity he knew.

They let him out of the hole for ten minutes each week so he could remove the pile of excrement from the corner. But he could not remove the stink. Not from the earth that surrounded him on all sides. Not from his skin.

It was humiliating, degrading, to be forced to squat in that fetid hole like some sort of dung beast, blind and dumb and helpless. He prayed for his freedom, for a weapon, for vengeance. Always for vengeance. And the hatred grew within him, taking root deep in his heart, choking the life from his soul.

There was no peace for him now, save in his dreams, vivid dreams haunted by a silver-haired maiden with soft, creamy skin and luminous green eyes. Ashlynne . . .

"It was awful, Magny. I've never seen anything so terrible in my whole life."

Magny nodded, her brown eyes sympathetic, yet alight with interest. "I heard Dain talking to my father about it. Were you scared?"

"Terrified. He looked so . . . so dangerous."

"Number Four. He's . . ." A flush tinged Magny's cheeks. "He's handsome, isn't he, Lynnie?"

"What difference does that make?" Ashlynne exclaimed, horrified to hear her own thoughts put into words. "He's a slave."

"But handsome, don't you think?"

"Well, yes," Ashlynne admitted. "He is that."

"I saw him the other day." Magny fell back on the bed, her arms spread wide. "My oh my, what a man."

Ashlynne shook her head. Magny was her best friend, but sometimes she just didn't understand her. Of course, Magny led a much freer life than Ashlynne. Magny had been to Enjine Base Nine several times; she had once confided to Ashlynne that she'd had an affair with a sky pilot from Riga Twelve, and that she still saw him whenever he came to Tierde. Sometimes Ashlynne envied her friend her freedom, but then she would think how awful it would be to have to live in the mine compound, surrounded by ugliness and condemned men. Magny's mother had left Tierde when Magny was only five, declaring she could no longer abide living there. She had promised to send for Magny when she found a place to live, but she never had. It was a subject she and Ashlynne never discussed.

Ashlynne picked up a comb and ran it through her hair. "What did they do to him? For attacking Dain?"

"He's in solitary." Magny sat up and ran a hand through her own hair, wishing it was long and thick and silver-blond like Ashlynne's, instead of short and impossibly curly.

"Oh. What is that, exactly?" Ashlynne asked, thinking it was probably like being locked in a closet or something. But as Magny began to describe it, Ashlynne realized it was far worse than anything she had imagined. What would it be like, to be confined to a hole in the ground, unable to stand up?

"And he has to stay down there, naked, in that hole, for a whole month." Magny wrinkled her nose. "It's awful. You can't imagine the smell. They let him out for a few minutes every week so he can muck out the hole." Magny shuddered as she grabbed an apple from the bowl beside Ashlynne's bed.

"He's all right, though?"

Magny lifted a knowing brow. "Worried about him, are you, Lynnie dear?"

"Of course not," Ashlynne said quickly.

"Uh huh. Then I guess you won't care that Dain beat him again."

"He did? Oh, Magny, why?"

"You know Dain. He doesn't need a reason. Let's talk about something more pleasant, shall we? I hear you're meeting Niklaus soon."

Ashlynne nodded. "Yes. I have to go to Trellis this summer. To meet him and his family, and discuss the wedding."

"Are your parents going?"

"No. Father said he can't leave the mine that long."

"Well, why doesn't Niklaus come here?"

"For the same reason. He can't leave. And since he can't come to me, I have to go to him."

She pointed at the picture of Niklaus on her dressing table. "How can I marry a man I don't even know?"

"Well, isn't that why you're going to Trellis? To get to know him?"

"Well, yes. But do you think one summer is long enough to get to know a man well enough to marry him?"

"I don't know, but I think he's dreamy," Magny said. "And just think of it, you'll finally get off this rock. You're so lucky."

"Lucky?" Ashlynne studied Niklaus's photograph. He was a handsome man, with wavy brown hair, brown eyes, a patrician nose. And yet, handsome as he was, she thought Number Four far more . . . not handsome, exactly, but there was something about him, something virile and extremely masculine that was lacking in Niklaus. "Would you want to marry a man you've never met?"

"I'd marry a Hordorian swine merchant if he could get me away from here," Magny declared. She tossed the apple core into the disposal unit and fell back on the bed again, her hands clasped behind her head. "Think of it, Lynnie, you'll get to travel to the far side of the galaxy, live in a big house, have anything you want."

"I already live in a big house," Ashlynne retorted. And she had almost everything she wanted. Except the freedom to marry whom she wished, when she wished.

"Well, if you don't want to marry Niklaus, I will," Magny said.

"What about your sky pilot?"

"Well, he's very exciting, but he'll never be rich."

"Wouldn't you rather marry for love than for money?"

"I suppose so."

"Oh, Mag, I don't want to get married and move to Trellis. I don't want to leave here."

"Why ever not?"

Ashlynne bit down on her lower lip. She had never lived anywhere else, never been anywhere else. She was afraid to leave the security of the only home she had ever known. But even that wasn't the real reason. She didn't want to marry Niklaus; she wanted to stay here, because *he* was here. But she couldn't tell Magny that.

"Do you think Number Four is the monster they say he is?"

Ashlynne looked up, startled. "What?"

"Number Four. Do you think he's as bad as everyone says?"

Ashlynne stared at Magny, wondering if her friend had been reading her mind, if Magny knew how obsessed she had become with Number Four. She thought about him constantly, dreamed of him at night.

"What difference does it make?" she asked, though she had often wondered the same thing herself. "He's a slave."

"I know." Magny sighed dramatically. "But have you seen his arms? I've never seen muscles like that. Don't you wonder what it would be like to have him hold you?"

"Magny!" Ashlynne exclaimed. She tried to look horrified, but failed miserably. She had wondered. Even though he was a slave, even though she hated him because he was rude and crude and insolent, she had noticed that he was a fine specimen of a man, and it embarrassed her. "Why did Dain beat him?"

Magny shook her head. "You know Dain. He has no patience. He ordered Number Four out of the hole, and Number Four didn't obey quickly enough. As soon as Number Four climbed out, Dain started whipping him. Dain enjoys inflicting pain far too much, I think."

"But he's all right?"

"Who?" Magny asked, stifling a giggle. "Dain?"

Ashlynne picked up a pillow and threw it at her friend. "You know who."

Magny caught the pillow in both hands and hugged it to her chest. "Oh, you mean Number Four. He's amazing," Magny said, her voice tinged with awe. "He just stood there, his hands clenched, while blood dripped down his back. You could see Dain getting madder by the minute. I don't know what he would have done if my father hadn't stepped in and put a stop to it. He took Dain aside later and reprimanded him. He told Dain if he caught him whipping a slave for no reason again, he'd lose his position."

"I've never liked him," Ashlynne said. "He has sneaky eyes."

Magny swung her legs over the edge of the bed. "Well," she said with an exaggerated sigh, "I've got to go fix dinner for my father." Rising, she dropped the pillow on the bed and headed toward the door. "If I see Number Four, I'll be sure to extend your regards."

"Mag!" Ashlynne called, running down the corridor after her friend. "Mag, don't you dare! Mag!"

"Can't catch me!" Magny ran out the front door and sprinted for the path that led to the mine.

"Magny! I'll never speak to you again!"

"Yes, you will. Bye, Lynnie," Magny shouted, and disappeared out the gate.

Chapter Four

The next month seemed interminably long. No matter where she was or what she was doing, all she could think of was Number Four. She couldn't imagine anything so awful as being shut up in a hole in the ground. Practically buried alive.

Finally, in need of a diversion, she begged her mother to let Magny spend the night. Her mother was usually reluctant, but this time she agreed. Ashlynne was sure it was only because her mother and father were going to be away at a counsel meeting most of the evening.

She looked up when Magny tossed the book she'd been reading aside.

"Well, that was dull," Magny exclaimed. "What shall we do?"

Ashlynne yawned. "I'm tired. I was thinking of going to bed."

"Bed! But it's still early. And your parents won't be home for hours. We can't go to bed."

Ashlynne rolled over onto her stomach. "Well, what do you want to do?"

Magny bounced off the mattress, her eyes sparkling with mischief. "How brave are you?"

"I'm not, Mag, you know that, so whatever you're planning, just forget it."

"Honestly, Ashlynne, you lead the most dull, boring life of anyone I know."

She wanted to argue, but she couldn't. It was true. Her life was boring. Routine. Regimented.

"Come on, Lynnie, you know you're dying to."

"All right, Magny, what am I dying to do?"

"Go swimming."

"What's so daring about that? I swim all the time."

"In the ocean."

Ashlynne's eyes widened. "You want to go swimming down there now? Tonight?"

Magny nodded vigorously. "The moons are full. It's a beautiful night. The water won't be too cold. Come on, let's do it."

Ashlynne bit down on her lower lip, her better judgment warring with the desire to do something wild and crazy. "All right. You can wear one of my bathing suits. Do you want the red or the yellow?"

"Neither, silly."

"You don't mean . . . ?"

Magny grinned. "You've got it. Let's go."

Like two thieves in the night, they crept down the stairs. Old Carday was in the living room. She had fallen asleep watching a vid. Like two schoolgirls playing hooky, Ashlynne and Magny slipped out the front door, ran down the path and out the side gate.

It was, indeed, a beautiful night. The twin moons hung low in the sky, bathing the landscape in a pale amber glow. Moonlight shimmered and danced on the water, sparkling like millions of tiny golden lights.

Magny dropped her towel on the sand and began to undress.

"Are you sure this is a good idea?" Ashlynne glanced up and down the beach. To the right, she could see the outline of the mine; far to the left began the tree line that marked the edge of the jungle.

"You're not going to back out on me now, are you?"

Ashlynne took a deep breath. "No, I'm not," she said, and before she could lose her nerve, she undressed.

She shrieked as a wave broke over her, then she dove into the water. She had never gone swimming in the ocean at night before, never gone swimming in the nude before, and it felt wonderful, deliciously wicked. She swam for several minutes, then floated on her back. Overhead, a million stars lit the sky as Brell chased Riasna. Would he ever catch her? she wondered.

"Oh, Magny," she exclaimed, "this was a terrific idea."

"Of course! Have I ever had any other kind?"

With a laugh, Ashlynne dove into the water again, amazed at how different it felt to swim wearing nothing at all. She shrieked as something slippery brushed against her leg, images of sea monsters jumping into her mind, but it was only a piece of sea kelp.

They swam and splashed until they were breathless, then sat on the shore, wrapped up in their towels.

Ashlynne gazed out at the dark green water, thinking how beautiful it was bathed in the moons' light, and how much she would miss this place when she was living on Trellis.

"Hey, Lynnie, got any adventure left in your soul?"

"Why?" she asked suspiciously. "What do you want to do now?"

"Why, go visit Number Four, of course," Magny said with a wink and a grin.

Ashlynne stared at her. "Are you crazy?"

"Maybe," Magny replied with a wave of her hand. "Well, do you want to?"

"Of course not," Ashlynne replied, but she was dressing as she spoke, her heart pounding, not at the very real possibility of getting caught, but at the thought of seeing Number Four again.

She began to have second thoughts as they drew closer to the mine. Her father would be furious, her mother appalled.

"Mag," she whispered, "I don't think this is such a good idea."

"Sure it is. Be careful, don't step in that hole."

Ashlynne followed Magny across the bridge,

all her senses alert. She jumped when one of the boards creaked, the noise sounding like thunder in her ears, gave a little shriek when a night bird flew in front of her face.

"Lynnie, be quiet!"

"Sorry." Ashlynne glanced over her shoulder. "What if we get caught?"

"We'll just say I forgot something at home and we came down to get it."

Magny turned right, skirting the edge of the compound, until they drew near the squat cells that housed the prisoners.

"This is silly," Ashlynne said, looking around. "We won't be able to see him anyway. There's no light in the hut."

Magny whirled around to face her. "And just how do you know that, Lynnie?"

Mouth agape, Ashlynne stared at her friend.

"Well?" Magny tapped her foot on the ground. "I'm waiting."

"I-I-I don't know. I'm just guessing. I mean, do they have lights in the huts?"

"Ashlynne Myrafloures, tell me the truth! You've been down here before, haven't you? When?"

"You won't tell?"

"Of course not."

"It was when my parents went to Partha the last time. I forgot you were gone, too, and I decided to come down for a visit."

"Go on."

"Well, I decided as long as I was here, I'd look around. I went to look in the cells, and I saw Number Four. It was right after he was brought here. He was wounded, remember? I heard him moaning and I made Dagan open the door for me."

Magny grinned at her. "Dagan thinks you're pretty, you know."

"What? Don't be silly."

"Go on," Magny urged, "what happened?"

"Nothing. He opened the door and I treated Number Four's wound and then I left."

"You call that nothing? Why didn't you ever tell me this before?"

"Why do you think?"

Magny laughed softly. "I think you're a lot braver than you think you are, my Lady Myrafloures, that's what I think. Come on."

Like thieves in the night, they crept along until they reached Number Four's cell.

"All right, we're here. Can we go home now?" Ashlynne whispered.

"Of course not. We look inside."

"Tell me again why we're doing this?"

"Because you think he's handsome. Go on, you go first."

Ashlynne rolled her eyes. The sooner she got this over with, the sooner they could go back home. Taking a deep breath, she stood on tiptoe and peeked in the barred opening, and found herself staring into Number Four's face, which was clearly visible in the moons' light.

With a gasp, she jumped back, and bumped into Magny.

"He's awake!" Ashlynne exclaimed, and turning on her heel, she ran for the bridge, and didn't stop running until she was on the other side.

Magny joined her a moment later. For a

minute, they just stared at each other, and then Magny burst out laughing.

"It's not funny!" Ashlynne said, and knew she would never forget the look of bitter despair on Number Four's face, or the way it had turned to anger when he saw her staring at him. As if he were an animal in a cage.

The laughter died on Magny's lips when she saw the expression on Ashlynne's face. "Are you crying?"

Ashlynne wiped the tears from her eyes. "No, of course not. Can we go home now?"

Chapter Five

"The pool needs cleaning," Jadeleine remarked at dinner several nights later. "Ask Parah to send one of the slaves up to take care of it, will you?"

"As you wish, my dear," Marcus replied.

"Actually, we could use a full-time slave in the compound," Jadeleine said, her brow furrowed thoughtfully. "Otry's getting too old to do more than care for the horses, and since Fiurmin left, there's no one to trim the shrubs or weed the flower beds on a regular basis."

Marcus grunted softly. "Are you sure you want one of the slaves?" He glanced at Ashlynne. "It might be wiser to hire someone from the city."

"Why spend good money for hired help when we have slaves at our disposal?" Jadeleine countered. "I dare say slaves are easier to control at any rate."

"Without doubt," Marcus said agreeably. "I shall go down tomorrow and look them over."

Ashlynne sat up in her chair, her foot tapping nervously as she listened to her parents' conversation. One of the slaves, here? She bit down on her lower lip, wondering if there was any way she could persuade her father to pick Number Four. Six weeks had passed since the incident with Dain. She wondered how Number Four had endured the long weeks of solitary confinement. Magny had told her that slaves sometimes went insane after being imprisoned in the hole for more than a week. How did anyone endure a month? Was he glad to be back in the mine? Did even his dismal cell seem welcome after four weeks of being buried alive?

She glanced around the room, its opulence unmatched anywhere on Tierde, and tried to envision being trapped in a dark hole in the ground, with nothing to see but darkness, no voice to hear but her own.

"We've never had a slave in the compound," she remarked casually.

"Does the idea bother you, daughter?" Jadeleine asked, her voice holding a faint note of concern.

"No, of course not," she replied quickly. "Will you pick him out yourself, Father, or let Parah make the selection for you?"

"I don't need anyone to make my decisions for me," Marcus replied. He looked at

Jadeleine. "I will, of course, take Parah's recommendation into account, since he is more familiar with the slaves than I."

Ashlynne smiled at her father. "Of course."

"I'll go tomorrow morning," Marcus decided. "I've been meaning to speak to Parah about the recent decrease in production."

Ashlynne sat forward, trying not to look too eager, too anxious. "May I ride with you?"

"To the mine?" Marcus asked, astonished. "Of course not!"

"But, I mean, I just thought how nice it would be if I could go with you. I could wait for you at the bridge, and when you're finished talking to Parah, we could take a ride along the beach." She smiled her most winning smile. "It's been months, Father, since we've had any time alone together."

"She's right," Jadeleine said. "You haven't spent much time with Ashlynne lately. I don't think it would hurt for her to accompany you, this one time."

Ashlynne held her breath, waiting for her father's decision.

"I'll be wanting to leave immediately after first meal," he said gruffly.

Jumping up, Ashlynne threw her arms around his neck and kissed his cheek. "I'll be ready! Thank you, Father."

Walking around the table, she bent down and hugged her mother. "Thank you," she whispered.

Ashlynne glanced at her father as they rode along the narrow tree-lined path that wound down the hillside to the mine compound. He was a handsome man. He wore his dark hair cropped close to his head. Clad in dark gray breeches, a light gray shirt, and black leather boots, he cut a dashing figure astride his favorite mount, a high-stepping black stallion. Both his horse and hers had been imported from Earth.

Her father had taught her to ride almost before she could walk. He was an excellent horseman. She knew he was proud of her, had overheard him bragging about her good seat and light hands. Her mother had been thrown when she was a child and as a result she had a deep-seated fear of horses. Marcus had bought her a gentle gelding, but Jadeleine refused to ride, declaring she much preferred her small shuttle cart, which had no mind of its own, didn't buck and didn't smell. But Ashlynne and Marcus went riding every chance they got.

"How's the new mare working out?" Marcus asked.

"Wonderful, Father. I love her. Thank you." The chestnut mare had been her father's gift to her on her seventeenth birthday six months before.

Ashlynne ran her hand over the mare's sleek coat. Before her birthday, she'd had to ride one of the native karu-atar, which, though pleasant to ride, had none of Artemis's speed or beauty. The karu-atar roamed wild up in the north. They were horselike in appearance, with long coarse hair, clawed feet, and a whiplike tail.

"You should start making plans for the wedding," Marcus remarked. "It will be year's end before you know it. Perhaps you should redecorate the two corner suites upstairs for our guests. I've asked his parents to stay on after the ceremony. It's been a long time since I've seen Rugen and Zahara."

Ashlynne nodded. "I'll talk to Mother about it."

"I know you don't want this marriage, Ashlynne, but Rugen is my closest friend."

"I know." Rugen and her father had fought together in the last Tierdian war years ago, and had pledged their children to each other when Ashlynne was born.

"Niklaus is a fine young man, with a brilliant career ahead of him."

Ashlynne nodded again. Few girls of her class were permitted to choose their own husbands. Women were pawns, traded for land, offered in marriage to secure peace between feuding families or forge alliances between worlds; or, in her case, to fulfill her father's pledge to his best friend.

"I want you to keep silent while I examine the slaves. Most of them haven't seen a woman in quite some time."

"Yes, Father."

Parah had been advised of their imminent arrival and he hurried forward to greet them. Marcus dismounted near the bridge and handed the reins of his horse to Ashlynne. From her vantage point on her horse's back, she watched her father and Parah cross the narrow wooden bridge to the compound that housed the prisoners. The small stone cells looked like blocks set in a row.

It was Sunday, and the prisoners were all locked inside their cells. On any other Sunday, they would have been toiling in the bowels of the mine, but not today. Today her father was going to look them over.

Parah started at the far end. Unlocking each door, he ordered the occupant to step outside. As soon as the prisoners emerged from their cells, the shackles on their hands and feet were activated, rendering them immobile. They were a motley crew, she thought sadly. Eyes empty of life, of hope, they stood like so many sheep waiting for the slaughter. Dressed in coarse leather breeches and sleeveless vests, their hair long and unkempt, they all looked alike.

Except for Number Four.

Ashlynne leaned forward in the saddle as the tall, dusky-skinned slave emerged from the darkness of his cell to blink against the early morning sunlight. She saw the way his jaw clenched as the bands encircling his hands and feet snapped together. They had not yet broken his spirit, she mused. Even after months of captivity and four weeks in solitary confinement, his eyes still blazed with anger and defiance.

She wished she could hear what was being said, what questions her father asked as he walked up and down the row of prisoners, what answers they gave. None of the prisoners dared to meet her father's eyes. Even Number Four looked properly subdued when her father stopped in front of him. She watched Number Four nod curtly, once, twice. Saw her father take Parah aside for a moment, and then her father was walking back toward her, his military upbringing obvious in the square set of his shoulders, the length of his stride, the self-confidence that was so much a part of him. She had always been proud of her father, proud of his many accomplishments, of the fact that he had been decorated for bravery above and beyond the call of duty.

She handed him the stallion's reins, and he swung into the saddle effortlessly, gracefully.

"Ready for that gallop on the beach?" he asked.

"Yes, sir!" She glanced back at the compound. The prisoners had been returned to their cells. "Did you make a choice, Father?"

"We'll talk of it later," he said, and touching his heels to the stallion's flanks, he raced over the bridge and headed for the beach.

With a wild cry, Ashlynne sent her mare after the horse, delighting in the heady sense of freedom that engulfed her as they raced across the hot golden sand, reveling in the wind in her face and the scent of the sea, the thundering power of the chestnut mare.

Leaning low over the mare's neck, she drummed her heels against the mare's flanks. "Let's go, girl!" she cried, and let out a shout as the horse jumped a large piece of driftwood.

Oh, to be free! To be able to ride forever. To be able to live her life as she pleased. To pick a man of her own choosing, a man with long black hair and eyes as turbulent as a storm-tossed sea . . .

Why couldn't she get that man out of her mind?

"Did you find a slave that suited you, Father?"

Her father had won the race, and now they were sitting on a patch of grass near the shore while the horses rested. It was a pretty spot. She loved the sound of the ocean, could sit for hours watching the waves lap at the shore. Tiny little birds with gold-and-black wings scurried along the sand, chirping merrily.

Marcus nodded. "I believe so. Parah tells me the man has caused some trouble in the past, but he seems fit and appears to have been brought to heel." He shook his head ruefully. "Not much of a choice, really. So many of them lose the will to live after a few months in the mine."

"Does the man you've chosen know horses?"

"He claims to."

Ashlynne plucked a long blade of grass and twirled it between her thumb and forefinger. There was no way to ask if it was Number Four, not without fear of revealing that she knew more about the man than she should.

"Well, shall we go?" Marcus asked. He stood up and offered Ashlynne his hand. "Midday meal should be ready by now, and you know how your mother hates for us to be late."

With a smile, Ashlynne took her father's hand and let him pull her to her feet. She would find out soon enough who her father had chosen. Until she knew, she could hope.

And then she frowned. What if her father did pick Number Four? And what if Number Four told her father about her little adventure with Magny the other night? Her father rarely got angry with her, but she had never forgotten the few times that he had.

She told herself she was worrying needlessly. There was no reason for Number Four to mention it, no reason at all, but try as she might, she couldn't put the thought out of her mind. Her father had warned her that she wouldn't be allowed to see Magny if they got into any more mischief. And she had a feeling that her father would consider sneaking down to the mine in the middle of the night much worse than any of their other pranks.

Suddenly, she hoped he hadn't chosen Number Four at all.

Chapter Six

Falkon stood in the center of the floor, his gaze roaming around the room. It was sparsely furnished, containing only a narrow bed covered with a light brown spread, a small square table and a single chair. The walls, painted a muted shade of sea green, were bare of any decoration. There was a small window covered with a dark green shade. Still, his new quarters seemed like an abode fit for a king compared to the cell he had left only a short while ago.

And yet it was still a prison.

He lifted a hand to the thick collar around his neck. And he was still a prisoner.

Muttering an oath, he began to pace the floor, his footsteps muffled by a deep brown carpet. He had been taken from the mine, bathed with a strong-smelling disinfectant, dressed in a pair of black breeches and a loose-fitting white shirt. His hair had been thoroughly washed, deloused, and trimmed. He'd even been fed a decent meal. It was the first time in months he'd had enough to eat. He had forgotten how good bread fresh from the oven tasted, forgotten the taste of coffee.

He swore again, remembering how the slaves had been lined up in front of their cells that morning so that the owner of the mine could examine them. The man had walked up and down the line, inspecting each prisoner, checking their teeth as he might have examined those of a horse he was thinking of buying.

It had been degrading, humiliating, and yet, with the bands at his wrists fused together and the overseer standing at the ready, lightly tapping the pommel of his whip against his hand, there had been little choice but to submit.

And now he was here, in a small square room located in the back wing of the main house. No longer would he toil deep in the bowels of the mine, deprived of sunlight and fresh air. His lot in life had improved, Parah had informed him. In the future, he would work in the mine owner's jinan, where he would be expected do whatever he was told, without question or complaint. Any attempt to escape would see him back in his cell, locked inside without food or water, until he died.

Falkon had nodded that he understood.

And now he paced the floor. The room was not large by any means, yet it was more than twice the size of his cell at the mine. It seemed odd to be able to take more than a few steps in

73

any direction, to look out the window and see the sun shining, to have a real bed to sleep in, clothes that weren't torn and stained, that didn't reek of his own sweat.

He heard footsteps in the hall, and then the door swung open and the owner of the mine stood in the doorway, one hand resting on the controller at his belt.

"I trust Parah has told you of the consequences should you try to escape?"

Falkon nodded.

"Your escaping is not my primary concern," Marcus said tersely. "The security walls are more than adequate to keep you in. Should you somehow manage to slip past them, the collar you wear will lead us to you." He paused, his expression hard. "My concern is for my family. I have a wife and an impressionable young daughter. Should you show either of them the slightest disrespect, should you dare to lay a hand on them, you will loose that hand, and then your life. Is that clear?"

"Quite clear."

"The last storm has played havoc with the foliage. Your first task will be to trim the shrubs and clean up the debris left by the storm."

Falkon nodded. He saw no reason to tell the man he had been here before, or that he had seen the man's daughter only a few nights ago, peeking into his cell in the middle of the night. He didn't know what the devil she had been doing in the compound, but he was reasonably certain she wasn't supposed to be prowling around the mine after midnight, or at any other time.

Marcus regarded the prisoner for a few moments. He wasn't sure why he had chosen this particular slave to work within the compound. The fact that the man appeared to be the youngest and the most physically fit of the prisoners had certainly been a factor. He had almost changed his mind when Dain had informed him of the prisoner's attack. When confronted, the man had not denied it. When asked why he had tried to escape, the prisoner had glanced at his surroundings, then looked Marcus in the eye and said, "Wouldn't you?"

At the time, Marcus had been impressed with the man's candor. He shook his head, hoping he hadn't made an error in judgement. "Come. I'll show you the way to the yard. You will stay there until someone comes for you. Is that understood, Number Four?"

Falkon choked back an angry retort. He wasn't an idiot. Hands clenched at his sides, he nodded curtly.

Without another word, Marcus turned and walked down the hall, confident the slave would follow.

Falkon rested his back against a tree and closed his eyes. It was good to be outside. He had removed his shirt, hungry for the touch of the sun on his skin, on his face. He took a deep breath, drawing the scent of sun-warmed earth and grass into his lungs. He had been working for several hours, trimming trees and bushes, raking leaves, cleaning debris from a small blue pond. Never in all his life had he seen a place such as this. Even the royal residence on Riga

75

Twelve paled in comparison. The house was of white stone that seemed to glow in the sun. There was a large pool surrounded by graceful ferns and flowers and small groups of tables and chairs. Birds with bright plumage chirped in the treetops; colorful fish swam in a small manmade lake on the far side of the grounds. There were flowers everywhere—large brightly colored blooms, delicate buds, lacy ferns. His home planet was a dreary place, plagued by wars and drought. And yet it was home, and he longed to be there, fighting for freedom with his kinsmen.

Freedom . . . He stared at the shackles on his wrists and wondered if he would ever be free again.

Muttering an oath, he followed the narrow path that led toward the main house, intending to weed the gardens that grew along the south side of the building.

Rounding a bend in the path, he came to an abrupt halt. The girl was sitting beside the pond, one hand dangling in the water. Dread welled up inside him when he saw the controller lying beside her.

Ashlynne looked up, suddenly aware that she was no longer alone. Seeing Number Four reminded her of the last time she had seen him. Instinctively, her hand closed over the controller.

Her gaze clashed with his, and time seemed to stop as they stared at each other.

Ashlynne frowned. Cleaned up, with his hair washed and trimmed, and clad in a decent pair

of breeches, he didn't look so wild and ferocious, yet he was a slave, a prisoner, and she
couldn't help being afraid of him. In all hon-
esty, she knew she would have been afraid of
this man no matter what he was. In her sheltered life, she'd had little contact with men, had
never associated with a man like this one. The
men who came to visit her parents were busi-
nessmen, diplomats, couriers; they weren't
warriors. They weren't fighters, like Number
Four had been. The number four branded on
his upper arm was clearly visible, another
reminder of the kind of man he was. Her fingers tightened around the controller.

Falkon watched the girl, unable to draw his
gaze away. Dressed in a bright yellow frock,
with her silver blond hair falling around her
shoulders, she looked like the sun come to
earth in human form. Her eyes, those beautiful
green eyes, stared back at him, filled with
undisguised fear and distrust. She held the
controller so tightly, her knuckles were white.

Damn, he thought, what the devil was she
doing here? His hand brushed the collar at his
throat, every muscle in his body tightening as
he waited for her to activate the pain reflex.

Ashlynne felt her breath catch in her throat
as her gaze slid down over his bare chest. His
shoulders were incredibly broad; his dark
bronze skin glistened with perspiration. She
swallowed hard, her mouth suddenly dry. He
was a big man, taller than her father, more
muscular than Parah. His tight black breeches
left little to the imagination.

77

Falkon cleared his throat, took a deep breath, and let it out in a long sigh. "Are you going to use that thing?"

Mesmerized by his darkening stare, Ashlynne glanced at the controller in her hand as if seeing it for the first time. "If I have to."

"Go into the house."

She blinked at him, momentarily taken aback by his audacity. Imagine, a slave telling her what to do! She shifted her hold on the controller, saw his expression grow suddenly wary. Reassured that she was the one in power, she shook her head. This was her favorite place and she would not be driven away by an insolent slave. "I want to sit here and read."

"And I have work to do."

"So, do it."

Muttering an oath, Falkon knelt in the dirt and began to weed the patch of spiky blue and lavender flowers that grew along both sides of the path. Anger churned deep inside him. He was a warrior, not a gardener. He had been born and raised to give orders, not take them. He was accustomed to fighting, not digging in the dirt like some Nardian farmer.

Fighting, he mused bleakly. If he hadn't been off fighting another man's battles, his wife and child might still be alive. He wondered if Maiya had gone to her grave hating him. Guilt and regret warred within him, flaying his soul. He had never been a true husband to Maiya. Waging war had been his life and what did he have to show for it? His wife and daughter were dead because of it, and he was a slave on a distant planet.

He thrust the bitter memories aside, only to become aware that he was being watched. Glancing over his shoulder, he saw the girl staring down at him, her eyes wide, as if she were studying some new species of Venusian earthworm.

He had a sudden urge to grab her, to draw her up against him and plunder those pouting pink lips, to prove to her that he was every inch the savage she thought he was, to prove to himself that he was still a man.

Disgust welled up within him and he turned away, ripping the weeds from the garden with a vengeance, wishing it was as easy to rip away the guilt that consumed him day and night. Not for the first time, he wondered if he wouldn't be better off to make them kill him outright and be done with it. Perhaps, in death, he would find the peace that had eluded him all his life.

After thirty minutes, he stood up to stretch the kinks out of his back and shoulders. Slowly, he turned around, hoping the girl would be gone, but knowing somehow that she was still there, still watching him.

Ashlynne felt her cheeks grow warm as her gaze met his again. She looked down at her book, but it was impossible to concentrate on the words. Always her gaze strayed toward the prisoner, to his broad scarred back, to the play of corded muscles rippling beneath his sun-drenched skin. He moved with such fluid ease, such strength. Just watching him did funny things to the pit of her stomach.

Their gazes locked, and for a moment she

couldn't breathe, couldn't think, could only stare into his eyes, those beguiling blue-gray eyes that seemed able to penetrate her very soul. A flush rose in her cheeks. No one had ever dared look at her with such insolence.

"What were you doing at the mine the other night?" he asked.

"Nothing. We were just . . ." She lifted one shoulder and let it fall. "Just having an adventure."

"Pretty stupid, wandering around in the middle of the night like that."

"I don't think it's any of your business what I do in the middle of the night, or at any other time," she retorted, and turned her attention to her book again.

He stared at her a moment. If he was smart, he would get the hell away from her. Spoiled, pampered lady of the manor, she was nothing but trouble, and he had trouble enough. "What are you reading?"

She looked up, her gaze meeting his once again. "Excuse me?"

"I asked what you're reading?"

"A book."

Before she could stop him, he plucked it from her hand.

"Give me that!" She made a grab for it, but he held it out of her reach. With a disdainful sniff, she sat down again. "You probably can't read anyway."

He glared at her, then glanced at the title of the book. "Poetry?"

She felt a flush rise in her cheeks. Meardon was an old-world poet, and one of her favorites. Her mother had forbidden her to read his works, declaring that most of his poetry was too suggestive for a girl her age, but Magny had bought her a copy the last time she went to Partha.

"What's wrong with poetry?" she asked defensively.

He shrugged. "Nothing. I like it."

"You?"

His gaze settled on her, a challenge in their blue-gray depths. "Why not me?"

"No reason, I just didn't think—"

"Didn't think what? That a barbarian like me could appreciate it?"

"Well, yes, something like that," she muttered, then felt her cheeks grow even hotter as he opened the book and began to read aloud.

> There are ways to feel love
> to touch
> and taste love
>
> I feel her
> with my soul
> I have tasted her kiss
> with a simple breath
> filling me
> moving across my heart
> she touches
> . . . so lightly
> sending waves of pleasure
> that pulse through my core
>
> she lifts my pain
> . . . with her gentle laugh

Amanda Ashley

a simple 'hello'
and my eyes fill with her sparkle

there are ways to feel love
. . . sharing a fear
holding a thought
. . . flowing in the softest silence
where only the soul hears

always with me is she . . .
thank you . . . my angel
for loving me. . . .

He looked at her over the edge of the book,
one dark brow raised, and then he turned the
page and began to read again.

His voice was low and husky, mesmerizing,
making her wonder what it would be like to
have him read those same words to her, and
mean them.

my whisper slips past
hiding desire
holding it fast

this need to have
this want
to feel
listen as you
move . . .
taste as you moan

I want you
please just once
let me know your passion

The Captive

take me into
your sweetest hold . . .

our whispers mix
with the night
let's dance
with pleasure
see if the love
covers as words
push inside
I love you
you know this is true . . .
so be with me
let
me
have you

Falkon swore under his breath as he closed
the book and tossed it back to her. If there was
one thing he didn't need, it was to waste his
time reading romantic poetry to remind him of
what he was missing, what he had lost.

Ashlynne caught the book, almost dropping
the controller as she did so. It occurred to her
that remaining in Number Four's presence was
the most dangerous thing she had ever done,
far more dangerous than going swimming at
midnight with Magny, or sneaking into the
mine compound. There had been a door
between them at the mine; nothing stood
between them here but a few feet of space.

It filled her with a sense of daring, being this
close to Number Four, even as she assured herself there was nothing to be afraid of as long as
she had the controller. Remembering how

quickly Number Four had turned on Dain, she hadn't put it down for a moment. It gave her a sense of power, rather like the feeling she had when she rode Artemis in a headlong gallop down the beach. The mare was bigger, stronger, faster, yet she controlled it.

Number Four's bold stare made her suddenly uncomfortable and she took a drink of water from the glass sitting on the rock beside her. Watching him over the rim of the glass, she saw him lick his lips and it occurred to her that he was probably thirsty. It was unseasonably warm, and he been working out in the hot sun since early that morning.

Slipping off the rock, she stood up and held the glass out toward him. "Would you like a drink?"

"No."

"You must be thirsty."

"I don't want anything from you or your people," he said brusquely. "Nothing except my freedom."

"You'll never be free again."

"And you'll never be anything but a spoiled, arrogant brat with too much time on her hands." He watched her cheeks grow red, felt himself tense in dreadful anticipation as her hand tightened on the controller. "Go ahead, do it," he challenged, and wondered what perverse devil had goaded him into saying such a thing.

Ashlynne's thumb hovered over the top of the controller, but the memory of the pain that Dain had inflicted on Number Four stayed her hand, though why she should care if this odious creature suffered was far beyond her comprehension. He was a slave, after all, an enemy to her people, to everything fine and decent. Surely he deserved whatever he got.

Nevertheless, that one moment of hesitation took the fire from her anger. With a wordless cry of annoyance at her own weakness, she flung the contents of the glass in his face.

He glared at her, water dripping from his nose and chin. Damn, in his own country, no one would dare treat him like this. He took a step forward, rage boiling up within him, only to halt in mid-stride as the sound of her laughter filled the air.

She was laughing at him! Had he been a free man, he might have laughed, too. But not now. There was no room in his life for laughter. There was no room for anything but soul-shattering hatred and bitter regret.

Turning on his heel, he stormed down the path.

He vowed not to speak to her again, not to look at her again. He would treat her as if she didn't exist.

And yet, somehow, she seemed to be everywhere.

If he was cleaning the stables, she was there, currying her pretty little chestnut mare.

If he was pulling weeds, she was at the other end of the garden, her nose stuck in a book.

If he was chopping wood, she was sitting at her easel, painting.

If he was exercising one of the horses in the corral, she was there, watching him through those wide green eyes.

And always, he was aware of the controller in her hand, of the absolute power of life and death it gave her over him, just as he was aware of the attraction that hummed between them whenever their eyes met. He wondered if she felt it, too, if she even knew what it was. *So be with me* . . . The words of that blasted poem seemed to echo in his head whenever he looked at her. *Let me have you.* Damn!

Today, he was mucking out the stalls. And she was currying her horse. The groom, Otry, was sleeping in one of the empty stalls. He was an old man who looked on Falkon's arrival as a godsend. Under other circumstances, Falkon would have liked the man.

In spite of all his good intentions, Falkon couldn't keep from watching the girl, couldn't help but notice the way her riding pants outlined her long slender legs and shapely thighs, couldn't ignore the swell of her firm young breasts, or the way her thick silver-blond braid swung back and forth as she brushed the mare's sleek chestnut coat.

He swore under his breath as he dumped a shovelful of manure into a barrel. It was just that she was a woman, he told himself, and he had been too long without a woman. It had nothing to do with the soft, slightly husky sound of her voice as she spoke to the mare, nothing to do with the faint flowery perfume that was noticeable even over the strong scent of manure and horseflesh that filled the air. He told himself that after months of enforced captivity and celibacy, he would have responded the same way to any woman, any humanoid female. Right now, even one of the green-skinned street walkers of Hodore would have looked good to him.

Seemingly unaware of his heated gaze, the girl tossed the currycomb aside and ran her hands over the mare's neck.

He watched each movement, each stroke of her pale slender hands, his imagination running wild as he imagined those slim fingers playing over his body, massaging his back, sliding seductively along his thigh. . . .

With a violent oath, he turned away, hating her, hating himself.

"You can put Artemis away now."

Her voice, feminine yet slightly husky, carried an inbred note of authority. Born to luxury, she was a young woman who was accustomed to giving orders and having them obeyed. Unfortunately, he was also accustomed to giving orders, not taking them. Months of slavery had taught him the futility of disobeying, but it had not made captivity any easier to bear. It was bad enough to take orders from the overseers and guards at the mine. He would not take them from her, as well.

Hands clenched, he turned around to face her.

She met his gaze squarely, then lifted one hand, offering him the mare's lead rope.

She frowned when he made no move to take it. "Well?"

"Well, what?"

"I'm through here, for now. You may put Artemis in her stall."

"May I?"

Ashlynne frowned. "Are you going to put my horse away, or not?"

Fighting the urge to grab the rope and wrap it around her pretty little neck, Falkon took a deep breath, then reached for the lead.

Ashlynne stared at Number Four's hand. His palm was calloused and smudged with dirt, his fingers were long and brown and strong, the nails broken and uneven. His fingertips brushed hers when he took the rope.

He saw her eyes widen in shock at his touch, and then she jerked her hand away. As if she had touched something incredibly vile.

Unreasoning anger roared through him. Without thinking, he took a menacing step toward her. The controller was in her hand in an instant, her thumb poised over the activation panel. One touch, and every muscle and nerve in his body would be screaming in agony.

Ashlynne tightened her hold on the controller, her heart pounding as he halted in midstride. His blue-gray eyes had darkened to the color of cold stone.

She drew herself up to her full height, irritated that she still had to look up to meet his gaze. "If you know what's good for you, Number Four, you will put my horse away."

"And if I don't?" He forced the words through clenched teeth.

She looked at him, obviously perplexed by his disobedience. "Why are you doing this?"

"Doing what?"

"Being so difficult."

"It's your horse. Why don't you put it away?"

"Because it's your job."

"Why? Because I'm a slave?"

She lifted her chin imperiously. "Yes."

"Go to hell."

"How dare speak to me like that! I demand that you do as I say."

"Say please, and I'll consider it."

Anger turned her eyes from sea green to deep emerald. "I will not!"

"Say it."

Her hand tightened on the controller. "Do as I say."

Falkon shook his head, his whole body tensing as he watched her. She was soft and spoiled but not easily intimidated. He had to know how far he could push her; needed to know if she had the guts to use that damnable weapon. Unfortunately, there was only one way to find out. Last time, she had let Dain unleash the controller's power. But Dain wasn't here now. It was just the two of them.

She took a deep breath. "I'm asking you for the last time."

"And I'm saying no, for the last time."

She hesitated, her expression uncertain, and Falkon took a step forward. If he could wrest the controller from her grasp, there was a chance, however slim, that he might be able to escape over the back wall. He was willing to risk whatever dangers the jungle might hold if it meant a chance at freedom.

His hands clenched. He'd never get a better opportunity, he thought, and made a grab for the controller.

Wild, unreasoning panic rose up within Ashlynne. Warnings went off inside her mind. He was the enemy. A mercenary. A man who had killed women and children without remorse.

Fear for her own life overrode every other thought as she jerked her hand back, and activated the control panel.

The controller's effect was immediate and irrevocable.

With a strangled cry, Number Four crumpled to the floor, his body turning and twisting, curling in on itself in an effort to escape the excruciating pain splintering through every nerve and cell of his being.

Transfixed, Ashlynne stared down at him. Horrified by what she had done, by the pain she had willingly inflicted, she lifted her finger from the control panel. But there was no stopping it once it had begun. Unable to watch any longer, she turned and ran out of the barn.

Gradually, his muscles relaxed. Badly shaken, his body still trembling, Falkon rose to his hands and knees. Head hanging, he gathered his strength, then lurched to his feet. He had underestimated her.

It was a mistake he wouldn't make a second time.

The following afternoon he was at work once again, trimming the branches from a tree near the side of the house. He could have used a ladder; instead, he had climbed the tree simply for the fun of it, something he hadn't done since he'd been a boy.

He climbed higher, and now he was on a level with the second story. Overcome with curiosity, he leaned forward and looked in the window, and knew immediately that it was Ashlynne's room. The walls were painted a soft pearlescent pink, the carpet, which seemed to be over an inch thick, was a deep mauve. There was a large round bed with a pink flowered spread and a matching canopy, a desk and chair, a shelf that held books and trinkets. The room was as pretty and feminine as the girl who lived there.

He drew back a little when the door opened and Ashlynne stepped inside. Closing the door, she sat on the edge of the bed and kicked off her shoes, peeled off her stockings. She fell back on the bed, lifted her arms, and stretched. Rising, she pulled her sweater over her head and tossed it on the bed.

Falkon felt his mouth go dry, thought he might fall out of the tree when she started to remove her skirt.

She turned abruptly, her eyes widening when she saw him staring at her. With a little shriek, she grabbed her sweater and yanked it over her head, then crossed the floor and opened the window.

"What are you doing? How dare you spy on me! When I tell my father, he'll—"

"I wouldn't tell your father if I were you."

"Well, you're not me! And I will tell him. And he'll have you flogged."

"No, you won't."

She lifted her chin defiantly. "I will."

He shook his head. "I wonder what Daddy would say if I was to tell him that his daughter and her friend were sneaking around the mine compound late one night."

She stared at him in horror. "You wouldn't!" she exclaimed, and then shrugged. "He wouldn't believe you anyway."

"No?"

"No," she replied firmly. But what if he did? She'd never be allowed to see Magny again if her father found out what they had done.

"I'll keep your secret," Falkon said, grinning impudently, "if you'll keep mine."

"Oh! You are the most . . . the most, oh, I don't have a word bad enough for what you are!"

"I could teach you one."

She glared at him. "I'll just bet you could!"

"In several languages," he said, laughing.

"Oh, you are the most incorrigible man I've ever met."

"But handsome," he said. "Don't forget handsome."

Embarrassment washed over Ashlynne as she realized he had heard them whispering about him outside the hut that night.

"Oh!" she exclaimed. "Why don't you go away!" And so saying, she reached out the window and gave him a shove.

She didn't push very hard, but it was hard enough to make him lose his balance. Muttering one of the words he had offered to teach her, he fell out of the tree. She felt her heart fall with him, blew out a sigh of relief when he landed on his feet.

Falkon looked up to find her leaning out over the windowsill. For a moment, he thought she looked concerned, but then she began to laugh.

Someday, he thought, glaring up at her. Someday . . .

Chapter Seven

Falkon prowled the confines of his room, as restless as any caged beast. He had come to hate this place as much as he had hated his cell in the mine, as he hated any place that walled him in. He yearned for his freedom, for news of the war on Taran Three. Had the Romarians overtaken the planet? And what of Daccar? Was his home still free, or had it fallen prey to the Romarian hordes?

He muttered a vicious oath. It seemed the leaders of Romariz wouldn't be content until they had enslaved the whole galaxy.

He stared at the wall in front of him; then, with a savage cry, he slammed his fist against it. His people were fighting for their lives and he was trapped here, forced to do menial work for the Tierdian royal family and their spoiled daughter. Their spoiled beautiful daughter.

Ashlynne, with hair the color of silver moonlight and eyes the color of a turbulent sea. Ashlynne, who had not hesitated to use that hellish controller.

In spite of his threat to reveal her midnight stroll, he had fully expected her to report his disobedience to her father. At best, he had expected to be whipped for his insolent behavior. At the worst, he had expected to be returned to the mine. Last night, he had paced his room, waiting for her father to appear to mete out his punishment. But none had been forthcoming, and he realized she hadn't said anything about what had occurred between them. He should have been grateful. Perversely, it only made him hate her the more. He had no desire to be in her debt.

He slammed his fist into the wall again, relishing the pain that exploded through his hand. How he hated her! How he would love to get his hands around her throat. How he would love to get his hands on her. . . . Thoughts of touching her drove the anger from his mind. What would it be like, to hold her in his arms, to taste those pouting pink lips just once?

He swore under his breath as visions of Ashlynne swam through his mind. He hadn't seen her for several days, but every night her image invaded his dreams, beckoning him, teasing him, smiling at him until he woke in a state of painful arousal, his heart pounding, his body bathed with perspiration.

He refused to acknowledge that he wanted her. It was merely that he needed a woman. Any woman. He didn't care if she had silver-blond hair, orange hair, or no hair at all. He didn't care if her lips were the pale pink of a wild rose or as black as the bowels of the mine, didn't care if her eyes were as green and clear as the depths of the ocean, or muddy brown and crossed. All he wanted was a female to ease his desire, a woman to sate his lust. Someone, anyone, who would drive the spoiled, pampered, damnably beautiful Lady Ashlynne from his mind and dreams.

He turned around as the door to his room slid open. Ashlynne's father stood there attired in a white silkspun shirt, a pair of gray woolen slacks, and a pair of calf-high leather boots polished to such a high shine Falkon could see his reflection in them.

"We are hosting a small dinner party tomorrow night," Marcus said. "I want the grounds to be in perfect order by then."

Falkon nodded.

"My wife has purchased several new flowering shrubs and trees to replace those lost in the last storm. They will need to be planted."

Again, Falkon nodded.

Marcus frowned, annoyed by the slave's mute insolence. "You will start first thing in the morning." Without waiting for an answer, he pivoted with military precision and left the room.

Falkon stared at the closed door; then, with a wordless cry of rage, he slammed his fists against the portal.

* * *

He was at work early the following day. Keeping his mind carefully blank, he planted the trees and shrubs the lady of the house had purchased, then pruned the hedges and trimmed the foliage.

To his dismay, Ashlynne was in residence in the garden, her nose buried in a book, the controller close at hand. He took one look at her and went to work in another part of the yard.

He spent all that day toiling in the vast yard and gardens, his mind carefully blank as he raked the leaves.

Late in the afternoon, his back weary, his body covered with perspiration, he paused to rest by the small man-made pond near the west wall. He was given water for washing each night; once a week he was permitted to take a bath in a small round tub barely large enough to hold him.

He stared into the deep blue pool for several moments and then, unable to resist its lure, he shucked his clothes and dived into the pond.

The water was cool, but not cold and he swam from one end of the pond to the other, reveling in the illusion of freedom it gave him. He swam for several minutes, then floated on his back, basking in the touch of the sun on his face and chest. He had hated being forced to labor down in the mine, hated never seeing the sun, never feeling its warmth on his skin. His people were a wild, untamed race who lived most of their lives outdoors.

Eyes closed, buoyed up in the arms of the water, he lost track of time and place, until a gasp of startled surprise brought him tumbling back to the present.

Treading water, he turned toward the sound, grimacing when he saw Ashlynne standing near the edge of the lake.

"What do you want?" he asked curtly.

"My privacy, if you don't mind."

He lifted one brow. "I'd like a little privacy myself if *you* don't mind."

"Who gave you permission to swim here?"

Falkon hesitated, wondering if a lie would serve him better than the truth, and then he shrugged. "No one. Have I broken another rule?"

She looked momentarily taken aback. "I don't know," she admitted, and then lifted her chin. "Probably. Yes, I'm sure my father would object if he knew a creature as vile as you was polluting our pond."

He scowled at her, annoyed.

"Well?" She tapped one sandal-shod foot impatiently. "I'm waiting."

"I'm not ready to get out yet."

"I don't care!" she exclaimed. "This is my pond and I wish to swim."

"Go swim in the pool." His gaze met hers, and he smiled a wicked smile. "Or you could join me in here."

Why did he bait her, he wondered? What perverse demon made him taunt her? She had only to report his insolence, and he would be severely punished. Just because she hadn't said anything the last time didn't mean she would be so forgiving this time.

Ashlynne glanced at his clothing, piled in a

heap on the ground. For one maddening moment, she wondered what would happen if she shed her robe and bathing suit and joined him. Magny wouldn't hesitate . . .

She thrust the thought aside before it was fully formed. For all that he was quite a handsome man, he was a murderer, an enemy to her people and to decent people everywhere.

"Get out of my pond," she demanded.

"Go back to the house."

"I will not! I have every right to be here."

"Whatever you say," he replied impudently.

Her eyes widened as he began to swim toward the shore. Her first thought was to flee for the safety of the house. Oh, wouldn't he love to see that, she mused angrily. How he would laugh! Determined that he would not think her afraid of him, she stood her ground, her heart beating wildly as he drew ever closer.

When his feet touched bottom, he stood up and began walking toward her. Drops of water trickled down his shoulders, his chest. Sunlight glistened on his blue-black hair, caressed his skin as he emerged from the water, rising from the quiet blue lake like some mythical water god. She couldn't help staring at his broad shoulders and chest.

She looked up at him, panic in her eyes, as the water covered less and less of him. When it barely reached his waist, he stopped.

"Are you sure you don't want to go back to the house?"

Her heart was pounding so loudly she was certain it could be heard in the bowels of the mine. She slid one hand into the pocket of her robe. The feel of the controller beneath her hand bolstered her courage. "Quite sure."

He took another step. And then another. And she knew she couldn't stay, knew she didn't have the nerve to stand there while he emerged from the water's concealing depths, naked as the day he had emerged from his mother's womb.

Angered by her own cowardice, hating him for refusing to treat her with the respect that was her due, she grabbed his clothing, then turned and ran for the safety of the house.

Falkon stared after her in disbelief, unable to believe she had done such a childish, spiteful thing.

Stepping out of the water, he stared through the foliage. He was sorely tempted to give chase. He had no doubt he could catch her. And it was that knowledge that kept him from going after her. Catching her would be like grabbing the proverbial tiger by the tail, with much the same results.

He gave her plenty of time to reach the safety of the house before he made his way to his room.

He found his clothes at the edge of the path that wound around to the back of the house. Slipping into his trousers, he picked up his shirt and boots, then continued on, grateful that he hadn't met anyone on the way.

As he did every evening, he turned and glanced at the wall that surrounded the grounds before he entered his room, a silent battle raging within him. He could scale the wall easily enough, perhaps lose himself in the thick jungle beyond before he was missed. He lifted a hand to the collar at his throat. There was no hope of escape, not as long as he wore the collar. Sooner or later, they would track him down. He had seen what happened to two men who had tried to escape. Their remains had been carried back to the mine, hung from a pole for all to see.

With a sigh, he opened the rear door of the house and made his way down the narrow corridor that led to his room, his prison.

As soon as he stepped inside, the door slid closed, automatically locking behind him, effectively sealing him inside for the night. A pitcher of hot water and a bowl awaited him. Stripping off his pants, he washed his hands and feet and face, then donned the clean shirt and breeches that had been provided. A short time later, a panel in the wall slid back. He took the tray that held his evening meal, then placed his soiled clothes and the pitcher and bowl on the retractable shelf. A moment later, the panel closed.

Muttering an oath, Falkon placed the tray on the small table beside his bed. The night stretched ahead of him, long hours with nothing to occupy his hands or his thoughts.

He ate to ease his hunger, hardly tasting the food, which was far better than he was accustomed to, and certainly better than the hard bread, bitter black tea, and lumpy gruel made from triticale and Horth grubs that passed for food in the mine. The grubs, found in the roots of the trees and plants on Tierde, were a cheap source of protein and carbohydrates. The taste was similar to the mushrooms found on Daccar and reminded him of home.

Tonight, instead of bringing him pleasure, the bounty spread before him only fueled his anger.

Setting the plate aside, he stretched out on the narrow bed and closed his eyes. But sleep wouldn't come. Rising, he began to pace the floor.

He jerked upright, startled when the door to his room slid open. In all the weeks he had been here, no one had come to his room once he had been locked in for the night.

"Number Four," Marcus said without preamble, "one of the servers has taken ill. You are to take his place. Report to the kitchen immediately. Meggie will tell you what do to."

Marcus regarded him a moment. "We have guests. I will tolerate no insolence, is that understood?"

Falkon nodded curtly.

"You will not speak, nor draw attention to yourself. If you cause me any embarrassment, I shall have the skin flayed from your back, and then you will be sent back to the mine. Do you understand?"

Again, Falkon nodded.

"Do you understand?"

"Yes, sir," Falkon answered tightly. "I understand perfectly."

"Very well. Follow me."

Meggie, the cook, was as round as she was tall, with a knot of gray hair, bright blue eyes, and a voice that brooked no nonsense. She looked Falkon up and down, scowled as she muttered something derogatory about his obvious lack of experience. She quickly explained his duties, then thrust a pile of clothing into his hands and sent him into the pantry to change.

Falkon emerged five minutes later attired in a form-fitting pair of dark blue pants and a collarless dark blue shirt. He took the large silver tray Meggie handed to him and carried it into the dining room.

He couldn't help staring as he entered the room. It was unlike anything he had ever seen. An enormous cut crystal chandelier hung from the vaulted ceiling. A profusion of artfully arranged tree-plants and ferns decorated one corner of the room, effectively screening the three musicians who began to play as the food was served. Heavily flocked gold-and-green paper covered the walls. Gauzelike curtains were drawn back from the window, affording a view of the lamplit gardens beyond.

Sixty men and women attired in costly raiment sat at two long black teak tables. None of them paid him or the other two servers the slightest bit of attention, except to snap their fingers when they wanted something.

None of them except Ashlynne. She was seated to the right of her father. Clad in a diaphanous gown of shimmering silver trimmed with star pearls, her hair artfully arranged in a mass of soft waves that fell to her waist, she took one look at him and hid a laugh behind her napkin, her eyes twinkling with amusement.

Humiliation burned through him. It was bad enough to labor in the gardens. Acting as servant to dozens of wealthy Tierdians was much worse. She summoned him to her side again and again. She bid him bring her a clean fork when she carelessly dropped hers on the floor, indicated he should refill her water glass, bring her more bread. And always he knew she was laughing at him. He fought the urge to refuse, knowing that to do so would accomplish nothing but a return to the mine, but in that moment he hated her. He had seen her kind from one end of the galaxy to the other— spoiled, selfish women who ate food they had not grown, wore expensive gowns they had not worked to buy, who lived in luxury, not caring that the ease of their lifestyle was purchased with the blood and sweat and humiliation of others.

He couldn't believe the number of courses that came from the kitchen, one after the other. He had never seen such an abundance of food and drink. While the guests ate, he was expected to stand at attention just behind Marcus's right shoulder in case one of the guests should want something—more wine, another canapé, a clean napkin.

Dinner lasted well over two hours. From the conversation he overheard, Falkon gathered that the guests were all high-ranking visitors from the Confederation planets of Swernolt and Andoria, as well as the neutral planets of Polixe and Cherlin Four. They had all gathered to celebrate the renewal of the peace treaty between Tierde and Romariz.

There were no representatives from Daccar, but that was to be expected. Daccar was not neutral, but unlike Riga Twelve, Ohnmahr, Inner Ohnmahr, and Cenia, it was still free of Romarian rule.

One of the guests rose and lifted his glass. "To peace!"

The words "to peace" were repeated around the table.

Ashlynne's father stood up, smiling. "I am pleased that we were able to come to terms with the Romarians so that we may continue to enjoy the peace we have enjoyed for the past twelve years. As some of you may know, there are those who believe we should allow Cenian ships access to our mine, now that they have agreed to withdraw their troops from Swernolt. My future son-in-law feels strongly that Cenia should be admitted to the Confederation, and has said so on numerous occasions. However, I am opposed to such a plan, and have said as much to the Romarian ambassador, as well as the Trellan ambassador. I do not believe the Cenians are interested in peace, or that they can be trusted."

"We are with you, Lord Marcus. The Cenians are a barbaric race, worse than the Hodorians. Their treachery is well known."

Murmurs of approval went around the table.

"The Romarian ambassador was not pleased," Marcus said, "but he has agreed not to interfere with our decision, at least for the time being."

The ambassador from Andoria stood up. "I was told the Cenians offered a rather substantial number of credits for the right to land here and fuel their ships."

"Yes, Ambassador Timoran, that's true," Marcus said, "but . . ."

Jadeleine tugged on her husband's sleeve. "Marcus, let us find a subject more pleasant, shall we?"

"Gentlemen, we will speak of this at a later time," Marcus said, and with a wry grin, he resumed his seat.

"My apologies, Lady Jadeleine." The Andorian ambassador bowed in her direction before he, too, resumed his seat.

When the last course was served, the guests retired to the ballroom to dance. Falkon had expected to be ordered back to his room; instead, Marcus informed him that he was needed to help serve drinks.

Though the dining room was opulent, the ballroom put it to shame. The ceiling was made of glass so that the guests had the illusion of dancing outside under Tierde's twin moons. The white marble floor, polished to a high sheen, reflected the glow of the stars. The walls were painted with scenic murals, interspersed with floor-to-ceiling mirrors. A small waterfall splashed playfully in one corner of the room. Long benches covered with plush red velvet cushions lined the walls; matching sofas and chairs were placed at regular intervals around the perimeter.

Falkon stood at attention near the entry, his gaze following Ashlynne as she twirled around the floor in the arms of one dashing young man after another. Her silver gown caught the light of the candles, reflecting all the colors of the rainbow. Eyes sparkling, cheeks flushed with pleasure, she put every other woman present to shame.

He watched, trying not to be jealous as a tall, blond young man claimed her for the next dance. It was an old-fashioned waltz. He tried not to imagine what it would be like take her in his arms, to gaze down into her eyes, to twirl her around the dance floor until she was laughing and breathless.

Muttering an oath, he turned away. It was none of his business what she did, or whom she did it with.

At Marcus's order, he went into the kitchen for more crushed ice. When he returned to the ballroom, there was no sign of Ashlynne or the young man.

Surreptitiously, he moved toward the doorway that led out to the balcony. In the light of the twin moons, he could see two figures standing face-to-face at the far end of the balcony. He scowled as the distance between the two decreased. The man placed his hands on Ashlynne's shoulders, bent his head, and captured Ashlynne's lips.

Falkon clenched his hands, fighting the urge to lay into the man who dared take such liberties with Ashlynne. He told himself he didn't care, that it wasn't his place to interfere. If she wanted to steal a kiss in the moonlight with some baby-faced boy, it was none of his business.

Falkon was about to turn away when he heard the sound of a scuffle. Looking back, he saw Ashlynne trying to twist out of the young man's arms, heard her muffled cry when he refused to release her.

Taking a deep breath, Falkon stepped out onto the balcony. "Lady Ashlynne, your father is looking for you."

The young man immediately released Ashlynne and put some distance between them.

"Thank you, Number Four," Ashlynne said.

Falkon walked toward them, his gaze fixed on the young man, who took one look at his face and disappeared around the corner.

When the man was out of sight, Falkon ran his gaze over Ashlynne. Her cheeks were flushed, his lips slightly swollen. "Are you all right?"

"Yes, of course."

She was close, so close. He took a deep breath, inhaling the scent of her perfume. His gaze moved to her lips. What would she do if he pulled her into his embrace and kissed her? Would she scream for help, or melt into his arms?

As though reading his mind, she looked away. "I'd better go see what my father wants."

"He doesn't want anything."

"What do you mean?"

"You looked like you needed some help."

She glared at him, eyes flashing. "I'll thank you to stay out of my personal life."

"Whatever you say, princess," he retorted.

"Oh, you are the most vile man!" she exclaimed, and lifting her skirts, she hurried back into the ballroom.

Falkon swore softly, then turned on his heel and returned to his post.

She sought him out late the following morning.

"Number Four?"

He looked up from the leaves he had been raking. She looked lovely, as always. Today, she wore a dark blue dress with a very short skirt and white knee-high leather boots. Her hair was gathered at her nape and held with a bright red ribbon. She looked very young and very innocent, and far too tempting for his peace of mind.

"I wanted to thank you," Ashlynne said, keeping her tone carefully polite. "For what you did last night." She tried not to stare at him, and failed. His skin was damp with perspiration, a lock of thick black hair fell over his forehead. She had dreamed of him last night, dreamed of those muscular arms holding her tight. The memory brought a flush to her cheeks.

Falkon shrugged. It annoyed him that he had gone to her rescue, but what was even more annoying was the surge of jealousy that had engulfed him when he saw her in another man's arms.

"Vache is a nice young man," she said. "He'd just had a little too much spring wine." He'd frightened her, with his hot, eager hands and hurtful kisses, but she wouldn't, couldn't, admit that.

Falkon grunted. "You don't owe me any thanks, or any explanations," he muttered.

"Maybe not, but I'm grateful just the same. And I'm also grateful that you never told my father about . . . about the night Magny and I were at the mine."

"Princess, I've got a lot more on my mind than how you spend your nights." Which was the truth, and a lie. He spent far too much time thinking about her, picturing her curled up on a nice soft mattress, with her hair falling around her face like a silver halo. "You never told your father about what happened in the barn, either, did you?"

"No, I didn't."

He nodded curtly. "So, now that we're all squared away, why don't you just run along and leave me to my work?"

"Why must you be so rude?"

"Why must you be such a pest? Go on, get out of here."

"You'll be rid of me soon enough."

"Oh?"

"I'm going away next week."

"Good. Maybe I'll be able to work in peace."

"Maybe you will," she replied sulkily. With a sniff, she turned and flounced away, wondering why he was always so mean and hurtful.

Falkon stared after her, felt a sudden, inexplicable sense of loss at the thought of not seeing her every day. In spite of his words to the contrary, he enjoyed her company. He looked forward to seeing her every day. Hell, he even enjoyed their verbal sparring matches. She was the only bright spot in his dismal life and now it seemed he was going to lose that, too.

Chapter Eight

"So," Magny said. "Where is he?"

"Who?"

"You know, Number Four."

"I think he's down at the stable."

"Well," Magny said, bounding out of her chair. "What are we sitting in here for?"

Ashlynne rolled her eyes. "Really, Mag, who did you come here to see, me or him?"

"Well . . ." Magny scrunched up her face as if she was giving it some serious thought, and then laughed. "You, of course. After all, you're leaving next week."

"Don't remind me."

"You may as well make the best of it," Magny said.

"I don't want to make the best of it!"

111

"I know, Lynnie. I'm sorry." Magny blew out an exaggerated sigh, her hands clasped over her heart. "It's so difficult being a woman."

Ashlynne burst out laughing, amused, as always, by Magny's theatrics. "What would I do without you?"

"I can't imagine."

"Me, either."

"Good. Now, can we go look for Number Four?"

They found him in the corral, exercising a new stallion Ashlynne's father had purchased from a breeder on Earth. It was her father's intention to breed Artemis and the stallion. It was a beautiful horse, seventeen hands high, with a sleek coat the color of burnished copper and the long clean lines of a Thoroughbred. But Ashlynne had eyes only for Number Four. As usual, he wasn't wearing his shirt, just a pair of indecently snug breeches, and a pair of scuffed boots. The sun seemed to caress his flesh, leaving a fine sheen of perspiration behind.

"Oh," Magny murmured. "Isn't he beautiful?"

"You mean the horse, of course," Ashlynne said dryly.

Magny elbowed her in the ribs. "Of course. But you must admit, the man is beautiful, too."

He was, but Ashlynne wouldn't have admitted it for anything in the world. The horse was still a little wild, and when Number Four urged the stallion into a lope, the horse began to buck.

They made quite a pair, she thought, the wild horse and the wilder man. Number Four stuck to the horse's back like a burr from a sticker bush, apparently anticipating every move the animal was going to make.

After several minutes of intense bucking, the stallion gave up the fight. With a toss of its head, it settled down and loped around the corral. It was a beautiful sight, she mused, the stallion moving with liquid grace, its stride long and smooth, its mane and tail flowing in the breeze. But it was the man who took her breath away. It was easy to see that he loved riding, that it gave him the same sense of freedom and exhilaration it gave her. He rode easily, his body moving in perfect rhythm with the stallion's. She hadn't felt like painting in weeks, but she would paint Number Four, she thought with growing excitement, paint him as he looked now, with his body sheened with perspiration and his long black hair flying wild. She tilted her head to one side, remembering a book of paintings in her father's library. One of them was a photograph of an Indian warrior from Old Earth. That was what Number Four reminded her of, a wild savage. And that was how she would paint him, she thought—bare-chested, with feathers in his hair and his face streaked with war paint.

Falkon reined the stallion to a walk, conscious of the two girls standing at the corral fence, their arms folded over the top rail. He spared hardly a glance for the dark-haired girl. Parah's daughter. She was a pretty thing, a constant reminder to the slaves in the mine of all they had lost. He had heard the other men whispering about her down in the mine from time to time, spinning wild fantasies of what they would do to her if they ever caught her alone. He hoped, for her sake, they never did.

But it was the silver-haired girl who drew his gaze. They were like day and night, he mused, and he preferred the heat of the sun to the cool of the night. It was the fair Lady Ashlynne who filled his every waking thought, the memory of her hands on his skin that kept him tossing and turning in his bed at night.

He reined the stallion to a halt in front of her, a challenge in his eyes. "Care to try him?"

"Of course," she replied.

"Lynnie, do you think you should?" Magny shared Jadeleine's fear and mistrust of horses.

"Oh, Mag, don't be silly." Ashlynne handed the controller to Magny and slipped through the rails.

Falkon dismounted, holding the stallion's reins while Ashlynne stepped into the saddle and settled her skirts around her.

She looked down at him, her insides all aflutter at his nearness. She clenched her hands to keep from reaching for him, tempted to run her fingers over his chest, to brush a lock of hair from his brow.

"Adjust the stirrups, Number Four," she ordered. "They're too long."

He regarded her insolently for a moment, then did as she asked.

When he was finished, she held out her hand and he passed her the reins. His fingers brushed hers, sending frissons of heat dancing over her skin.

"He's a little skittish," Falkon remarked, "and a little hard-mouthed."

"I don't need you to tell me that," she retorted, her voice frosty.

Falkon gave the horse a gentle slap on the rump. "Well, don't say I didn't warn you."

He rested one shoulder against the corral as she clucked to the stallion. With a shake of its head, the horse broke into a trot.

Falkon watched her, wondering if he should have let her ride. She looked incredibly tiny on the back of the stallion, yet he had to admit she looked very much at ease in the saddle as she put the big stud through its paces. She was, he thought, a natural-born horsewoman.

Ashlynne reined the horse to a halt in front of Magny. "Are you sure you don't want to try him?"

Magny shook her head. "Not me."

"Mag, it would be such fun if we could go riding together. You could ride the old nag my father bought for my mother. He's too old and lazy to do anything but walk."

Magny shook her head again. "No. I like having my feet on the ground, thank you very much."

With a sigh of exasperation, Ashlynne wheeled the stallion around and touched her heels to its flanks. Just then, old Otry came out of the barn, shaking the dust out of one of the horse blankets.

The sudden flapping noise, combined with the waving blanket, spooked the stallion and it raced toward the opposite side of the corral, bucking wildly all the way.

Falkon swore under his breath as the stallion made a quick turn; he felt his heart plummet as

Ashlynne toppled over the horse's rump. The stallion fled to the far side of the corral, head high, eyes wild.

"Lynnie!" Magny ducked through the rails, only to be pulled up short by Falkon.

"Stay here," he said brusquely. "Otry! Get that damn blanket out of here!" He was running toward Ashlynne as he spoke, his heart pounding with fear as he knelt beside her. Damn!

She was lying facedown, unmoving, her eyes closed. His hands were trembling as he ran them over her arms, down her legs. Nothing seemed to be broken. He tunneled his fingers through the heavy mass of her hair, marveling at its softness as he checked her head for swelling.

He was wondering if he should try to turn her over when her eyelids fluttered open.

Ashlynne blinked and blinked again, felt her cheeks grow hot as she realized what had happened. She had been thrown. And he had seen it.

She started to get up, but Number Four placed a hand on her shoulder, holding her down. "Are you all right? Do you hurt anywhere?"

"Of course I'm all right." She pushed his hand away and sat up, her heart pounding at his nearness.

"Here now! What the hell is going on?"

Falkon glanced over his shoulder, swore under his breath when he saw Ashlynne's father striding toward them, his face contorted with rage.

"She was thrown, Mr. Myrafloures," Magny explained quickly.

The anger on Marcus's face turned to concern as he entered the corral and ran toward his daughter. "Ashlynne!"

"I'm fine, Father." She held out her hands and her father lifted her to her feet.

"Are you sure you're not hurt?" he asked anxiously.

"It was all my fault, Lord Marcus." Otry shuffled into the corral, his rheumy old eyes filled with fear as he faced his employer.

"It's all right, Otry," Ashlynne said, brushing the dirt from her clothes.

"What happened, Otry?" Marcus asked.

"Father, it wasn't his fault at all. I should have been paying more attention." And she would have been, if she hadn't been showing off for Number Four. "I'm fine, really." She looked up at her father and smiled. "Nothing badly bruised but my ego."

Marcus frowned at her, and then laughed. "Come along, let's go up to the house." He brushed a bit of dirt from her cheek. "You'll want to clean up before dinner. And for goodness sake, don't say anything about this to your mother."

With a nod, Ashlynne slipped her arm around her father's waist and they left the corral.

Magny fell into step beside them. "See, Lynnie?" she said. "See why I don't ride? You could have been killed."

"Don't be silly, Mag. That's not the first time I've fallen off a horse, and it probably won't be the last."

Marcus looked at Magny and grinned. "We'll get you on a horse one of these days," he predicted. "Just wait and see."

Ashlynne fought the urge to glance over her shoulder. She could feel Number Four watching her. Warmth flooded her cheeks as she recalled the touch of his hands skimming over her arms and legs, the touch of his fingers moving ever so gently in her hair.

Maybe it was a good thing that she was going to Trellis next week, she mused, before she did something really stupid, like throw herself into his arms. She had a feeling Number Four was far more dangerous to her health, and her peace of mind, than a stallion that was still half-wild.

Chapter Nine

"You want me to do what?" Falkon stared at Ashlynne, unable to believe what he was hearing.

"I want you to pick me a bouquet of flowers and ferns."

"I don't have time for that. Pick them yourself."

"Do as I say, Number Four, or I shall report your insolence to my father, and you'll find yourself back in the mine." It was an empty threat, and they both knew it.

"Don't you have anything better to do than torment me?"

"No." She looked up at him through wide green eyes. "Life was really quite dull here until you came along."

Falkon glared at her. He had the feeling she

was laughing at him, that she was, indeed, telling the truth, and that he had become her greatest source of amusement.

"A large bouquet." She picked up a blade of grass and twirled it between her thumb and forefinger. " 'Twill look lovely on the table at dinner."

Muttering an oath, Falkon tossed his shovel aside and stalked toward the vast flower beds that grew along the south wall. Flowers!

He made his way along the narrow brick-lined paths that wound through the flower beds, randomly plucking the blooms that caught his eye. He had to admit that whoever had arranged and planted the gardens had an eye for color and design. He'd never seen anything quite so pretty. He had never had much time to notice such things, and didn't know what most of the flowers were called, but they were beautiful, bright reds and blues and pinks and yellows. Butterflies large and small and in bright rainbow colors flitted from bush to bush. Sparrows sang in the treetops, and he felt his anger dissipate as he continued on. The sky was blue and clear, the sun was warm, the air was filled with the sweet fragrance of the flowers, of earth and grass.

"You're not supposed to pick them all."

He turned around, surprised to find the girl trailing after him, a smirk on her face.

"You said you wanted a large bouquet." He thrust the flowers he had gathered into her hands. "Damn, girl, you're harder to get rid of than a case of the plague," he muttered irritably.

"Admit it," she said. "You were having a good time."

"Don't be ridiculous."

"I saw the look on your face. I'll bet it's the first time you ever picked a flower in your whole life."

"You're imagining things."

"Why are you so stubborn?"

"Why are you following me?"

She shrugged. "Nothing else to do."

He took a deep breath and blew it out slowly. "How long did you say you were going to be gone?"

"I didn't say, but if you must know, I'll probably be gone the whole summer. I guess that makes you happy, doesn't it?"

Falkon nodded, but it was a lie. He was going to miss her when she was gone, he thought. Her every move seemed to tempt him. Her mere presence was a constant reminder that it had been far too long since he'd had a woman. Woman, he thought. She was hardly that. She was young, far too young and far too innocent for the likes of him, yet even now he felt his body hardening, reacting to her nearness.

He clenched his hands in an effort to keep from reaching for her. She'd kept quiet about his spying on her in her room, but he doubted even his threat to tell her father about her sneaking down to the mine would be enough to guarantee her silence if he kissed her. But he wanted to, by the stars, he wanted to, even though he knew it would be the biggest mistake he had ever made.

She looked up at him and licked her lips. In

any other female, it would have been a blatant invitation, but Ashlynne wasn't experienced enough to play games. He could teach her, he thought, teach her how good it could be.

"Damn!" All thoughts of her delectable body fled his mind as he heard a low rumble.

"What's that?"

Falkon lifted his head, listening. The noise came again, louder and closer this time.

He frowned. It sounded like sky cannon.

He glanced over his shoulder, swore under his breath when he saw a cloud of thick black smoke rising from the direction of the mine. A moment later, he felt the ground beneath his feet shudder. There was an explosion, and a hole big enough to ride a horse through appeared in the far wall.

"What's happening?" Ashlynne asked.

"We're under attack!"

She shook her head. "No, that can't be."

He heard the low whine of incoming sky cannon. Grabbing Ashlynne by the arm, he began running toward the opposite end of the yard, dragging the girl behind him. The flowers tumbled from her hands, leaving a colorful trail in their wake.

They were nearing the edge of the gardens when there was a violent explosion. Ashlynne screamed as the house exploded in flames.

"Let me go!" she shrieked. She tried to wrest her arm from Number Four's grasp, but he held her tightly.

"You fool! What do you think you can do?"

"My parents are in there!"

"Then they're dead." His words were harsh,

deliberately cruel. "Come on," he said, tugging on her arm. "We're getting out of here."

"I'm not leaving them!" she shrieked. "You can't make me! Let me go!"

"Like hell."

She glared at him, her eyes glittering like chips of cold green glass as she pointed the controller at his chest. "Let me go."

He hesitated for the space of a heartbeat, wondering if he could snatch it from her hand before she could activate it.

"Let me go!"

Her thumb moved to the top of the controller, and he dropped her arm.

As soon as he released her, she ran toward the blazing inferno that had once been her home.

Muttering an oath, Falkon turned away. If she wanted to commit suicide, that was her business, but he was getting the hell out of there while the getting was good. Everyone else would be too busy looking after their own skins to come looking for one prisoner. With any luck, they would think he had died when the house exploded.

He continued down the path that led to the damaged section of garden wall and crawled through the opening. Standing there, he could see the mine below. A battle cruiser hovered over the mine, the black-and-gold shield of Hodore plainly visible on the ship's underbelly. Several small hovercraft lined the beach. Hodore. There was no reason for them to attack the mine, he thought, frowning. They were already getting their fair share of crystals.

Hatred flooded his soul as he stared at the black-helmeted men swarming over the mine. The familiar stench of cannon smoke and seared flesh reached his nostrils, sickening him. For a moment, his mind went back in time and he saw it all again—the ruins that had once been his home, the charred remains of his daughter's favorite doll. . . .

His eyes narrowed as he glanced at the battle cruiser, then at the figures moving around near the mine's administration building. Had Drade persuaded Hodore to attack Tierde? Was he down there, even now, strutting back and forth while he decided who lived and who died? Drade . . .

Falkon's hands clenched and unclenched as he imagined his hands at Drade's throat, squeezing, squeezing. . . .

A high-pitched scream scattered his thoughts. Turning, he peered back through the hole in the wall and saw Ashlynne running across the yard, her skirts billowing behind her. Taking a step forward, he saw two men garbed in the black-and-gold uniforms of Hodore pursuing her.

Rage rose up within Falkon, hot and swift and impossible to ignore. Adrenaline pumping, he stepped through the break in the wall and gave chase.

Ashlynne screamed as she felt a hand close on her arm. A moment later, she was jerked to a halt, then shoved to the ground. Before she could so much as blink, the man was straddling her hips, one of his hands imprisoning both of hers.

She stared past him to the second man, her eyes widening as he began to unfasten his pants.

"No!" She screamed the word. "No! No!"

The man holding her down slapped her across the face, hard, effectively silencing her.

Cheek throbbing, she stared at the man straddling her hips. She had never seen a Hodorian. The skin of his hand was a pale green covered with fine green hair. He was dressed in the uniform of the Hodorian army. A black-visored helmet covered his head. It was a nightmare. It had to be. She closed her eyes. This couldn't be happening. She was Ashlynne, daughter of the ruling house of Tierde. No one had ever laid a hand on her in anger or violence.

She opened her eyes as the man lifted her skirts. She stared at him in horror. They were going to rape her.

It had to be a nightmare. That was all, just a nightmare. She rocked her head back and forth, praying that she would awake before it was too late.

"No!" She screamed as she felt the man's callused hand on her thigh. Her nails raked his neck, his arms, as she struggled to free herself from his grasp. "Let me go!"

She was sobbing now. Tears of anger and fear and revulsion clogged her throat. And then, out of the corner of her eye, she saw Number Four. He was creeping up behind the two men like a spring-cat, his footsteps muffled by the thick grass, his blue-gray eyes narrowed to angry slits. He carried a thick tree branch in his hands.

Was he coming to help her?

She renewed her struggles, kicking and screaming with all her might. She felt a sense of exhilaration as her knee caught one of the men full in the groin. He dropped to the ground, gasping for air.

And then Number Four was there. The branch in his hands came down hard across the back of the man straddling her hips. With a grunt, the Hodorian rolled off her.

Ashlynne scrambled to her knees, screamed "look out!" as she saw the second Hodorian reach for his blaster.

Number Four pivoted on his heel and swung the branch at the man's head. There was a loud *smack* as the wood hit the man's helmet, knocking him over backward.

Falkon was reaching for the man's weapon when he felt the searing heat of a laser blast scorch his right arm near the shoulder.

The man's second shot went wide.

Muttering an oath, Falkon grabbed Ashlynne by the arm and sprinted for cover behind a huge flowering vine. "No, this way!" Ashlynne cried, tugging on his hand. "Hurry!"

He followed her through a maze of greenery, stood panting for breath while she searched for the hidden panel that opened a door in the wall.

"Where does this come out?" Falkon asked as he followed her through the opening into a dark tunnel.

"I'm not sure, exactly. All I know is that it comes out in the jungle somewhere. My father . . . my father told my . . . my mother and me that we should use it if we were ever attacked." She closed the door, plunging them into total darkness. "I've never been in here before."

"Give me your hand."

"Why?" He heard the suspicion in her voice.

"So we don't get separated. You want to go first, or should I?"

"You," she said. She felt his hand slide over her shoulder, down her arm, then close around her hand.

She followed behind him, her free hand wrapped firmly around the controller in her skirt pocket.

Step by careful step, she followed him blindly through the tunnel. She tried not to think of what might be living in the tunnel, but visions of spiders burrowing into her hair and snakes crawling up her legs flooded her mind.

She breathed a sigh of relief when a faint gray light appeared at the end of the passageway.

Minutes later, Number Four came to a stop.

Ashlynne peered around him. The tunnel opening was camouflaged behind a twisted mass of snowberry bushes. Beyond them stretched miles and miles of uncharted jungle.

"Do you see anyone?" she whispered.

"No. Apparently they concentrated their attack on the house and the mine." He swore under his breath, cursing himself for having mentioned the house.

A small sob rose in the girl's throat. Her parents were dead; her home had been destroyed. He knew how she felt, and a brief, unwanted flicker of compassion swept through him.

"What are we going to do now?" she asked, her voice quivering.

"I think we should spend the night in here."

"In here?" She glanced over her shoulder, unable to stifle a shudder of revulsion.

"You got any better ideas?" he asked curtly.

Ashlynne shook her head, hating him because he was alive and her parents were dead. She peered through the bushes. The sky was turning dark. It would be night soon.

"I'm going to try to get some sleep," Falkon said.

Turning away from the opening, he walked back a few feet from the entrance and sat down, his back to the wall of the tunnel. He winced as he explored the laser wound on his arm. The numbness was wearing away and now it throbbed relentlessly. But he could live with the pain. Better that than losing his arm entirely.

He looked up at the girl, who was still standing near the tunnel's opening. "You'd better get some rest while you can," he suggested wearily.

Ashlynne shook her head. "Surely you don't expect me to sleep on the ground?" She looked at him as if he had just asked her to eat a slab of raw meat.

Falkon lifted one inquisitive brow. "Why not?"

"Because . . . because I can't. It's dirty."

Falkon snorted. "Suit yourself."

Slowly, she pulled her hand from her pocket, revealing the controller.

"What are you going to do with that?" he asked suspiciously.

"Secure your hands and feet, of course."

He glared at her as she activated the controls. The manacles on his wrists and ankles made a dull clanking sound as they locked together. He swore as the movement sent a fresh wave of pain through his arm.

"I'm sorry," she murmured.

"Are you?"

"Sorry, but not stupid," she retorted. "You're a prisoner, after all."

"I just saved your life."

She had the decency to look ashamed, but she didn't unlock the manacles.

With a weary sigh, he stretched out on the ground, though with his hands and feet shackled, it was next to impossible to get comfortable.

Ashlynne watched him carefully, unable to believe he was actually going to sleep. But there would be no rest for her, she thought. Even with his hands and feet shackled, she didn't trust him. The minute she closed her eyes, she knew he would be on her, and once he had the controller, she would be at his mercy.

She stared at him for a moment, then gazed at the sky again. It was full dark now, and she was hungry and tired. And alone with a slave. Her fingers tightened on the controller. She would use it if she had to. Just because he had saved her from the Hodorians didn't mean he could be trusted. He was a slave, a man sentenced to live out the remainder of his life in the mine.

Suddenly the strength went out of her limbs and she sank down to the ground. Tears stung her eyes. Her throat felt tight and thick. Burying her face in her hands, she wept bitter tears, crying for her parents, for Magny, for the loss of everything she had ever known, everything she had loved. All her life, she had been loved and cared for. She had never wanted for anything. She'd had the best education available, the finest clothes money could buy, the security of a good family. And now, none of it meant a thing. Better she should have learned how to survive in the wilderness than how to paint a landscape or sculpt or entertain foreign diplomats.

Falkon's jaw clenched as he listened to the girl's sobs. He had a ridiculous urge to go to her, to gather her into the circle of his arms and assure her that everything would be all right. She was such an innocent, she would probably believe him. At least until tomorrow.

He knew about the jungles of Tierde, about the slime-pits and the blue fire-sand. While imprisoned in the mine, he had heard numerous tales of men, slave and free alike, who had been lost in that jungle, never to be seen again, heard a dozen grisly stories of the cannibals and renegades who hid in the depths of its green heart, heard of the wild animals and wilder men who preyed upon the weak, the foolish, the unwary.

With a sigh, he closed his mind to the sound of the girl's tears. He had no comfort to give her or anyone else. All he wanted was his freedom and five minutes alone with Drade.

He fell asleep, a smile on his lips, as he contemplated squeezing the last breath of life from the man who had destroyed his home and murdered his family.

Chapter Ten

Niklaus Hassrick scowled at the tele-screen. "Dammit, Drade, what the hell happened?"

The image on the screen shrugged. "We made a mistake."

"A mistake! A mistake! Is that what you call it? You damn fool, you were supposed to wait until she was here."

Drade shrugged again. "What's done is done."

"That's all you have to say? Is that what you want me to tell Lord Brezor? I'm sorry, but what's done is done?"

"You'll think of something."

"You'd damn well better hope I do, because if I go down, I'm taking you with me. What's happening there now?"

"Everything's under control. The mine itself

131

is undamaged. As far as everyone knows, it was an unprovoked attack by the Hodorians." Drade frowned. "Two of my men were found dead a short distance from the house."

"What happened to them?"

"I'm not sure. I think one of the servants must have killed them and escaped through the back wall. I wouldn't worry about it, though. The jungle will take care of whoever it was."

Niklaus ran a hand through his hair. This whole thing had gone from bad to worse. It had all seemed so simple at the beginning. He swore under his breath. There had to be a way to make it work. A forged letter from Marcus, perhaps, bequeathing him ownership of the mine? Or papers alleging that he had bought half the mine? One way or another, he had to gain control of the mine; it was the only way to fulfill his bargain with the Cenian ambassador, the only way to save himself from ruin.

"Hassrick?"

"You're sure she's dead?"

"The house was leveled. No one could have gotten out."

"Someone killed your men."

"Yeah, but I'm willing to bet it wasn't the girl."

Niklaus grunted softly. At the sound of his father's voice, he muttered a quick goodbye and broke the connection.

He would find a way out of this mess somehow.

His future, his reputation, depended on it.

Chapter Eleven

Falkon sat up, his body tense, his ears ringing with the sound of a woman's scream. *Maiya* . . .

It took him a moment to realize the scream had come from Ashlynne. "What the hell's wrong with you?" he asked gruffly.

"A . . . a spider."

"What?"

"There was a spider on my arm. It . . . it scared me. I hate spiders."

Falkon grunted softly, then turned away. A spider. "How about releasing me?"

She hesitated a moment, then activated the release mechanism.

Falkon stood up. After stretching his arms and legs, he walked to the tunnel's opening and peered through the bushes. Dawn was breaking over the distant mountains. The rising sun splashed the sky with brilliant streaks of ocher and fiery shades of crimson. He heard the trilling of birds, the rustle of the leaves on the trees outside the tunnel, the shriek of some wild animal.

He glanced over his shoulder at the girl. Her hair fell in a tangled mass of silver-blond curls down her back; her face was smudged with dirt. Her dress was ripped along the neckline, revealing one softly rounded shoulder and a tantalizing glimpse of smooth creamy flesh. She didn't look so high and mighty now, he mused. "Let's go, princess."

"Is it safe?"

Falkon shrugged. If there were men prowling the jungle, the birds wouldn't be singing. Indeed, the moment he stepped out of the tunnel, the jungle grew silent, almost as if it were holding its breath.

Ashlynne stepped warily to the mouth of the tunnel, the hand in her pocket fisted around the controller. She saw Number Four standing a few feet away, his head cocked, as though he were listening to something only he could hear, and then he began walking east.

She felt a peculiar lurch in her stomach as she looked at him. He wore only a pair of tight-fitting breeches and a pair of black boots. The early morning sunlight cast blue highlights in his long black hair. She stared at his back, pity rising within her when she saw the ugly marks left by the lash. His arms and legs were long and well-muscled.

The thought of those arms, the strength of them, made her tighten her hold on the controller. She would have to be on her guard every minute, she thought, lest he overpower her and wrest the controller from her grasp. She would be helpless then, completely at his mercy.

Falkon looked over his shoulder, frowning when he saw the girl staring at him. "I'm leaving," he said, "with or without you."

"I don't think so."

"I know so."

Slowly, Ashlynne drew her hand out of her pocket, the controller pointed at his back. "You will wait for me."

Falkon glanced at the controller, then back at the girl. He had no doubt she would use the thing. She had done so before. "Right."

Arms crossed over his chest, he watched her step out of the tunnel. The hand holding the controller was trembling. A muscle twitched in his jaw. One slip of her thumb and he would be writhing on the ground at her feet.

He choked back the anger that rose in his throat like bile. It was maddening, humiliating, degrading, to be at the mercy of another and even more so to be at the mercy of a mere girl. There was a good chance he could jump her and wrest the controller from her grasp, but not now. He would bide his time for just the right moment.

"You've been injured!" She gestured at his arm with the controller, felt the nausea rise in her throat as she stared at the ugly black burn across his right biceps.

"Yeah." He glanced at the wound. The skin of his upper arm was raw and red, black around the edges.

"Does it—does it hurt very much?"

"Damn right." He took a deep, calming breath. "Are you ready to go now?" He forced the words through clenched teeth.

"Shouldn't we—your arm. Shouldn't we tend it first?"

"I don't know how, unless you've got a medi-kit hidden in your pocket."

Ashlynne shook her head.

"Let's go, then."

"I'll follow you. Mind you, go slowly. I won't hesitate to use this if I have to."

"I have no doubt of that," he muttered. Pivoting on his heel, he started walking, slowly.

Gradually, his anger melted. It was the first time in months that he had been outside the mine compound or the jinan. The sun felt warm, soothing, on his back. A deep breath filled his nostrils with myriad scents—earth and trees, the perfume of wildflowers, the stink of a rotting carcass, the heavy smell of damp tree moss.

Falkon walked steadily toward the rising sun. If he remembered correctly, there was a star base located on the eastern strip of Tierde. He could leave the girl there. With any luck, he would be able to steal a cruiser and get the hell off this rock. Free, he thought. Soon, he'd be free again. He lifted a hand to his throat. With any luck, he'd soon be free of the heavy collar and the shackles, too.

The laser burn on his arm seemed to throb in time with his footsteps, increasing as the day went on until it was a constant pulsing pain.

At noon, they stumbled onto a deep green

pool surrounded by gigantic blue ferns and a profusion of flowering vines.

Falkon paused at the edge of the pool, his mouth watering as his gaze swept over the surrounding area.

Ashlynne licked her lips. "Do you think it's safe to drink?"

Falkon nodded. "Probably." Judging from the variety of animal tracks, the pool appeared to be a watering hole.

She started to take a step forward, but he held her back. "Hold on."

Years of training as a sky pilot had taught him never to rush into unknown territory, but to wait, to study the lay of the land.

Ashlynne looked at him, annoyed. A flash of movement caught her eye and she glanced at the pool to see a small reddish-brown spring-cat approach the edge. The animal scented the air, then lowered its head and began to drink.

Falkon let out a sigh of relief when the cat disappeared into the forest. He'd been pretty certain the water was safe; the cat confirmed it. Hurrying forward, he dropped down on his belly and buried his face in the pool, then drank deeply. The water was cool and sweet. He was aware of the girl kneeling beside him, taking delicate sips of water from her cupped hands.

When he had quenched his thirst, he lowered his wounded arm into the pool, closing his eyes as the cool water eased the burning ache.

When she finished drinking, Ashlynne scooted away from Number Four. His nearness made her nervous. He looked dark and dangerous sitting there beside the pool. Water glistened on his bare arms and chest, his jaw was shadowed with the beginnings of a beard, his trousers hugged his long, muscular legs like a second skin. She wondered what it would be like to explore the hard muscles of his arms, to run her fingertips over his flat muscular stomach . . . She shook her head, horrified by the direction of her thoughts. He was a mercenary, a killer. She would do well to remember that.

Glancing up, she saw him watching her, a bemused expression on his face. Mortified, she realized she had been staring at his chest. A rush of heat flooded her cheeks. Her first instinct was to look away. Instead, she lifted her chin and met his gaze.

"You want to see the rest?" he drawled. "I could strip down for you."

"I'm sure I don't know what you mean!" The lie tasted sour in her mouth. Impossible as it seemed, she felt her cheeks grow even hotter.

"You own me," he said, his voice tinged with bitterness. "Are you sure you don't want to see it all?"

She had never been so humiliated in her life. She wanted to die, to disappear, to never see him again.

"Ready to go, princess?"

"Yes," she replied curtly, "as soon as I wash this stuff from my hands."

"What is it?"

"I don't know." Frowning, she scrubbed at the flaky greenish substance under her fingernails. It looked like paint, but it couldn't be. "And stop calling me princess."

He rose fluidly to his feet and held out his hand, his dark eyes dancing with amusement.

He was laughing at her! Ashlynne glared up at him. Refusing his offer, she stood up and wiped her hands dry on her skirt.

"Afraid of me?" he asked.

"Of course not."

"Uh-huh."

"I'm hungry," she said imperiously.

"Well, I'm sure that's a first. Come on, let's go."

It was true—she had never been hungry before. The gnawing ache in her belly helped keep her mind off the humiliation she had endured at the pool. It was bad enough to realize she had been staring at him, wondering what his bare skin would feel like beneath her fingertips. It was positively mortifying to know that he had been aware of her thoughts.

It seemed as though they had been walking for days when he finally found a place to rest. Ashlynne's legs felt like rubber as she sank to the ground. Her hand ached from holding the controller, yet she dared not put it down. It was the only protection she had.

She felt her cheeks grow warm as her stomach growled loudly. She was hungry and thirsty and tired. She wanted something to eat, a glass of sweet wine, a warm bath, a soft bed to sleep in. She wanted her parents. . . . Hot tears burned her eyes. They were dead, and she would never see them, or her home, again.

Sunk in the depths of her own misery, she began to cry. Unconsciously, her hand tightened on the controller.

A sharp cry of pain penetrated her grief.

Looking up, she saw Number Four writhing on the ground, his body straining, every muscle taut.

Instantly, she released her grip on the controller. "I'm sorry," she cried. "I didn't mean it. It was an accident!"

She watched helplessly as he continued to writhe in agony, her own anguish forgotten. His body twitched uncontrollably as hundreds of tiny electrical shocks pulsed through him.

Gradually, the spasms stopped. Eyes closed, he lay on the ground, his body bathed in sweat, his breathing harsh and uneven.

"I'm so sorry," she murmured contritely. "So sorry."

"Why?" Just a single word, filled with condemnation.

"It was an accident. I didn't mean to."

He opened his eyes to stare up at her. She flinched at the pain and contempt she read in his expression.

"I'm sorry," she said again.

"No need to be. I'm just a slave. You could kill me and no one would care." With an effort, he sat up. He wiped his sweaty brow on his forearm, then sat there, staring at her, until his body stopped trembling and his breathing returned to normal. "I don't suppose you'd consider giving me that thing? Or throwing it away?"

"No."

"I didn't think so." He stood up slowly and took a deep breath. When he looked at her, his eyes were cold. "If you ever use that damn thing on me again, I'll break your neck."

Ashlynne scrambled to her feet and backed away from him. "I said it was an accident."

"Yeah. Let's go."

"But I'm hungry. And tired."

"So am I, princess." Without another word, he turned his back to her and started walking.

There was nothing for her to do but follow him.

At dusk, he found a shallow stream. The bank was crisscrossed with animal tracks. Ashlynne sat on a stump, the controller in her lap, watching Number Four fashion a snare from a sturdy brown vine. "Do you think that will work?"

"You'd better hope so."

He put the finishing touches on the snare, covering it with a thin layer of leaves. "Come on." Without waiting to see if she followed him or not, he moved away from the stream, taking cover behind a stand of timber.

"How long will we have to wait?"

"I don't know." He sat down with his back against a tree, his legs drawn up, his arms resting on his bent knees. He had never been so tired. The wound in his arm throbbed monotonously. "As long as it takes, I guess."

After a moment, Ashlynne sat down across from him. Silence stretched between them. It made her uncomfortable. "Do you have a name?"

"You mean besides Number Four?"

She flinched at the bitterness in his voice. How degrading it must be, she thought, to be called by a number instead of your name. What if she had been imprisoned? What if no one

141

called her Ashlynne anymore? Using a number instead of a name was so cold, so impersonal, almost as if that person was no longer human. For the first time, it occurred to her that stripping a man of his name was like stripping him of his identity, his dignity. Why hadn't she realized that before?

"I'd like to know it," she said.

"It's Falkon."

Falkon. She repeated it in her mind. It was a strong name, one that suited him perfectly.

"And yours is Ashlynne." His voice, deep and rich, caressed her name like a prayer.

"Yes."

"I'm sorry about your parents."

"Thank you."

Silence dropped between them again.

Ashlynne stared into the distance, fighting the urge to cry. Everything she had ever loved was gone. Her parents, her home, her best friend, her pretty little chestnut mare, the security she had taken for granted all her life. They were all gone, wiped out in a blast of laser fire, and she was alone and afraid, more afraid than she had ever been in her life.

She slid a surreptitious glance at Falkon. Dark bristles shadowed his jaw. She saw him touch his arm and wince. What if the wound became infected? Even though she didn't trust him, even though she was afraid of him, she didn't want him to die, didn't want to be out here alone, at the mercy of the jungle and its inhabitants.

"Why were you sent to the mines?"

He turned to look at her. His blue-gray eyes

seemed to be weighing her, judging the reason for her interest. "I went to Riga Twelve to fight the Romarians."

"Why would you do that? It wasn't your fight."

"Wasn't it? I had friends on Riga Twelve."

She heard his emphasis on the word *had* and knew his friends were dead.

"Riga Twelve isn't the first planet they've conquered," he said bitterly, "nor will it be the last."

"The Romarians are trying to bring peace to the galaxy."

"Who told you that?"

"I heard my father talking about it."

"The Romarians are determined to conquer the galaxy, to force everyone to believe as they do, or be destroyed," he declared, his voice bitter.

"And what of Daccar?" Ashlynne exclaimed. "There is no more warlike people in the galaxy."

"That's true," Falkon allowed, with a small measure of pride. His people were the bravest and fiercest fighters in the galaxy. "But we've never tried to force our beliefs on other worlds. We may fight among ourselves, but we don't take our wars to other planets."

"You were a mercenary," she said scathingly. "If the price was right, you'd probably fight your own people, too."

Anger blazed in his eyes. "You don't know a damn thing about me," he said, his voice brittle. And then the anger faded from his eyes, replaced by a deep inconsolable sadness.

He blew out a deep breath. "I've no doubt the Romarians are the ones behind the Hodorian attack on the mines. Romariz will come in now and clean up the mess, and then they'll claim Tierde, and the mine, for their own." And when that was done, they would be in control of the last free black baneite crystal mine in the galaxy.

"But we're at peace with Romariz," she said. "And Hodore, too."

"Not anymore."

"But my father signed a treaty."

"Did he? Hell of a lot of good it did him." But even as he spoke the words, he knew none of it made sense. Romariz was already getting its share of crystals from the mine; Hodore, too. The girl was right. There was no reason, no logic, behind the attack.

She looked up at him, her eyes like bruises in her pale face. Then her gaze slid away from his, and he wished he had kept his mouth shut. He hadn't meant to hurt her, or to remind her of what she had lost.

"I'm going to check the trap," he said quietly, and, rising to his feet, he left her there.

Ashlynne licked the grease from her fingers, then wiped her hands on the hem of her skirt. Falkon's snare had caught a fat black rabbit. No matter what else he might be, he knew his way around in the woods, knew how to survive. He had managed to light a fire, spit the beast, and roast it to perfection. Even Meggie, the cook, couldn't have done it better.

Thinking of Meggie brought thoughts of

home to mind again. She wondered if her parents had suffered before they died.

"Ashlynne."

She looked up at him.

"Go ahead and cry."

Not wanting him to think her weak, she started to tell him she didn't need to cry, that she was fine. But she wasn't fine. Her heart was heavy, her throat thick, and suddenly tears were running down her cheeks and she was sobbing, crying as she hadn't cried since she was a child.

Falkon watched her a moment and then, unable to help himself, he drew her into his arms. He knew how she felt, knew the guilt of surviving, the pain of losing those one loved. She burrowed against him, seeking his warmth, needing the comfort and reassurance of a human touch.

He tried not to think of how small she was, how right she felt in his arms. It was only because he hadn't had a woman in a very long time that made holding her feel so good. He tried not to notice how soft her hair felt against his cheek, or how warm her breasts felt pressed against his chest. He tried not to notice the way she fit into his arms, as if she had been made especially for him.

He swore under his breath, wondering at the foolish notions creeping into his thoughts. She was no different from any other woman, no softer, no sweeter, no more desirable . . . ah, but she felt so very good nestled in his arms.

Shoulders shaking, she wept until she had no tears left. And still he held her, until her breathing returned to normal and she sat quiet in his embrace, her face still buried in the hollow of his shoulder.

"Feel better now?" he asked kindly.

Feeling embarrassed, Ashlynne nodded. "Thank you." She drew back, wiping her eyes with the hem of her skirt.

"We should be moving on."

She nodded again, not trusting herself to speak.

She watched as he smothered the fire and buried the rabbit's bones.

"Ready?" he asked.

"Yes."

With a curt nod, he took her hand and pulled her to her feet, then turned and started walking eastward, cursing himself for his weakness. He never should have taken her in his arms. She was the enemy. He cursed softly. He had been so caught up in comforting her, so busy thinking about how good it felt to hold her in his arms, he had missed the perfect chance to lift the controller from her pocket.

"Falkon?" She spoke his name aloud for the first time, liking the sound of it.

"What?"

"Where are we going?"

"Enjine Base Nine."

"The star base? Why?"

"Why not?"

Ashlynne considered that for a moment. "You're going to try to steal a cruiser or something stupid like that, aren't you?"

"Right the first time." He didn't know if the base had been attacked, didn't know which army might be in control, but it didn't matter. One way or another, he was getting the hell out of there.

"You'll never get away with it."

She was probably right. The base would be heavily guarded. After the recent attack, security would be tighter than usual. But it was his only chance. "I've got to try."

"What about . . . what about me?"

"I'll leave you there. You can get a transport to wherever you want to go."

"Oh." With a shock, she realized she didn't want to be parted from Falkon. She felt safe with him in a way she had never felt with anyone else. And that was strange, she thought, because she didn't trust him at all.

Chapter Twelve

Ashlynne sighed. It seemed as though they had been walking forever. Her feet hurt. She was hungry again. Tired from a restless night spent on the hard ground. Every passing shadow, every sound, had brought her to full wakefulness.

She stared at Falkon's back. In spite of his protests, she had activated the shackles the night before. She knew he hated her for it, but she was afraid to trust him, afraid if she left his feet free, he would run off in the night and leave her behind. She knew she was slowing him down, knew he considered her a burden. She didn't mean to be. It wasn't her fault she wasn't used to tramping through the jungle. She couldn't help it if she was afraid of spiders and snakes, if she didn't know how to skin a rabbit, or cook the meat over a fire. Never, in her wildest dreams, had she imagined she would need to know such things.

Today, it wasn't fear for herself that worried her. It was fear for Falkon. The wound in his arm was festering. It was swollen and red, oozing with thick yellow-green pus. He had told her not to worry, he was fine, but he wasn't walking as rapidly today, and she noticed that they rested more often. He needed help, and soon.

She fought down a rising sense of panic. If he died, so would she. She had no way of defending herself in this horrid place. She was dependent on him for food and shelter and protection.

They came to a small water hole and he dropped to his stomach, drinking greedily. She knelt beside him, alarmed by the heat she could feel radiating from his body. Lifting a tentative hand, she placed it on his arm. He flinched away from her touch, but even that brief contact was enough to tell her he was burning with fever.

Slowly, he turned to face her. "Guess you'll soon be rid of me," he said.

"No!"

"I can't go any farther." He rested his forehead on the ground. The damp earth felt cool against his heated flesh. "Keep going east. Sooner or later, you'll reach the space port."

"You can't give up."

He closed his eyes. "Sorry, princess. I wish . . ."

"Falkon?" She shook his uninjured shoulder.

"Falkon! Wake up." She shook him again. "Don't do this to me! You can't die. I need you." She shook him again. "Please wake up!"

But it was no use. She sat back on her heels, staring at him. Numb with fear, she glanced around the jungle. It would be dark soon. The animals that slept through the heat of the day would be rousing, coming to the pool to drink. She had to find a place to hide. And to think she had once wanted to be independent, rebellious, even! Hah! She would be content to be ordered about for the rest of her life if she could just go back home and find everything as it had been before.

She rose on shaky legs, glancing frantically around, trying to decide what to do. She had never had to make any decisions before, at least none more serious than what dress to wear or how to spend her day. East. Falkon had told her to go east.

Squaring her shoulders, she took a few steps, then looked backward. She couldn't just leave him lying there, prey to wild beasts. The least she could do was drag him away from the water.

That, she soon found, was far easier said than done. Try as she might, she couldn't budge him. Tears of frustration rose in her eyes. She couldn't leave him, but she was afraid to stay near the pool. Night was falling rapidly. Already, she could hear stirrings in the underbrush.

And then she heard voices. Male voices speaking a language she didn't understand. She glanced around, poised for flight, but before she could locate a hiding place, they were there. Six dark-skinned men clad in rough skins, their hair adorned with bits of fur and feathers and bone. She had heard of them, the wild men of the jungle, men who refused to surrender the old ways, men who still hunted with spears and clubs. Men who were rumored to be cannibals.

She stared at them and then, overcome by fear and fatigue, she slid to the ground, praying that she would be dead before they ate her.

Falkon woke to a raging thirst and the sound of drums. For a time, he lay still, eyes closed, trying to determine where he was.

He heard footsteps, muffled conversation, the crackle of flames.

Hands gripped his shoulders, holding him down. He gasped as agony splintered through his wounded arm, opened his eyes to find himself surrounded by a half-dozen painted faces. He'd heard stories of them in the mine, the cannibals of Tierde.

Damn, were they carving him up alive? He glanced at his arm, swore again as one of the men made a slit in his flesh. A trickle of dark red blood and greenish-yellow pus spurted from the cut. He groaned as pressure was applied to his arm, forcing more pus from the wound.

When only bright red blood ran from the cut, the witch doctor held Falkon's arm over a wooden cup until it was almost full, and then he slapped a hot poultice over the wound. The pain was excruciating. With a groan, Falkon pitched headlong into oblivion.

When he woke again, it was night. He glanced around, but could see nothing in the dark hut. He licked dry lips, threw off the rough blanket that covered him. He was hot, so hot. He tossed restlessly, plagued by a relentless thirst. He couldn't feel any pain in his arm and he wondered, morbidly, if they had cut it off. He had a vague memory of a painted face hovering over him, filling a wooden cup with his blood. The thought of someone drinking from that cup made him sick to his stomach. He took a deep breath, then reached across his body, relieved to find his arm still there.

Water. He had to have a drink.

He groaned as he rolled to his side, then to his hands and knees. The movement made him dizzy.

"Falkon?"

Choking back his nausea, he lifted his head and looked toward the sound of the voice. "Ashlynne?"

"Help me."

He blinked into the darkness. "What's wrong?"

"They tied me up."

He grunted softly; then, gathering what little strength he possessed, he crawled slowly toward her, only to go sprawling facedown across her lap when he bumped into her thigh.

"Are you all right?" she whispered.

"Oh, yeah, fine." He lay there a moment, his head pillowed in her lap. Sleep, he thought, it would be so nice to close his eyes and go to sleep with his head in her lap.

"I'm scared."

"Yeah, me too." He struggled to sit up, then reached behind her and fumbled with the rope binding her wrists. It seemed to take forever, but finally he managed to loosen the knots.

"Hurry, we've got to get out of here." She shook off the rope and began to massage her wrists, wincing as the blood began to circulate again. "They're cannibals, aren't they?"

"Yeah."

She shuddered. She had been hoping she was wrong. "They're going to eat us, aren't they?"

He didn't care what they did, so long as they gave him something cold to drink first.

"We've got to get out of here," she said urgently.

"Yeah." It was an effort to think. All he wanted to do was close his eyes and sleep.

"Wake up! Falkon, wake up!" She shook his arm. "Come on, we've got to go."

"You go." He was tired and thirsty and hungry and right then, he didn't care if he lived or died.

"Falkon! Damn you, wake up."

In spite of everything, he felt himself smiling at her use of profanity.

"Falkon." Her voice, close to his ear. "If you don't wake up, I'm going to use the controller."

That got his attention. "What do you want from me?" he asked.

"I want you to get me out of here. Now." She cocked her head to one side. "I don't hear anything. Maybe they're all asleep." She stood up, tugging on his arm. "Let's go. Hurry."

He rose on legs that felt like warm rubber

and staggered toward the door of the hut, wondering at her bravado. Not too long ago, she had been afraid of a harmless spider, now she was ready to fight off a tribe of bloodthirsty cannibals.

He opened the hide flap that covered the doorway and peered outside. All was quiet. Dark. Low clouds covered the moon and blotted out the stars. A few raindrops splattered his face, promising a downpour before the night was out. The cool air revived him a little, clearing the cobwebs from his mind. She was right. They had to get out of there.

"Stay close," he whispered, and slipped outside.

It was to their advantage that the hut they had been in was located a short distance away from the others. Keeping to the shadows, he ghosted around the corner of the shack. The jungle rose up in front of him, dark, silent.

He glanced over his shoulder to make sure the girl was behind him, then slipped into the underbrush.

Ashlynne followed close on Falkon's heels. She hadn't thought anything could be more frightening than seeing her home destroyed, but one look at the cannibals who had captured them had changed her mind. Fear could be a powerful impetus, and she had been terrified. She had watched in horror as the medicine man had drained Falkon's blood into a cup. He had taken a swallow, nodded, and handed the cup to the man behind him, who had taken a drink and passed it to the next man. That act alone had banished any doubts

she'd had about her captors, and she had
known that, somehow, she had to get away.

She had fought with a ferocity she hadn't
known she possessed when they tied her up,
but all her struggles had been in vain. They had
bound her hands, then stood around her, talking softly. One man had run his hands over her
arms and legs, nodding and smiling, and
though she hadn't been able to understand his
words, she had known he was thinking of all
the ways to cook her.

She didn't know how long she had sat there
after the savages left. Before the interior of the
hut had grown dark, she had glanced around,
searching for something she could use to cut
her hands free, but all she had seen were skulls
and shrunken heads and a pile of bones.
Human bones.

She had stared at Falkon, lying on the
ground across from her, willing him to wake up
before it was too late. She had heard the
natives singing and dancing, swallowed back
the bile that rose in her throat as she imagined
them dragging her outside, stripping her of her
clothes, tossing her into a pot of boiling water.

But no one had come for her. Gradually, the
drumming had ceased and the night had
grown silent.

And now she was following Falkon deeper
into the jungle. All the stories she had heard
when she was a child rose up to haunt her, tales
not only of the cannibals, but of wild animals,
of slime pits and burning sands, of a lost city
that had once been inhabited by a race of
giants. She had always thought such tales to be

nothing but fiction, but if the cannibals were real, might there not also be bottomless pits of slime and sands that burned like fire? What if the jungle housed giants, as well?

She tripped over a log, gasping as pain exploded through her knee. For a moment, she lay where she had fallen, too weary to move. What difference did it make if they escaped the cannibals? There were probably a thousand other worse ways to die waiting for them in this great green hell. Snakes and wild beasts and poisoned water. Suddenly, she didn't care. She just wanted it to be over.

"Ashlynne? Are you hurt?"

"Of course I'm hurt! And I'm hungry and tired and scared."

He looked at her a moment and then, with a low groan, he hunkered down on his heels beside her. "What happened to that spitfire who practically dragged me out of the cannibals' camp?"

"I don't know." She looked up at him, tears making wet trails through the dirt that covered her face. "We're going to die out here, aren't we?"

"Not if I can help it. Come on, you can't give up now."

"Yes, I can. I'm tired."

"I know. Come on, just a little farther."

"No."

"Come on, princess, I can't carry you." He smiled grimly. "Hell, before the night is over, you may have to carry me."

She couldn't help it—she laughed.

156

"That's better." He held out his hand. "Come on."

With a sigh, she put her hand in his and let him help her to her feet. "Do you know where we are?"

He jerked his chin. "All I know is that east is that way, and that's where we want to go. Ready?"

She nodded, and he turned and began walking. Far ahead, she could see a tall, slender mountain. Enjine Base Nine was at the foot of the mountain.

She was certain things couldn't get worse when it began to rain. Not a light mist. Not a spring shower. But a heavy rain that quickly soaked her to the skin.

She had never been so cold or so miserable in her whole life.

It seemed they walked for hours, but the mountain never got any closer.

At dawn, Falkon found a place for them to rest, a small, dark cave that smelled of dung and dust and something long dead.

Falkon went in ahead of her. He reappeared a short while later, a dead animal in his hands. He tossed the carcass away, then shrugged. "Your castle awaits, princess."

"I hate you," she murmured. "I really do."

"Yeah," he said, following her inside. "I know."

It was dark and cold. She stood in the middle of the cave, her arms wrapped around her body, shivering uncontrollably.

"Get out of those wet things."

"No."

"Do it," he said. She heard the scrape of cloth over skin and knew he was removing his boots and breeches. "Dammit, Ashlynne, get out of those wet clothes."

She turned her back to him and undressed, grateful for the cave's sheltering darkness. She gasped when he grasped her arm and drew her down beside him.

"Relax, I'm not going to hurt you. Just lie close to me. We'll be warmer that way."

She would have protested, but she could already feel his heat seeping into her everywhere they touched, save for one cold, damp area around his buttocks, and she realized that he was not totally naked.

They lay back-to-back on the ground. Too tired to think or feel, she closed her eyes, asleep between one breath and the next.

The shriek of laser weapons slowly died away. The air was pungent with the smell of smoke and charred flesh. Falkon stood outside the house that had once been his, watching as two men wearing the green and gold of the Romarian Army emerged from the wreckage bearing what was left of his wife and child.

With a roar, he turned on Drade, his manacled hands reaching for his enemy's throat, but Drade slipped through his fingers like swamp fire. The manacles on his wrists turned to lynaziam shackles and he collapsed on the ground as Drade stood over him, laughing maniacally as he activated the controller, sending shards of pain splintering through every nerve and muscle of his body.

He screamed with pain and outrage, screamed his hatred, his grief, screamed until his throat was raw. . . .

"Falkon! Falkon! Wake up. Please, wake up."

Ashlynne shook his shoulder, shook it again, as hard as she could, in an effort to wake him, to silence his cries. Finally, in desperation, she hit his wounded arm.

With a harsh cry, Falkon bolted upright, his eyes wild. His hands closed around her throat and he had her pinned to the ground between one heartbeat and the next.

"Don't!" she cried, gasping for breath. "It's me."

"What the hell?" He released his hold on her and sat back. "What happened?"

"You were having a nightmare. You cried out in your sleep. I tried to wake you, but I couldn't. I was afraid someone would hear you."

He rubbed his wounded arm, wondering why it hurt so much.

"I'm sorry," Ashlynne said. "I didn't know how else to wake you."

He stared at her a moment, puzzled, and then nodded as comprehension dawned. "You did the right thing." He would have welcomed any pain to escape the hell of that nightmare.

Pale sunlight filtered into the cave. He noticed that she was dressed and he wondered how long she had been awake. Her clothes were badly wrinkled, her hair fell in disarray

159

over her shoulders and down her back. Her face was smudged with dirt.

"It must have been awful," she said, not quite meeting his eyes. "Your dream."

"Yeah," he said gruffly. "Awful."

He took a deep breath, blew it out in a long, slow sigh. Always the same nightmare, he thought bleakly, reminding him of what he had lost, of his hatred for the man who had once been his friend. In the bowels of the mine, shackled hand and foot, shut away from the sun, he had given up all hope of vengeance. When he had been sent to work for Ashlynne's father, a small spark of hope had begin to burn deep within him—hope of escape, hope of achieving vengeance. And now . . .

He felt the spark within him kindle into a blaze. He was free now, and the possibility for revenge was closer than ever. He snorted softly as he fingered the collar on his neck. As free as he could be while Ashlynne held the controller, he mused, and wondered why he hadn't taken it from her the night before.

Sooner or later they would reach Enjine Base Nine. He had no doubt of his ability to steal a ship. When that was done, he would go to Romariz, in disguise, and find Drade. He smiled as he thought of what it would be like to confront his enemy, to put his hands around Drade's throat and slowly, slowly, squeeze the life from his body. It would be far easier, and certainly much safer, to kill the maggot from a distance, but that would not do. He wanted Drade to know who it was who took his life. Drade would know why.

"Falkon, do you think we could find something to eat?"

Slowly, he turned to look at the girl. Lost in dreams of vengeance, he had completely forgotten about her.

"I'm hungry," she said plaintively.

"Yeah." He blew out a deep sigh. "Me, too." He pulled on his breeches and boots and then stood up, hands braced against his thighs while he gathered his strength. He wondered briefly if the cannibals would come looking for them, but the pain in his arm and the hunger rumbling in his belly were more urgent concerns at the moment.

Taking a deep breath, he left the cave and headed east.

Ashlynne followed him, surprised that he had the strength to walk. There were dark shadows beneath his eyes. She knew his arm pained him, knew he must be as hungry and thirsty as she, yet he never complained, only kept walking, stubbornly putting one foot in front of the other.

It grew hotter as they walked. She heard the deep-throated roar of some huge beast, tried not to think of the hundreds of slimy, creepy creatures and poisonous snakes and spiders that inhabited the jungle. Surely they were just as afraid of her as she was of them. Weren't they?

She felt faint with happiness when Falkon stopped beneath a tree and plucked a large bunch of small blue bananas. He handed her half of them. She peeled one with fingers that shook in her haste, then sighed with pleasure as she bit into the sweet blue fruit. She devoured it in two bites and quickly peeled another, and then another. Never had anything tasted so good.

Falkon picked two more bunches, and then they started walking again.

With the edge taken from her hunger, she peeled another banana. She ate slower this time, savoring the sugary sweet taste, remembering how she had loved to have them for breakfast at home . . . home.

Despair washed over her. She would never see her home or her parents again. Why, she wondered, why had the Hodorians attacked them? They had been at peace. She had known little of politics, been aware of little beyond the high walls of the jinan. Magny and Artemis had been her only friends. She had been spoiled and pampered her whole life, until now. She stared at Falkon's broad, scarred back. He would not pamper her. He didn't even like her. She was nothing but a burden to him, an inconvenience.

She felt the sting of tears behind her eyes and dashed them away. No matter what happened, she wouldn't cry in front of him again. She wouldn't!

A short time later, she heard a dull roaring sound, and then, as they pushed their way through a tangle of thick vines, she saw a waterfall.

She stood there, gaping in awe, as she watched the water cascade over the side of a mountain to fall hundreds of feet into an enormous lake. Several small overflow pools surrounded the lake.

Ashlynne could only stare, thinking she could drink her fill at last, that she could step into one of those shallow pools and bathe away the dirt and perspiration that clung to her.

She started forward, only to be stayed by Falkon's hand on her arm. "Just wait," he said.

She frowned at him. "Why?"

"Hush." He stood there, motionless for a full ten minutes, all his senses attuned to his surroundings, before he stepped out of the cover of the jungle.

Ashlynne hurried after him. They stopped at the first pool, dropped to the ground, side by side. Falkon sniffed the water, took a small sip, then buried his head in the pool.

The water was cold and sweet, refreshing, intoxicating, and she drank and drank and then, feeling wonderful, she fell back on the grass and closed her eyes.

Falkon stared at her, surprised to discover that she was asleep.

Shaking his head, he walked toward one of the other pools. There were a dozen of them, a few meters apart. He had thought them all to be overflow pools from the waterfall, but the water in the nearest one had steam rising from it. A hot spring.

Filled with anticipation, he stripped off his boots, breeches, and briefs and slid into the shallow pool, sighing as the wonderfully warm water closed over him. Far in the distance he could see the tip of the mountain that housed

Enjine Base Nine. He wondered just how far away it was, and how long it would take them to reach there.

But somehow, sitting in the warm embrace of the pool, his head back, his eyelids growing heavier by the minute, he no longer cared.

Ashlynne woke with a start. Sitting up, she looked around, panic rising within her when she found she was alone. She clutched the controller in her hand, wondering why he hadn't taken it from her. Leave her out here alone, would he? Well, he wouldn't get any farther! She stood up, about to activate the controller in her pocket, when she saw him reclining in a pool a few yards away.

Chin up, shoulders back, she marched toward him, determined to remind him that, no matter what had happened, he was her slave.

As she drew closer, the first thing she noticed was his clothing lying in the grass. That meant . . . Heat flooded her cheeks. He was naked.

And asleep. He was leaning back against the side of the pool, his arms resting on the edge, his head back. His hair gleamed like wet ebony. She stared down at him, at his dark head and broad shoulders. She had a foolish urge to run her fingers over his beard. He looked peaceful, lying there. Steam rose from the water; even from where she stood, she could feel its inviting warmth.

Biting down on her lower lip, she watched him for a moment. He was sleeping soundly, she had no doubt of that. Did she dare?

She glanced back at the other pools. She could bathe in one of them, she mused, but the water in the pool she had drunk from had been cold. She looked down at Falkon again. The warm water in this pool was much more inviting.

Before she could change her mind, she removed her dress, petticoat, and shoes, and slipped into the pool, as far away from Falkon as she could get. She would rinse the dirt from her hair, soak for a few minutes, and get out before he woke up.

The water felt like heaven. It was bathwater warm and effervescent, bubbling like champagne. Keeping a wary eye on Falkon, she rinsed the dirt from her hair. He continued to snore softly, so she lingered in the water, enjoying the warmth, letting it soothe her weary muscles. She had never walked so far in her whole life.

She looked up at the sky, wide and blue, and thought of how quickly her life had turned upside down. One day she was the pampered heir to a black-crystal mine, and the next she was an orphan with no home and no family, forced to rely on a slave for her very existence.

Surely the gods must be laughing.

She looked over at Falkon to make sure he was still asleep, only to find him watching her.

"You're awake!" she exclaimed, and quickly crossed her arms over her breasts.

"So are you."

She stared at him, wondering if he was trying to make a joke. He didn't look like a man who laughed often. "Turn around so I can get out."

"What if I don't want to?"

She reached behind her, delving into the pocket of her dress. "I won't ask you again."

Falkon cursed softly. One way or another, he was going to have to get that damned controller away from her. Why did he always think of it too late? He wondered if, in some perverse corner of his mind, he liked being her slave.

"You win," he muttered, and turning his back to her, he stood up.

She couldn't help staring at him. His broad back and shoulders were both scarred by the lash. She chided herself for staring at him, but couldn't seem to draw her gaze away. She had seen so few men in her life. She remembered the first time she had seen Falkon. He had been nearly naked then, too, lying facedown in a pool of his own blood. She had a sudden urge to go to him, to run her fingers over the scars on his back, to apologize for every hurt and humiliation he had endured in the mine.

"You dressed yet?"

She jerked her gaze from his back and scrambled out of the pool. She had nothing with which to dry herself. She tugged her undergarments up over her wet flesh, then pulled her dress over her head.

"All right," she said. "When I tell you to—"

But he didn't wait for her permission to get out of the water, didn't wait for her to turn her back. He stepped out of the pool, water sluicing down his body. His skin glistened like wet bronze in the sunlight.

Like a rabbit mesmerized by a snake, she could only stand there, staring. His broad back tapered to a trim waist, firm buttocks, and long, well-muscled legs. Only when he started to turn around did sanity return. With a squeal, she hastily turned her back toward him. And then, eyes shut tight, she wished she'd had the nerve to look.

Falkon grinned as he stood there, letting the sun bake him dry. Shy little virgin, he mused. She had probably never seen a naked man in her whole life. No doubt she would faint dead away if he walked over there and took her in his arms. . . .

Where had *that* thought come from? Where, indeed, he thought ruefully. He had wanted her ever since the first time he laid eyes on her, when she'd looked down her nose at him as if she were a queen and he some lowly maggot. And that, he thought, just about summed it up. She was royalty, and he was a mercenary, and he would be wise to remember it.

Grabbing his clothes, he stepped into his briefs and breeches, then sat down and tugged on his boots. He drew in a deep breath and then, blowing out a long weary sigh, he stood up. "Let's go, princess."

Ashlynne didn't argue. She glanced over her shoulder to make certain he was dressed, then fell into step behind him, wondering if the nightmare she found herself in would ever end.

Chapter Thirteen

"Are we going to stop soon?"

"At dusk."

"How much longer till then?"

"About an hour."

Another hour. It seemed they had been walking for years. It had been two days since they'd left the pool. They walked and walked, and yet the distant mist-covered mountain that housed Enjine Base Nine never seemed to grow any closer. Her legs ached, her back ached, her head ached. She was hungry and tired and thirsty. And dirty. Her shoes and stockings were splattered with mud, she was sticky with perspiration, her hair fell over her shoulders and down her back in a tangled mass of snarls.

She glared at Falkon's back. Didn't he ever get tired or hungry or thirsty?

The Captive

Left, right, left. She put one foot in front of the other, too tired to think. She was almost asleep on her feet when she bumped into Falkon, who seemed to have stopped for no apparent reason.

She peered around him, surprised to see a dozen men huddled around a campfire a short distance ahead. A delicious aroma rose from several cook pots suspended on a rod over a small, cheery fire.

A faint rustle sounded behind her and she glanced over her shoulder to see a man coming toward her, weapon in hand. Another man appeared from the left.

She heard Falkon swear, only then realizing that the men were wearing the colors of the Tierdian army. They might be his enemies, she thought, but they were her salvation.

"Hello," she said, relief evident in her voice.

"Who are you?" the nearest man demanded.

"Lady Ashlynne of the house of Myrafloures," she said imperiously.

The two men exchanged glances, then both bowed their heads in a gesture of respect. "My lady," they murmured.

She waved a hand in Falkon's direction. "This is my slave, Number Four. To my knowledge, we are the only survivors of the attack on the mine." She thought of Magny and Parah and Carday, of Meggie and Otry, of Dain and Dagan. Of her parents. Always her parents. "Have you heard of any others?" she asked, hoping for a miracle, hoping they would tell her that her mother and father and all the others had miraculously survived.

"No, my lady," one of the men replied. "We have made a thorough sweep of the area. The attack was concentrated on the mine and . . ." His voice trailed off and he gestured at the campfire. "Come, warm yourself. We have food and drink."

"Thank you."

The men at the campfire stood up at her approach, their lusty glances quickly turning to respect when they learned who she was. In minutes, she was wrapped in a warm blanket and seated near the fire, a plate of food in her lap. She took several bites. It was rough fare, but tasty and filling.

A tall, slender man with short brown hair and a sweeping moustache came forward and introduced himself. "Commander Lyle Casman, at your service, my lady."

Ashlynne smiled at him, then waved a hand in Falkon's direction. "Could you please see that my slave is given something to eat?"

"Of course, my lady." Casman grunted softly. "He looks familiar. What's his name?"

Ashlynne glanced at Falkon. He shook his head imperceptibly, a warning in his eyes, or was it a plea?

"I don't know," she said. "Does it matter? We call him Number Four."

"I guess not," Casman said. "How long have you owned him?"

"He's been in our family for several years," she said. "My father bought him from a merchant on Nardia. Is something wrong?"

"No." Casman studied Falkon intently for a moment, then shrugged. "He reminds me of someone I used to know. So, my lady, where are you headed?"

"To Enjine Base Nine. I was hoping to get a transport to Trellas."

"Do you have relatives there?"

"A friend of my father's lives in the capital. Rugen Hassrick? Perhaps you know him."

"Of course. My men and I are heading in the general direction of Enjine Base Nine. It would be an honor to see you safely there. One of our scouts received a transmission saying that the Romarians have arrived at the capital. The Hodorian army has been routed and the Romarians have sent a unit to the star base to maintain the peace."

"Thank you, Commander." She smiled up at him. "If you don't mind, I should like to rest now."

"Of course. Please, use my shelter."

"Thank you." Setting the plate on the ground, Ashlynne stood up and beckoned for Falkon to follow her.

"Do you have the controller for the collar?" Casman asked when they reached his shelter. "If not, we can find some restraints."

"I have it," Ashlynne said, reaching into her pocket. "Sit, Number Four." She refused to meet his eyes as she activated the shackles on his wrists and ankles, but she could feel his angry gaze burning into her back.

"That's better," Casman said. "One can't be too careful."

Ashlynne nodded. "Yes, that's what my—" She took a deep breath, fighting the urge to cry. "What my father always said."

Casman cleared his throat, clearly disconcerted by her tears. "Rest well, my lady."

"Thank you for everything, Commander," she said, and ducked inside the small shelter. Left alone, she sank down on the cot and let her tears flow. She would be safe now. Casman would see her safely to Enjine Base Nine, where she could get a transport to Trellas. Niklaus and his family would take care of her. For some reason, that thought only made her cry harder.

"Ashlynne?"

She sat up with a start at the sound of Falkon's voice. "Leave me alone."

"What's wrong?" he asked gruffly.

"Nothing." She sniffed back her tears.

Falkon stared at the door of the shelter. He could picture Ashlynne sitting inside, her eyes red and swollen. His first thought at the sound of her tears had been to let her cry. Spoiled princess. How quickly she had fallen back into the role of lady of the manor! Asking Casman to feed him as if he were some stray dog she had picked up along the way instead of the man who had saved her life.

He swore softly. "Ashlynne? Release me."

He could almost hear her thinking about it. A moment later, the manacles separated.

Certain he was making a mistake, he entered the shelter. She was sitting in the middle of a pile of blankets, silent tears washing down her cheeks. He should hate her, he thought. He should wring her pretty little neck, grab the controller, and make a break for it. With any luck, he could get away unseen. Instead, he drew her into his arms. She stiffened in his embrace, then relaxed against him, crying softly. Her tears fell like warm rain on his chest.

She hiccuped as her tears subsided, then drew back to look at him. "Why didn't you want me to tell Commander Casman your name?"

"We went to flight school together. He's a stickler for obeying the letter of the law. He'd probably execute me on the spot if he knew who I was."

"You don't think I would let him do that, do you?"

"I don't think you could stop him. Shh."

"Lady Ashlynne?"

"Yes, Commander?"

"Your slave is gone."

"No. He's in here, with me."

There was a pause. "In there?" She could hear the suspicion, the disapproval, in Casman's voice.

"Yes. I—" Ashlynne grabbed the controller and activated the manacles on Falkon's wrists. "I thought I saw a . . . a . . ."

"Snake," Falkon whispered.

"I thought I saw a snake in here."

Falkon grinned at her, then turned and scuttled out of the shelter, careful to keep his head down so Casman couldn't see his face.

"Should I come in?" Casman asked.

"No, thank you, Commander." She forced a laugh. "I feel so silly. It was just a . . . a stick."

"Goodnight, then, my lady."

"Goodnight."

The sentries were posted, the fire was extinguished, and silence joined the darkness of the night.

Falkon gazed into the distance, weighing the wisdom of trying to make a break for it with his hands bound together. He cursed softly as Ashlynne activated the shackles on his feet, thereby making the decision for him.

Staring up at the sky, his hands and feet effectively hobbled, he cursed the spoiled young woman in the shelter until sleep claimed him, and he dreamed of freedom, and revenge.

They broke camp early the following morning. Ashlynne sat in the front of the shuttle, beside the commander, who was, in Falkon's opinion, overly solicitous, fawning and fussing over her as if she were as fragile and helpless as she thought she was. Falkon rode on the floor in the back of the shuttle, his back braced against the rear wall, his hands and feet bound at the commander's insistence.

They reached Enjine Base Nine two hours later. Ashlynne released the manacles on Falkon's ankles so he could walk, and he followed her and Casman down the narrow corridor that led directly from the shuttle landing bay into the base. Everywhere he looked, he saw the hated dark blue uniform of the Romarians. They had already taken over, he thought, and wondered again why they had sent the Hodorians to attack Tierde. Try as he might, he could find no logical reason for it. Tierde had been a neutral planet, sanctioned as such by the Confederation.

The Captive

Casman escorted Ashlynne to his private quarters and bid her make herself at home.

"You," he said, beckoning to Falkon, "will come with me."

"Where are you taking him?" Ashlynne asked.

"No need to worry your pretty head," Casman said. "He will be well taken care of."

Ashlynne bit down on her lower lip, not liking the look in the Commander's cold gray eyes. "He is not to be hurt," she warned. "He is my property, and I will not have him abused."

"I know how to handle slaves," Casman said.

"I think I would rather he stayed here, with me," she decided, and, with a wave of her hand, commanded, "Sit there, Number Four."

Choking back a sharp retort, Falkon sat on the floor where she indicated, careful to keep his head lowered.

"You spoil him, I think," Casman said.

"He saved my life," Ashlynne reminded him. She smiled sweetly. "For all his rather fearsome appearance, he is quite harmless." She bit back a smile. "Almost a eunuch."

Casman grunted. "I'll post one of my men outside the door, just in case. There is a bathing salon off the bedchamber at the end of the hall."

"Thank you. You've been very kind. Would it be possible for me to get in touch with Ambassador Hassrick?"

"Certainly." He gestured at the comport. "My home is yours."

"Thank you."

He bowed over her hand, kissed her fingertips, and promised he would return in an hour with a change of clothing. Then, with a last disdainful look at Falkon's bowed head, he left the room.

As soon as the door slid shut, Falkon stood up and held out his arms. "Release me."

"I don't think so."

"Dammit, woman, turn me loose!"

She shook her head. "You had best behave yourself," she warned.

"Or what? You'll sic Casman's hounds on me?"

She drew the controller from her pocket. "I don't think that will be necessary."

Falkon glared at her, his hands flexing. He had large hands, capable of breaking her in half. "I'm warning you," he said, his voice a low growl, "don't use that damn thing on me again unless you intend to kill me."

Ashlynne glared back at him. "Don't threaten me."

"I'm not threatening you. I'm warning you."

"I should have let Commander Casman take you away."

"Why didn't you?"

"I don't know. But it isn't too late."

"Go ahead, then, call him back."

Ashlynne blew out a deep breath. "Why are you being so difficult?"

"I'm not the one being difficult, princess."

"I'm trying to help you. And stop calling me that."

"Then turn me loose, dammit."

"No." She lifted the controller, intending to

activate the shackles on his feet. "I'm going to make a call and then I want to take a long hot bath."

"Dammit, at least leave my legs free."

She hesitated, frightened by the anger in his eyes. "But I want to bathe."

"So bathe! I'm not going to stop you, or spy on you." He glanced longingly at the bed in the next room. "All I want to do is get some sleep."

Her thumb hovered over the controls. "I don't trust you."

"Dammit, princess, I don't have any designs on you. I just want some sleep."

"Very well." She watched him walk into the bedroom and sink down on the bed.

With a sigh, she went to the comport. Moments later, Niklaus appeared on the screen.

"Ashlynne!" His eyes widened with surprise. "Is that you?"

"Yes." Sitting down, she put the controller on the table beside her.

"Where are you?"

"Enjine Base Nine."

"I thought—that is, we heard Tierde had been attacked, and the jinan had been destroyed. Leveled." He shook his head.

"Yes, yes, it was awful."

"But you're all right?"

She nodded.

"And your parents?"

Ashlynne shook her head, not wanting to say the words aloud.

"I'm sorry, Ashlynne."

"Thank you."

"At least you are safe. I'll come for you as soon as I can."

Maybe he did care, she thought. "Thank you, Niklaus, but that won't be necessary. Commander Casman has already arranged for transport to Trellis."

"Good. Good." He smiled at her. "Get here as soon as you can."

"Yes, I will."

She bid him goodbye and broke the connection. She had never wanted to marry Niklaus; now, just knowing she had somewhere to go gave her a measure of peace. He had seemed genuinely glad to know she was alive, anxious to have her join him. Maybe everything would work out after all.

Overhead lights came on when she entered the bathing salon. She closed and locked the door, then turned on the faucet, punching in her selection for vanilla-scented bubbles. Hot, fragrant water gushed from the tap.

She undressed quickly and stepped into the tub, a sigh of pleasure escaping her lips as the hot water closed over her.

She let the water run until the tub was filled almost to the brim, then she lay back, her eyes closed, at ease for the first time since the attack.

The cooling water woke her. She lathered herself with a bar of scented soap, washed and rinsed her hair, then stepped out of the tub. She wrapped up in a large fluffy green towel, then dried her hair.

Ah, it felt wonderful to be clean again! She looked down at her dress, reluctant to put it back on. It was dirty and torn, a constant reminder of all she had lost.

"Lady Ashlynne?"

"Yes?"

"I've brought you something to wear. When you're dressed, perhaps you'd like to go get something to eat. We have a rather nice dining room."

"Yes, thank you, Commander."

"I'll wait for you outside."

"I won't be long."

She heard muffled voices, the meaty sound of a fist striking flesh, the opening and closing of a door. Frowning, she opened the bathroom door a crack and peered out. Casman was gone, and so was Falkon.

Gone where? She dressed quickly, anxious to find out what had happened.

The gown Casman had chosen for her was blue, with a high waist and a long flowing skirt with two deep pockets. There was a pair of matching sandals. She wondered idly how Casman had known her size. He had thoughtfully provided a brush and she ran it through her hair, wondering where the two men had gone.

She was about to leave the room when she noticed the controller wasn't where she had left it. She glanced around the room, but it was nowhere in sight. Remembering the sound of a struggle, she wondered if Falkon had overpowered the commander and escaped.

She felt a sharp twinge of regret at the thought of never seeing Falkon again. And hard on the heels of regret came a surge of anger. After all they had been through, how could he just leave her without so much as a goodbye? Yet even as the thought crossed her mind, she wondered if it wasn't for the best.

Lyle Casman was waiting outside the door. He looked quite handsome in his dress uniform. There was a dark bruise on his left cheek. He offered her his hand, and she noticed a cut across his knuckles.

He smiled at her, his gaze warm with approval. "Ready?"

"Yes. Have you seen Number Four?"

"He's fine."

"He's here?"

"Of course. Where else would he be?"

"I don't know. I thought . . . where is he?"

Casman laughed indulgently. "He's in the brig, being bathed and fed."

"I seem to have misplaced the controller."

"I took it," Casman said easily. He smiled at her. "I hope you don't mind, but it was necessary. You understand."

"Of course." She bit back the angry words that rose to her lips. It wouldn't do to make too big a fuss over a man who was a slave. But, one way or another, she would get Falkon out of the brig. She owed him that. A life for a life, she thought.

Casman offered her his arm. "Shall we go?"

Ashlynne smiled as she placed her hand on his arm. "Yes, I'm starved."

Falkon prowled the confines of the cage that imprisoned him. He had been stripped of his breeches, hosed off, given a pair of ill-fitting black trousers and a coarse cotton shirt, allowed to shave, and thrown into a cell that was only a little larger than the one he had occupied at the mine. A guard the size of a small mountain had brought him a bowl of soup and a hunk of brown bread.

Now, clean and reasonably full for the first time in days, he paced the floor. Damn her! He clenched his hands into tight fists, wishing they were around her pretty little neck.

He came to a halt at the sound of footsteps, stepped back into the shadows as Casman came into view. Damn.

Casman moved close to the bars and peered inside. "Come here where I can see you."

"Why?"

"Because I'm telling you to."

There was no point in refusing. Taking a deep breath, forcing himself to at least appear relaxed, he stepped into the light.

"Falkon. I thought it was you."

He shrugged.

"I'll get a promotion for this."

"Where is Lady Ashlynne?"

"In her room. I've arranged transport to Trellis. She leaves tomorrow. I'd give a month's pay to see Drade's face when I tell him you're here." Chuckling softly, Casman headed for the door.

Hands clenched, Falkon stared after Casman. Once Drade arrived, Ashlynne would be rid of him. Permanently.

Chapter Fourteen

Ashlynne stood at the window, watching the activity in the distance. Enjine Base Nine was a busy station, with transports and cruisers coming and going at all hours of the day and night.

Commander Casman had told her that several cities in the area had been destroyed, but Partha, which was the capital of Tierde, had been spared. The Romarian army had driven the Hodorians away and taken up residence at the mine, which was still operational. All the slaves had been killed in the attack, so the army was working the mine until a new shipment of slaves arrived. She wondered why the Hodorians hadn't destroyed the space station as well.

With a sigh, she turned away from the window. Casman had arranged for transportation to Trellis. She should be relieved, she mused. In a few days, she would be safe again. No more trekking through the wilds, wondering where her next meal was coming from, no more sleeping on the ground, drinking from rivers and pools like a wild animal. No more verbal sparring with Falkon. Niklaus's family would look after her until the wedding.

Niklaus was a wealthy man. His family owned a large house in Arkata, which was the capital city of Trellis. She would want for nothing . . . except love. And independence. She would be nothing more than a decoration in Niklaus's house, of no real importance, of no value other than looking pretty on her husband's arm and providing him with an heir.

Her thoughts turned to Falkon, and she shied away. She didn't want to think of him, or of the fate that awaited him. At dinner, Commander Casman had told her that Falkon would most likely be executed. She had argued that he was her property, but Casman had told her someone high up in the Romarian command wanted the prisoner dead. It would be foolish to challenge the Romarians over a slave.

Feeling suddenly sick, she wrapped her arms around her stomach and closed her eyes. She tried to tell herself she didn't care, that she was well rid of him, but she was only lying to herself, and she knew it. He had saved her life, offered her solace and a shoulder to cry on, made her feel safe when she'd been frightened. She couldn't let him be executed, couldn't even imagine a world without him in it, and it had nothing to do with the fact that he had broad shoulders and tawny skin, that he was by far the most handsome man she had ever seen, that he made her feel vibrant and alive. Nothing to do with the shivery feelings that he aroused in her. Nothing at all. And even as the thought crossed her mind, she knew she was lying to herself again.

Muttering an oath she had heard on Falkon's lips, she left Casman's quarters and stepped into the hall. A small sign indicated that the Detention Level was on D1.

Head high, shoulders back, she walked briskly toward her destination, hoping she looked as if she had every right to be there.

A uniformed guard was posted at the door. "Your business?" he asked curtly.

"I'm here to see my slave."

"Do you have clearance to be here?"

"Of course," she replied in her haughtiest tone.

"May I see it?"

"Are you doubting my word? I am Lady Ashlynne of the House of Myrafloures. My father is Lord Marcus. I have Commander Casman's personal authorization to see my slave. Now, stand aside. The commander is expecting me in his quarters in ten minutes. I have no time to waste arguing with you."

Indecision showed in the guard's eyes.

Drawing herself up to her full height, Ashlynne looked the guard in the eye. "I am not accustomed to being questioned. I shall speak to Commander Casman about this."

She started to turn away, her heart pounding, wondering if he would call her bluff.

"Lady Ashlynne, wait."

She turned slowly. "Yes?"

"My apologies, my lady." The guard unlocked the door and stood aside.

She didn't bother to say thank you, merely inclined her head and swept past him.

A second guard sat at a large desk. Engrossed in something on the tele-screen, he spared her hardly a glance as she passed by.

She moved into the long corridor that led to the cells, her nose wrinkling with distaste. The place smelled worse than the slime pits. Her heart pounded in her chest as her gaze darted from side to side. All the cells were empty, save the last one.

He turned at the sound of her footsteps. She had expected him to be pleased to see her. He wasn't.

"What the hell are you doing here?" he asked. "Come to gloat?"

"I came to get you out of here," she retorted.

He snorted. "How do you plan to do that?"

"With this." She slipped her hand into her pocket and withdrew a small weapon.

"Where the hell did you get that?"

"I stole it from Casman's quarters."

He grinned at her. "Do you know how to use it?"

"No. Don't you?"

"It's not much different from the controller," Falkon said. "Squeeze the front trigger, and it will paralyze. The second trigger will kill."

The weapon fit neatly into her palm. She

curled her finger around the front trigger, then looked at Falkon. "Now what?"

He grinned at her. "Call the guard."

She did as he asked, her whole being quivering with nervous tension.

Moments later, the guard who had been sitting at the desk appeared. "Is there a problem?"

"Yes," Ashlynne said, smiling sweetly. "This door appears to be locked."

The guard frowned at her.

"Unlock it, please."

"I can't do that without written authorization, my lady. I'm sorry."

Ashlynne lifted her hand until the weapon was pointed at the guard's chest. "I think you can."

He grunted, clearly amused. He took a step forward, his hand reaching for the weapon.

"What are you waiting for? Shoot!"

Ashlynne took a quick step backward, her gaze darting toward Falkon. "Shoot?"

"Shoot, dammit! Pretend it's me."

With Falkon's voice ringing in her ears, she squeezed the trigger. A burst of brilliant white exploded from the muzzle of the weapon, wrapping around the guard like strands of light. He dropped to the floor and lay still.

"Is he dead?"

"No. Get the key. Hurry! The effect will fade in a few minutes."

"Where is it?"

"Look in his pockets."

She didn't want to touch him. Hesitantly, she went through the guard's pockets. Unable to move or speak, he stared up at her, his gaze malevolent.

"It's not here," she said.

"Try the desk."

Dropping the stun gun into her skirt pocket, she ran down the corridor. In the light of the tele-screen, she saw a ring of keys on the desk top. And the controller beside it. She grabbed the keys, thrust the controller into her pocket, then hurried back to the cell. She tried to fit one of the keys into the lock, but her hands were shaking so badly, she couldn't manage it.

Muttering an oath, Falkon grabbed the key ring from her hand. The third key unlocked the cell door. Stepping out of the cell, Falkon grabbed the guard under the arms, dragged him inside the cell and locked the door.

"Have you got the controller with you?"

"Of course."

He crossed his wrists. "Okay, activate the damn thing."

"What?" She stared at him a moment, then nodded. Pulling the controller from her pocket, she activated the manacles on his wrists, then opened the door that led out of the cellblock.

The guard outside frowned when he saw Falkon. "I'm afraid I can't let you take the prisoner."

"And why not? This man is my personal slave. He was detained at my request, and now I'm taking him with me."

"I'll have to get clearance from my superior."

Ashlynne glanced at Falkon, who nodded.

"Of course," she said. "We'll wait."

With a nod, the guard turned to pick up his communicator.

As soon as he turned his back, Ashlynne pulled the stun gun from her pocket and squeezed the trigger.

The guard hit the floor with a dull thud.

"Release me," Falkon said.

For once, she didn't argue.

When his hands were free, Falkon removed the gun from the guard's holster. He handed it to Ashlynne, then dragged the guard into the cellblock. Stripping the guard of his coat, Falkon put it on, as well as the man's helmet and boots. Leaving the cellblock, he closed the door.

Ashlynne gasped as a man emerged from the cellblock a few minutes later, then sighed in relief when she recognized Falkon beneath the black helmet.

"All right," he said, taking the guard's weapon from her hand, "let's get the hell out of here."

She had expected him to try to be inconspicuous, to keep his head down, but Falkon walked arrogantly down the center of the corridor, head high, eyes looking up and out, as if he had nothing to hide. She followed close behind him, trying to look as if she belonged there. Surprisingly, no one paid them any attention.

He paused at an intersection where four corridors came together, then turned right.

They walked down a long narrow passageway. Ahead, Ashlynne saw a dozen or so spacecraft. Several men clad in dark gray overalls milled about, talking and laughing as they worked on a sleek-looking fighter.

"Stay close," Falkon whispered. He nodded to one of the men they passed, moving down the line until he came to a two-man cruiser. It was a small ship, used mainly for short hops between space stations. He would have preferred a fighter, but the cruiser offered living quarters, which might come in handy. If they were lucky, it would be stocked with food and water.

He glanced around, then climbed aboard. Turning, he shoved the gun into his pocket, then reached down to help Ashlynne up the ladder.

When she was inside, he secured the hatch and moved into the cockpit. Removing his helmet, he tossed it on the floor, then slid into the seat. "Hope this baby's fueled and ready to go," he muttered. "Or this is gonna be a mighty short flight."

He ran an instrument check, muttering under his breath as he familiarized himself with the controls.

"Are you sure you know how to fly this thing?" Ashlynne asked as she slid into the copilot's seat.

Falkon shrugged. "It's a little different from what I'm used to, but I think I can manage."

"You think?"

"Here we go," he said, and opened the throttle.

As soon as the cruiser lifted off, the com deck crackled to life. "Cruiser twenty-two. You have not been cleared for takeoff. Please report your identity and destination."

Falkon looked over at Ashlynne and grinned. "Hang on," he said, and goosed the throttle to full ahead.

Ashlynne shrieked as the cruiser shot forward, skimming over the ground. Everything passed by in a blur, and then they were rising, soaring skyward like a bird of prey in flight. The thrill was unlike anything she had ever known—exhilarating and frightening, like the man sitting beside her.

His face was set in determined lines as he piloted the sleek craft.

The radio crackled to life again. "Cruiser twenty-two, you are not authorized for flight. Return to base immediately. I repeat, return to base immediately."

Falkon looked at the instrument panel, and she heard him swear softly.

"What's wrong?" she asked.

"We might be in trouble?"

"Trouble? What kind of trouble?"

"There are two fighters on our tail."

"What?" She leaned forward. At first, all she saw was a jumble of multicolored blinking lights, and then she saw what looked like two green arrows moving side by side across the view screen.

She jumped when the radio crackled to life yet again. "Cruiser twenty-two, return to base immediately or we will fire."

Ashlynne grabbed his arm. "Turn around! They're going to shoot us."

"No way, sweetheart. I'm not going back."

"Are you crazy? Didn't you hear what they said? They're going to start shooting at us."

"Sit back and hang on."

"Turn back!"

"Not a chance."

Delving into her pocket, she withdrew the controller. "Turn back," she warned.

He looked over at her and grinned a roguish, devil-may-care grin. "You gonna use that now?"

"If I have to. Turn this ship around before it's too late."

"It was too late the minute we climbed aboard, princess. Now put that damn thing away."

"I'm not bluffing."

Falkon sat back, his arms folded across his chest. "Go ahead. But who's gonna man the controls when I'm writhing on the floor like a snake on a hot rock? You?"

She stared at him, fear and anger and helpless rage smoldering within her. She slammed her hand on the armrest, wishing she dared slap that insufferable grin off his face.

"Sit back, princess, and enjoy the ride."

With a wordless cry, she shoved the controller back in her pocket, locked herself into the seat, and screamed as the cruiser rolled over and then shot straight up.

"Damn!" Falkon muttered. "That was a close one."

Looking out the window, she saw a brilliant flash of blue light. "What was that?"

"They fired on us."

She was going to die. She knew it. Closing

her eyes, she tried to pray, but she was too afraid. It wasn't fair. Her life was going to be over before it had even begun. She would never get married, never have children, never see the triple waterfall of Demurre, or the dragons of Riv.

She shrieked as the cruiser rolled left, then right, then plummeted downward. They were going to crash. She squeezed her eyes tightly shut. *Please*, she thought, *please let it be quick*.

The cruiser shuddered and bounced before it skidded to a bone-jarring stop. Ashlynne opened her eyes slowly, amazed to discover the ship was still in one piece. That she was still in one piece.

She looked over at Falkon to find him grinning at her.

"Hell of a ride," he said.

She scowled at him. "Where are we?"

"Darned if I know. I checked the charts, but there's nothing listed at these coordinates."

"So we're on a planet that doesn't even exist?"

He grinned. "Something like that."

Ashlynne looked out the window at what appeared to be a swamp. Tall trees trailing fingers of silver moss rose up all around them. Spiny brush with bloodred blossoms sprang up here and there, along with spiky clumps of blue-green grass. She saw a pool a short distance away, shrouded in a hazy blue-gray mist.

Falkon shut down the engine, then rose to his feet. "Wonder if there's anything to eat on board," he mused.

How could he think of food at a time like

this? She drew back as a long brown-and-yellow snake, its body easily as thick as her upper thigh, slithered down one of the trees. What other creatures lurked out there?

She could hear Falkon moving around in the back of the ship. Curious, she slid out of the seat and went into what she assumed was the kitchen. It was small and square and gray, hardly large enough for the two of them.

Falkon looked up. "We're in luck. You hungry?"

She shook her head. She was too scared to be hungry.

He punched a number into a small panel on the wall; a moment later, a tray slid out of a slot at the bottom. The aroma of roast karu-atar and coffee filled the small cabin.

He sat down at the small table that was attached to one wall. "Sure you don't want something?"

She shook her head.

"Well, sit down and keep me company."

She slid into the seat across from him, her hand folded around the controller in her pocket. "How long are we going to stay here?"

He shrugged. "I don't know. At the moment, it seems like a safe port."

She thought of the enormous snake she had seen outside. "Safe?"

"Sure. As long as we keep still and quiet, they can't track the ship."

"But I want to go to Arkata."

"Arkata? That's on Trellis, isn't it? What's there?"

"My fiancé." She had never been eager to

193

marry. Niklaus was, after all, not only a man she had never met, but fifteen years her senior. But now he was her only refuge in the world. He would marry her and protect her.

Falkon stared at her. "You're engaged?"

"Yes." She lifted her chin defiantly. "Why?"

"Just surprised me, that's all."

"He's a wonderful man. Very handsome. Very rich."

"Rich," Falkon said with a sneer. "I could have guessed that."

"There's nothing wrong with being rich," she snapped.

"How'd he get rich?"

"His family owns a factory that produces laser cannons."

"Ah."

"You're nothing but a mercenary. Who are you to judge him?"

"I'm not judging him. After all, if it wasn't for men like him, the Romarians couldn't have firebombed my house." He didn't add that laser cannons had destroyed her home and family as well. She seemed to have put it out of her mind for the moment and he saw no need to remind her. There was enough pain in the world already.

Ashlynne bit down on her lower lip, silenced by the anger in his eyes, by the certainty that he had lost more than a house. "Are you . . . have you family somewhere?"

"Not anymore." Falkon pushed the tray away, his meal unfinished. "My wife and daughter were in the house when they burned it."

She had a sudden, horrible image of her own

home going up in flames, felt again the loss of her parents. "I'm sorry," she said quietly, and knew in her heart that the words were inadequate, that there were not enough words in the galaxy to ease his pain. Or hers.

"Yeah," he muttered. "Me, too." He stood abruptly. "I'm going outside to have a look around."

"Do you think that's a good idea?"

Falkon shrugged. "Beats staying cooped up in here."

"But you don't know what's out there. I saw a snake."

"I'm not afraid of snakes."

She tilted her head to one side, her expression thoughtful. "What are you afraid of?"

"That controller in your pocket."

"I'm serious."

"So am I."

"What am I supposed to do if something happens to you?"

"Learn how to fly, I guess."

"That's not funny."

"Am I laughing?"

"Darn you, Falkon."

"I'm going. You can come with me, or stay here, but I'm going out."

Ashlynne glanced around. "You don't like small places, do you?" she remarked, thinking of the tiny cell that had imprisoned him. It hadn't been much larger than the galley.

"Not much." He moved past her, opening doors as he went. There were two cabins, fore and aft, a head, the galley, and a small combination storage area and closet.

She trailed behind, her hand caressing the controller.

Falkon opened the closet and pulled out a fur-lined jacket. It was more to his taste than the coat he was wearing. "Nice," he muttered as he removed the guard's coat and slipped the jacket on. "There's another one in here. You want it?"

She was torn between staying inside where it was relatively safe and going outside with him. In the end, being alone was less appealing than being with Falkon. The knowledge surprised her.

She held out her hand, scowling when he grinned at her.

"Guess that means you're going with me."

"I guess so," she said curtly.

"Where's the stun gun you took from Casman?"

"In my pocket."

"Well, keep it handy."

"Do you think I'll need it?" she asked, and then she remembered the snake.

Slipping on the jacket he handed her, she followed him down the companionway and out into an uncharted world.

Chapter Fifteen

Ashlynne shivered as a blast of cold air seemed to slap her in the face. Huddling deeper into her jacket, she followed Falkon down the ladder.

A gray mist seemed to hover in the air, its cold fingers slipping inside her collar, crawling up her legs. She shivered again and moved closer to Falkon. Why hadn't she stayed inside? At least it was warm there. And safe.

"What now?" she asked.

"We go exploring."

Ashlynne watched as he pulled the gun from his coat pocket and thrust it into the waistband of his trousers.

"Easier to get to, just in case," he explained.

His words did nothing to ease her nerves.

"Ready?"

Amanda Ashley

She nodded. "I guess so, though I still think this is a mistake."

"Won't be the first one I've made," he muttered.

"Well, that's comforting," she retorted. "Let's hope it's not your last."

With a grin, Falkon started walking.

Ashlynne took a deep breath, her gaze darting right and left as she followed him. What kind of place was this? Even the ground felt strange, sort of soft and springy, as if it was going to give way beneath her at any moment. Tall trees rose up everywhere, branches heavy with gray-green moss. There was an abundance of plant life with spiked leaves and sharp thorns.

There seemed to be no wildlife other than the snake she had seen from the window. Remembering that, she glanced quickly behind her, wondering where the thing had gone. She hurried after Falkon, moving cautiously. Where there was one snake, there was bound to be more. And the snakes had to eat something . . .

"What are we looking for?" she asked.

Falkon shrugged. "Just looking."

"What if we get lost?"

"I never get lost."

"We're lost now," she muttered.

"We're not lost. I just don't know where we are."

They walked for what seemed like miles and miles, and the scenery never changed. Tall slender trees dripping moss, spiky plants and ferns; ferns, spiky plants and tall slender trees dripping moss.

She was about to suggest that they turn back

198

when she heard a dull roaring sound. "What's that?"

Falkon shook his head. "I don't know. Sounds like a waterfall."

Curious, she quickened her steps as she followed him through the thick underbrush.

It was, indeed, a waterfall, but unlike any she had ever seen. It tumbled down the face of an enormous mountain, a foaming cascade of rainbow-hued water splashing into a churning pool, which gradually quieted and became a wide river.

It was beautiful, breathtaking, like something out of a fairy tale of old.

She started to speak, but Falkon lifted a finger to his lips to silence her and then pointed across the river.

At first she didn't see anything, and then, slowly, the creature took shape. She stared in disbelief. It couldn't be. But it was. A blue unicorn, a creature of myth and legend. It stood at the river's edge, delicate ears flicking back and forth, silver horn shining in the sun, its gray muzzle testing the wind before it stepped out of the dappled shadow of the trees and lowered its head to drink.

Ashlynne gasped as a small cream-colored foal moved up beside the unicorn and began to nurse.

The mare's head went up. With a flash of its tail, it disappeared into the underbrush, the foal close at its heels.

"Oh!" Ashlynne exclaimed in disappointment. "Weren't they beautiful?"

"Yeah, beautiful." His hand caressed the butt

of the gun in his waistband. "Wonder if they're good eating."

Ashlynne stared at him in horror. "You're not serious!"

"If we stay here long enough, we'll be needing fresh meat. The supplies in the ship won't last more than two or three days."

"I don't care. You can't kill the unicorn. It's beautiful. Why, people spend their whole lives hoping to see such a creature."

Falkon grunted thoughtfully. "Maybe you're right. Maybe it would be worth more alive."

"What do you mean?"

He shrugged. "I imagine I could find someone willing to buy a unicorn if I could catch it."

"Only a mercenary would think of that."

"Right now I'm thinking about you and me." He stared across the river, his expression gloomy. "I'm on the run. I've got no credits. We need to find a safe port . . . I need to get back to Daccar." He regarded Ashlynne through narrowed eyes. "You said you were engaged to a wealthy man."

Alarmed by the speculative look in his eyes, she took a step back, her hand delving into her pocket to clasp the controller. "Yes."

"He'd probably pay a pretty hefty sum to get you back."

"What are you saying?"

"You're a lot easier to transport than a unicorn. And probably worth a lot more."

"What do you mean?" she asked suspiciously.

Falkon shrugged. "I mean, when we get to Arkata, it might be worth my while to call your fiancé and see how much he's willing to pay for your safe return."

"What do you mean, my safe return?"

"I'll tell him that you've been kidnapped, but I know where you are, and that for the right price, I'll deliver you safe and sound."

"You're despicable."

"You sound surprised."

She stared at him, wondering, hoping, that he was just joking.

"What's the matter, princess?"

"Nothing. And stop calling me that!" She turned away, the beauty of the scene lost on her now. How could she have been such a fool, to think he actually cared what happened to her? He was nothing but a scoundrel. "I'm going back to the ship."

"Can you find your way?"

"Of course." She started off briskly, eager to get away from him. Sell her, would he! Well, she'd see about that. He'd wish himself back in the mine when she got through with him. She'd . . . she'd . . . what would she do? Her fingers stroked the controller. She could cause him pain, but what would that accomplish? He was her only hope of getting to Trellis. The thought of Falkon using her as a means to an end stung her pride. Even though Niklaus could well afford to pay any amount Falkon might demand, she refused to be a part of it. She would just leave him once they reached Trellis, she decided, because there was no way she was going to let him use her to make a profit. The cad! And to think she had actually started to care for him, to feel that he would protect her. He had probably been planning to hold her for ransom all along.

Once they landed on Trellis, she would activate the shackles on his hands and feet and leave him in the ship. With his feet bound, he wouldn't be able to follow her. Once they were on Trellis, she would have no trouble finding transport to Arkata.

She was so busy imagining what it would be like to get the best of Falkon, she forgot to pay attention to where she was going. She cried out as she tripped over a gnarled root and went sprawling facedown in the dirt.

"Oh, blast that man!" she exclaimed as she sat up and examined the cut on her leg. "This is all his fault."

She wiped the blood from her knee with the hem of her skirt. Grimacing, she stood up and continued on her way, somewhat surprised when she actually found the ship.

Climbing up the ladder, she went into the galley and poked around until she figured out how to get something to eat out of the servidor.

She was sitting at the table, sipping a cup of hot tea, when Falkon entered the ship a short time later. As soon as she heard the hatch close behind him, she drew the controller out of her pocket and activated the manacles.

The sudden closing of the shackles on his feet caused him to fall. She grinned as she heard him curse.

Rising, she left the galley.

Falkon was sitting up, his back against the

bulwark, his face dark with anger. He lifted his arms. "Turn me loose."

"No." She took a step backward.

Falkon glared at her. "Turn . . . me . . . loose."

She shook her head. "No. I don't trust you."

"Why the hell not? Dammit, I haven't done anything to you." His eyes narrowed. "Oh, I get it. You're mad, aren't you? Mad because I said I was gonna ransom you to your rich boyfriend."

She didn't deny it.

"It's the only way you'll get to him," he said, his voice suddenly calm.

"I'm going to bed." She had checked the cabins earlier, noting that the larger one had a good strong lock on the door.

"Wait a minute, dammit!"

"What do you want?"

"My freedom," he said.

"No. Goodnight."

"How about getting me something to eat, then?"

She hesitated, then went into the galley and punched the control panel, wishing it was his face.

Falkon stared at the tray she placed on the floor beside him. Karu-atar steak, crisp potatoes, blue corn, a cup of black coffee. He looked up at her. "How do you expect me to eat with my hands like this?"

"That's your problem," she replied airily. "I'm going to bed."

She stepped past him, shrieked as his hands closed around her ankles. He gave a sharp tug and she fell facedown, her arms trapped

203

beneath her body, the air whooshing from her lungs.

She yelped as her cheek struck the floor. "Get off me!" She bucked beneath him, but it was like trying to move a mountain. He weighed far more than she did.

"Turn me loose." His voice was an angry whisper in her ear.

"No," she gasped. "Get off of me! I can't breathe."

"And I can't eat with my hands shackled."

"You can eat on your hands and knees like the cur you are!"

He swore a violent oath, the words singeing her ears.

Falkon turned her over. As soon as her arms were free, she swung at him. He swore again as her nails raked his cheek, tearing the skin. She wriggled out from beneath him and scooted away on her hands and knees, shrieking as his hands closed on one of her ankles yet again. She kicked backward with her free leg, heard him grunt as her heel struck him in the face. She didn't wait to see how badly he was hurt. Lunging to her feet, she ran down the companionway, flew into the room she had chosen and closed and locked the door.

Breathless, she stood in the middle of the floor, one hand pressed to her heart. When her breathing returned to normal, she put her hand in her pocket, needing the reassurance of the controller.

With a sinking feeling, she realized it was gone.

* * *

Falkon sat up, his head tilted back in an effort to stop the blood oozing from his nose. He lifted his bound hands to his cheek, wincing as his fingers came away wet with blood. Damn her! Yet even as he cursed her, he had to admire her spunk. His princess had claws and wasn't afraid to use them.

He closed his eyes and took a deep breath, his nostrils filling with the aroma of steak and potatoes, no doubt cold by now.

Opening his eyes, he regarded the tray on the floor. He had eaten without utensils before; he could do it again. He was reaching for the tray when he saw the controller.

A slow smile curved his lips as he reached for it. A moment later, he was free, truly free, for the first time in months.

Chapter Sixteen

Ashlynne hardly slept that night. All she could think about was the whereabouts of the controller. Had Falkon found it? She started at every sound, expecting him to come bursting through the door and . . . what? Ravish her? Tie her up? Make her pay for the pain and humiliation she had caused him?

She pulled the covers up to her chin and stared into the darkness. The bed was narrow, the mattress hard and unfamiliar. And it was quiet, so quiet. The thought had no sooner crossed her mind than she heard a horrible shriek from somewhere outside. What kind of animal made such a sound? Or had it been an animal? They hadn't seen any signs of human habitation. She shivered, remembering the cannibals they had encountered in the jungle on Tierde.

Tierde. The only home she had ever known. The seasons would be changing now. The Season of Mists had always been her favorite time of year. She had always loved the heavy rains that watered the ground, the oddly eerie greenish light of the twin moons as Riasna and Brell rose in tandem. She had been five or six the first time her mother had told her the story of the twin moons. Tears slid down her cheeks as she thought of her parents. Had they suffered much? Did they know she was safe? She would never see them again. She wished now that she had told her mother and father more often that she loved them. She thought of Magny, her best friend, her only friend, and the days and nights they had spent together, laughing and sharing secrets, planning for the future. . . .

Her tears came faster, and she dashed them away. She would not cry! But she couldn't seem to stop. A sob rose in her throat as she wept for all she had lost: her loved ones, the security of a home, the sense of belonging, her piano, the beautiful chestnut mare her father had given her. Gone, all gone, destroyed in a moment's madness, and her childhood with it.

She took a deep breath. She had never wanted to marry Niklaus; now, he represented safety and shelter. Without him, she would truly be alone. She wondered if Commander Casman had informed Niklaus of Falkon's escape. She wondered if Niklaus was concerned about her, or even cared. They had never met in person; all their communications had been by mail or comport, formal, polite. He had expressed his willingness to have her for his bride, but no real enthusiasm. No doubt he viewed their upcoming marriage as a duty to be fulfilled, just as she had. Perhaps he would consider himself well rid of her.

She froze as she heard a knock at the door. There was no need to ask who it was. "What do you want?"

"Are you all right in there?"

"Yes." She sniffed. "I'm fine."

Silence stretched between them. She tensed when she heard him try the door, wondering if he would break it down.

She was still wondering when she fell asleep.

Falkon sat in the cockpit, his left leg draped over the arm of his chair. Gazing into the darkness, he weighed his options. Returning to Daccar was risky. By now, Drade would know of his escape from Tierde. No doubt spies were already in place at his usual haunts, listening, waiting. He could go into hiding somewhere until things cooled off. Once he turned Ashlynne over to her fiancé, he would have enough credits to live in style for a good long time. He could rent a place on some out-of-the-way planet, stock it with food and drink, hire a little housekeeper who would be willing to take care of all his needs, and take a well-earned vacation.

He grunted softly, wondering what Ashlynne's fiancé was like. Probably as spoiled and rich as she was. A perfect prince for a perfect princess. Well, he was welcome to her—welcome to put up with her pouts and her tantrums—to run his fingers through that gorgeous hair, kiss those pouting pink lips, run his hands over that delectable body . . .

Damn! Maybe he should just forget about the reward and keep her for himself. He closed his eyes, imagining the two of them living on some peaceful planet raising blue corn and silver-haired kids.

Muttering an oath, he made his way to the back cabin. He wasn't a farmer, he was a fighter pilot with a score to settle, and he damn well meant to settle it. Drade had not seen the last of him, that was for damn sure.

Ashlynne woke with a start, her heart pounding as she glanced around the room. With a sigh, she realized it had all been a dream. A nightmare, really. As bad as reality was, her dream had been far worse. She had been Falkon's slave, had felt the weight of the lynazium collar around her throat, had been subject to his every whim as he dragged her from one end of the galaxy to the other. He had used her and humiliated her in every way possible, determined to pay her back in kind for every hurt and humiliation he had endured.

Her stomach clenched, rumbling with hunger. Sitting up, she slid her legs over the edge of the bed. Was he awake?

Rising, she went to the door and pressed her ear to the panel. If he was still asleep, she might be able to get to the galley, grab something to eat, and return to the safety of her room without his knowing.

She listened for several moments, but heard nothing. Taking a deep breath, she unlocked the door and peered up and down the companionway. All was still and quiet.

She eased the door open a little farther, every muscle tense as she stepped into the narrow corridor and tiptoed toward the galley.

She was reading the menu when she sensed him behind her.

"Morning, princess," he drawled.

She turned slowly to face him. The first thing she saw was the controller in his hand.

He grinned at her as he tossed it lightly from hand to hand. "Look what I found."

"Give it back to me." She held out her hand, as if she expected him to obey. "It's mine. And so are you."

He laughed. "Not anymore, princess."

She lowered her arm to her side. She hadn't really thought he would obey.

"Get yourself something to eat," he said, "and then bring me some ham and scrambled eggs and a cup of coffee, black."

Before she could voice the protest that rose in her throat, he left the galley. "Insufferable man," she muttered.

She punched her selection into the servidor. A tray slid out a few minutes later and she carried it to the table and sat down. She ate slowly, wondering what he would do if she simply refused to do as he asked.

She rose with a sigh, feeling much put upon. What right did he have to expect her to wait on him? She stared at the servidor and then, with a grin, she selected another entrée and carried it into the cockpit.

She found Falkon hunched over the console, studying a star chart.

"Here." She thrust the tray into his hands.

Falkon stared at the food on the tray. Wheatmeal and soft-cooked eggs. And a cup of weak black ginger tea. He looked up at her, his expression grim.

"Anything else I can get for you?" she asked sweetly.

He looked at her a minute, then shook his head. "No, this is fine."

He ate it while she watched. It was all she could do not to laugh as he choked down the bland wheatmeal, grimaced as he swallowed the eggs. She hadn't really expected him to eat it. He downed the tea in two gulps.

When he was finished, he handed her the tray, muttered, "Thanks," and went back to studying the chart on the screen.

Feeling somewhat guilty for being so spiteful and childish, she carried the tray into the galley and dropped it in the bin. He had saved her life. The least she could have done was to give him a decent meal.

She stayed in the galley for a few minutes, her fingers drumming on the tabletop and then, because she was bored and lonely, she went back to the cockpit and sat down in the copilot's seat.

Falkon looked over at her and frowned. "You want something?"

Ashlynne shook her head.

"Does that hurt?" he asked, pointing at the bruise on her cheek.

"A little." She pointed at the scratches on his cheek. "Does that?"

"I've cut myself worse shaving." His fingers caressed the bruise. "I'm sorry," he said gruffly.

"Me, too."

His gaze met hers and she felt suddenly like smiling without knowing why.

"What are you looking for?" she asked.

"Just looking." He tapped the screen. "We're here." He dragged his finger across the map. "Trellis"—he looked up and met her gaze—"and your fiancé, are here."

Trellis. It was depicted as a large shimmering orange planet on the star chart. Her gaze moved over the chart. Daccar was a small blue planet; Tierde was a rich, dark green. Tierde. She wondered if she would ever see her homeland again.

"Tell me about him," Falkon said.

"Niklaus?"

Falkon nodded.

Ashlynne lifted one shoulder and let it fall. "He is his father's only son. He has two sisters, both of whom are older and married. He graduated in the top five percent of his class. He has been running the family business for the past two years, and will eventually take over full control."

Falkon grunted softly as she related facts, nothing but facts. There was no affection in her voice, none of the glow or sparkle a woman in love should show.

"Are you in love with him?

"No. How could I be? We've never met."

"Never?"

She shook her head. "I was supposed to go to Arkata this summer to meet him."

"Why would you want to marry a man you've never met?"

"Our parents arranged it, of course," she replied. "Isn't that how things are done on Daccar?"

Falkon shook his head. "No." He thought of Maiya, of the first time he had seen her. It had been at a dance his last year at the Academy. Maiya had been dancing with Drade, laughing at something he said. One look, and Falkon had known she would be his. He had cut in on Drade, and spent the rest of the night with Maiya. He had wooed her with the same single-mindedness with which he fought a battle, refusing to consider defeat. They had been married a week later. And a week after that, he had left her the first time. They had been married for five years and in all that time, she had never complained of the long separations. She had maintained their home, made him welcome when he returned, put up a brave front when another war took him away. Maiya . . .

"Falkon?"

He looked up, seeming startled to find her there. "What?"

"What were you thinking about?" she asked.

"Nothing."

Ashlynne sat back in the chair and looked out the window of the cockpit. Whatever he'd been thinking of, it had not been a happy thought. She felt a twinge of regret that he wouldn't confide in her, and then wondered why she cared. All she wanted was to go to Trellis and get on with her life.

"How soon are we leaving here?" she asked.

"A day or two."

"Why can't we leave now?"

"I need some downtime."

"Downtime?"

"R and R. You know, rest?" He laughed softly. "Maybe you don't know. When have you ever worked?"

"It's not my fault your life has been so horrible," she retorted.

"No, I guess not."

She glared at him. "You're probably glad all this happened, aren't you? Glad that the mine was destroyed, that my parents were murdered . . ."

"Ashlynne."

"Everything I ever knew is gone." She looked at him, her eyes filling with tears. "But you don't care, do you? You don't care about anything but yourself!"

Jumping up, she ran out of the cockpit. A moment later, a light flickered on the control panel, indicating that she had opened the hatch.

Falkon swore. Surely she wouldn't be foolish enough to go outside alone. Even as the thought crossed his mind, he saw her walking into the jungle, following the route they had taken the day before. He knew somehow that she was going to look for the unicorn. He checked the exterior temperature gauge. At least she had a good day for it, he mused, warm and clear.

Ashlynne pushed her way through the jungle, her vision blurred by tears. And to think she was starting to like him! She must have been out of her mind. He was nothing but a coarse, crass, vulgar man who didn't care about anything or anyone but himself. How had she ever thought otherwise?

Blinking back her tears, she walked toward the sound of the waterfall. There had been a break in the foliage yesterday. She stopped and looked around. Where was it?

She ducked under a tree branch, pushed through the greenery, and found herself at the edge of the river. The tranquil water shimmered with all the colors of the rainbow.

Dropping to her knees, she put her hand in the water. It was warm to the touch, soothing, inviting. A nice long soak was just what she needed.

After a quick look around, she undressed and slid into the water, sighing as it enveloped her. It was effervescent, she thought, almost alive, as if dozens of tiny fingers were running over her skin, soothing away her fears, easing her tension.

She waded deeper, enchanted by the feel of the frothy water on her skin.

Time lost all meaning as she floated there, her eyes closed, her mind empty of everything except the touch of the water and the warmth of the sun on her face.

Peace. Contentment. A stillness broken only by the chirping of a bird, and . . .

A loud splash.

Ashlynne's eyes flew open, her first thought that Falkon had followed her. But it wasn't Falkon. It was a very large catlike creature with thick brown-and-black-striped fur and large slanted yellow eyes, and it was swimming rapidly toward her from the opposite bank.

With a cry, she scrambled out of the water, gasping in pain as her toe struck a rock. She glanced over her shoulder. The cat had almost reached the shore now.

What to do? What to do? Panic engulfed her and she began to run, hoping she could find a place to hide. A growl sounded behind her, adding wings to her feet. She flew through the underbrush, oblivious to the spiky fronds that scratched her arms and legs and caught at her hair. Why had she left the safety of the ship?

She ran blindly, afraid to stop, afraid to look back for fear she would find the cat at her heels.

She screamed when she slammed into something hard and unyielding.

"Ashlynne! What the hell!"

"Falkon! Thank God."

He was about to ask her what she was doing running naked through the jungle when the big cat leapt into view. Thrusting Ashlynne behind him, Falkon yanked the gun from his waistband and fired.

The blast struck the cat full in the chest, killing it instantly.

Falkon turned to Ashlynne. Her eyes looked

huge in her pale face. "You damn fool. What were you thinking, coming out here alone?"

She stared up at him, too frightened by what had happened to speak.

He shook his head. She was shivering badly. Nerves, he thought.

"Don't do that again," he said quietly. He wiped a streak of blood from her cheek with his thumb.

"I—" She let out a long shuddering sigh. "If . . . if you hadn't followed me . . ." A huge tear rolled down her cheek and he brushed it away.

"Try not to think about it." He glanced at the cat. If he'd arrived a few minutes later, he would have been too late. The thought of her being attacked, ripped to shreds by those long black claws, twisted his gut in knots. She could have been killed, and it would have been his fault.

He swore softly as he shoved the gun into his pocket, then drew her into his arms and held her close. "Shh. It's all right now," he said. One hand drifted down her back. Her skin was soft and warm, so warm. Lifting her into his arms, he carried her back to where she'd left her clothing.

Ashlynne buried her face in his shoulder, embarrassed by her nudity, by the fact that she had behaved so stupidly. If Falkon hadn't come after her, she would be lying dead back there, torn to pieces by a wild animal. The thought drove everything else from her mind.

"Don't think about it," he repeated, his breath warm against her cheek. She was aware of his hands on her body, rough, callused hands that held her gently.

Her arms tightened around him. Thank the Maker for Falkon. He might be a mercenary and a renegade, but he was the strongest, bravest man she had ever known.

When they reached the river, he put her down. She would have turned away, but he caught her by the arm, his gaze moving over her.

Only then was she aware of the numerous cuts and scratches she had sustained in her wild flight. Fright had numbed the pain. Falkon's shirt front was stained with her blood.

He jerked his chin toward the river. "Go and rinse the blood off."

She wasn't anxious to go back into the river, but it offered her a way to cover her nudity and she waded into the water, her gaze darting up and down the bank. If there was one cat, there might be another. She sighed as the water closed over her. It felt wonderful, its warmth soothing, easing her pain.

She might have stayed in there the rest of the day if Falkon hadn't called for her to come out.

Knowing it was useless to refuse, she waded out of the water. Heat scorched her cheeks as he removed his shirt and began using it as a towel to dry her off.

"I can do it," she said.

With a nod, he thrust his shirt into her hands and turned his back, knowing that her image had been forever burned in his brain, from her full, pink-tipped breasts to her long, slender legs. Burned was the perfect word, he mused, because he was on fire for her. He stared at the water lapping gently against the shore. Stripping off his boots and breeches, he plunged in, hoping a cold swim would cool him off.

But even that was denied him. The water was warm. Nevertheless, it soothed him, easing the last bit of fear he had experienced when he saw the cat chasing her, taking the edge off the ache in his loins.

He swam for several minutes, then floated in the middle of the river, regarding Ashlynne through half-closed eyes.

She hadn't wasted any time getting dressed, and now she sat on the riverbank, scrubbing the blood from his shirt. She spread it out on a rock to dry, then ran her fingers through her hair. She looked like an angel sitting there, he thought, her skirt spread around her, the sun shining in her hair.

She looked up as he swam toward the shore. A flush rose in her cheeks as he stood up, and then, at the last minute, she turned her back to him.

He was grinning when he stepped out of the water. He pulled on his breeches and boots, then slung his damp shirt over one shoulder.

Ashlynne refused to meet his gaze on the walk back to the ship, and he wondered which bothered her more, the close call she'd had with the cat, the fact that he had seen her naked, or regret because she hadn't had the nerve to satisfy her curiosity.

Chapter Seventeen

There was an air of tension between them that hadn't been there before. Something had passed between them at the river, something for which she had no name, but Ashlynne felt it keenly as she sat in the copilot's seat staring out into the night.

Falkon sat in the pilot's seat, muttering under his breath as he studied a star chart of the galaxy. She was surprised that he didn't have it memorized by now.

Upon returning from the river, she had gone to her cabin to take a nap. Sleep, however, had been elusive, and she had lain there, wrapped up in a blanket, trying not to think about Falkon, about the gentleness of his touch as he had wiped the blood from her cheek, the way he had looked emerging from the river, rivulets of water dripping from his bronzed skin, his muscles rippling with every movement. She had been sorely tempted to see all of him but at the last minute, her cheeks burning with embarrassment, she had turned away.

Dinner had been a quiet affair. She had found herself looking at him surreptitiously time and again. His long black hair fell to his shoulders, giving him a roguish look that was accented by the faint white scar on his cheek.

Looking at him now, she wondered what he was thinking as he studied the chart on the screen.

He turned his head then, his gaze meeting hers. She looked into his eyes, blue-gray eyes that seemed to hold all the secrets of the universe, that promised answers to every question she'd ever had, if she would only trust him.

Time ceased to exist as he leaned slowly toward her, until they were little more than a breath apart. He didn't speak, only continued to look at her, and now there was a question in his eyes, a question she answered by closing the distance between them.

His lips were warm and firm, his kiss feather-light, barely more than a touch. A shivery feeling slid down her spine. She scooted over, her eyes closing as his lips sought hers again.

There was no hesitation in his kiss. He knew what he wanted, and he took it. His lips played over hers, flooding her with warmth. His hands slid around her waist and then he was lifting her out of her chair, settling her in his lap so her thighs straddled his. Her eyelids flew open in surprise.

"Relax, princess," he murmured.

His voice moved over her like black velvet, warm and soft, making her think of long dark nights, of bodies entwined on silken sheets. She felt his breath on her face. Excitement bubbled up inside her as his hand cupped the back of her head and his mouth slanted over hers once again while his other hand traced ever-widening circles over her back.

She should have pushed him away, but her curiosity was far stronger than her sense of propriety. Growing up in the jinan, surrounded by high walls and protective parents, she'd had little interaction with men, little chance to experiment, to flirt and be flirted with.

And so she closed her eyes and let Falkon kiss her again. It was, after all, just a kiss, she thought. Surely there could be no harm in it.

But this kiss was different from the last. His lips moved with tantalizing slowness over hers, evoking sweet sensations deep within her. His tongue slid over the seam of her lips. She gasped as his hand slid over her buttocks, drawing her hips closer to his.

She put her hands against his chest, thinking to push him away, then slid her arms around his neck, holding him tighter as he deepened the kiss still more. Her heart was pounding now; her breathing was erratic. A moan rose in her throat. When he slid his tongue across her lips again, she welcomed him inside.

She had never known passion before, never dreamed it had such power. She was on fire, burning, flaming, and all from a kiss.

She clung to him, wanting to be closer, her

hands restless as they moved up and down his back and over his shoulders, sliding down his arms to measure the muscles quivering there. A quick image of Falkon emerging from the river flashed through her mind, his body gleaming wetly in the sunlight.

Falkon drew Ashlynne closer. Just one more kiss, he told himself, and then he would let her go. But one kiss became two, and then three. She was fire and honey in his arms, warm and sweet, so damn sweet. Her skin was soft and smooth beneath his hands. She moaned softly as his thumb inadvertently stroked the curve of her breast. It had been months since he had lain with a woman, tasted one, caressed one. Need and desire swelled within him, urging him to take what she was offering. Except she didn't really know what she was offering. She was pure and untouched, a virgin in every sense of the word, and he had no right to defile her, no right to take that which rightfully belonged to her future husband.

He had done a lot of things in his life that he wasn't proud of, but he had never deflowered a virgin, especially one who was betrothed to another man.

Letting her go was the most difficult thing he had ever done.

She blinked at him, her lips slightly swollen, her beautiful green eyes cloudy with passion. Stifling a curse, he placed her on her feet and then stood up.

"You're engaged," he said with a tight smile. "One of us needs to remember that. Your fiancé might not be willing to pay for damaged goods."

His words had the desired effect. Anger chased the passion from her eyes. A rush of color flooded her cheeks. With a wordless cry, she slapped him across the face, then ran out of the cockpit. A moment later, he heard the door to her cabin slam shut.

He grinned as he rubbed his cheek. For a little thing, she packed a hell of a wallop.

Chapter Eighteen

She slept late after a long and restless night. Waking or sleeping, her thoughts had been of Falkon. Always Falkon. He was like a fever in her blood, an addiction for which there was no cure. One minute she was sure she hated him, the next she wanted to be in his arms, wanted to feel his mouth on hers, taste the forbidden pleasures promised by his knowing smile and roguish grin.

Rising, she dressed quickly, determined to pretend nothing had happened between them the evening before.

She was on her way to the galley for breakfast when she happened to look out the port. Frowning, she realized they were in space.

Changing direction, she went into the cockpit. "Where are we going?"

He looked at her as if she wasn't very bright. "Trellis."

"How long will it take to get there?"

Was it his imagination, or did she sound less than enthusiastic that they were finally on their way?

"We'll be there late tomorrow night." He was taking her to her fiancé. Being with her, holding her, was far too seductive, far too dangerous, for his peace of mind.

Last night, holding her in his arms, he had been tempted to forget about Drade, to forget about avenging the deaths of his wife and daughter. Last night, he had wanted nothing more than to take Ashlynne away somewhere and spend the rest of his days loving her.

He fingered the collar at his throat, felt his anger stir to life once again, and with it his need for vengeance. Drade would pay for every day he had toiled in the mine, for every night he had spent locked in a cold, damp cell, for every minute he had spent in solitary, for every humiliation he had endured, every stroke of the lash.

Ashlynne felt a sudden chill as she looked at Falkon. His eyes were cold; a muscle throbbed in his cheek. She wondered what he was thinking, sincerely hoping that she was not the cause of the anger seething inside him.

She spent the day moving between her cabin and the galley. She stayed out of the cockpit, except to take Falkon his meals, which he acknowledged with a curt nod. She hadn't intended to wait on him. Why should she? He could get his own food if he was hungry. But it was a good excuse to go to the cockpit. She wanted to ask him what was wrong, why he was so angry, but she lacked the nerve to break the brittle silence between them.

In her cabin later that night, she tried to recall Niklaus's face, but it was Falkon's image that sprang readily to mind, the memory of Falkon's kiss that followed her to sleep.

When she rose in the morning, he was sitting as she had left him the night before. Dark bristles shadowed the line of his jaw.

With a sigh, she went into the galley and fixed two cups of coffee, one black, for him, one with cream, heavy on the sugar, for herself. She carried them into the cockpit and sat down.

"Here." She handed him one of the cups.

"I'm sorry," he muttered.

"So am I. What are you going to do after you drop me off?"

"I have an old score to settle."

"What do you mean?"

He rubbed his hand over the collar at his throat. "Do you know how to get this damn thing off?"

She shook her head. "Maybe there's a release on the controller. Did you look?"

"Yeah." He had looked, very carefully, afraid he might accidentally trigger the damn thing. He wondered what kind of man had invented such a barbaric contraption.

"How much ransom are you going to demand for me?"

Falkon shook his head. "I'm not."

"Oh? What changed your mind?"

"I decided it would be too risky. I'd have to arrange a meeting, and I'm sure your fiancé would inform the authorities." He shook his head. "I'll drop you off near his residence, and then you're on your own."

She nodded. She had never been on her own before. There had always been someone near-by she could call on, someone to watch over her, take care of her.

The hours passed slowly. She dozed in her chair, woke, and dozed again; her dreams were fragmented, confusing, filled with fuzzy images of her parents and Magny. And Falkon. Always he was there, a dark presence lurking in the background, both fearsome and reassuring.

It was after midnight when they reached their destination. Falkon landed the ship at a free port near the south end of the city.

Ashlynne looked out the window. Lights burned in a building off to the left. Three men were working on a Romarian league cruiser in a nearby hangar.

She looked at Falkon. With a pang, she realized that he would soon be gone from her life and she would never see him again.

He turned, his gaze meeting hers. "Well, princess, we're here."

She nodded, unable to speak past the lump in her throat. He was her last link with her old life, with home.

"Ready?"

"It's late. Maybe we should wait until morning."

"I thought you were anxious to get here?"

"I was. I am. But . . ." She looked down at her dress. She didn't want to meet Niklaus looking like this, wearing a gown and sandals that were dirty from traipsing through the jungle of an uncharted planet.

"Let's go find lodging," she said. "I need to clean up."

"Lodging, princess?" Falkon shook his head. "I'm broke."

"I'm not."

He frowned at her. "What do you mean?"

"I have credits in an account."

"Why didn't you say so sooner?"

She shrugged. "I didn't think of it, till now. It's just a small account, twenty thousand credits. My mother didn't want me be totally dependent on Niklaus. She said a girl should have a little something of her own to fall back on, so she opened an account for me. I wasn't to touch it until after I was married."

Falkon shook his head. Her parents had been rich indeed if twenty thousand credits was considered a small amount. "You ready?"

She nodded.

"All right, this is what we're gonna do." He took the controller out of his pocket, blew out a sigh of resignation, and handed it to her. "We don't have any papers. When we get to the check-in point, I want you to tell them what happened on Tierde, tell them we stole a ship and escaped. They'll have heard about the attack by now. Have you got that stun gun with you?"

"Yes."

"Good." He pulled the gun he had taken from the guard on Enjine Base Nine out of his pocket. "Hang on to this, too. All right, activate the manacles on my wrists, and let's go."

There were two guards clad in Romarian garb when they reached the port of entry.

"I'll need your documents," the taller of the two men said, holding out his hand.

"Documents?" Ashlynne said. She pressed a hand to her heart. "Oh, dear, I'm afraid I don't have any."

"Who are you, and where are you coming from?"

"I'm the daughter of Lord Marcus of Myrafloures. My father owned the mine on Tierde. We were attacked several days ago. My slave and I were the only ones to escape. We managed to steal a ship and get away."

"We heard of the attack," the second guard said. "Damned green-skinned, black-hearted Hodorians. They can't be trusted."

Ashlynne nodded. Tears pricked her eyes, and she let them fall. "My parents were killed. I'm on my way to Arkata. My fiancé, Niklaus Hassrick, lives there."

The Hassrick name worked like magic. The guards stepped back and opened the gate. "We're sorry for your loss, my lady," said the first.

"Thank you. Can you tell me where I might find lodging for the night?"

"I can do better than that. I'll have one of my men take you there."

"Thank you, that's very kind."

The guard smiled at her. Picking up a communicator, he summoned an amphibious surface transport craft and gave the driver directions.

Ashlynne smiled her thanks as the guard handed her into the ASTC. "Come along, Number Four," she said in her best lady-of-the-manor voice.

Keeping his face carefully blank, Falkon

took his place in the rear seat of the four-seat vehicle.

"Have a pleasant stay," the guard said.

"Thank you," Ashlynne replied. "You've been very kind."

"My pleasure, my lady," he said.

"My pleasure, my lady," Falkon muttered as the guard closed the door. He stared at the manacles on his wrists, and wondered if putting himself at her mercy had been such a good idea.

They found lodging in a glass-fronted, four-story building. Falkon watched Ashlynne sign for the room, then followed her into the elevator.

As soon as the doors closed, he held out his hands. "Turn me loose."

She hesitated a moment, making him wonder if he was going to have to try to wrest the controller from her again, when she pulled it from her pocket and released his hands.

Their room was on the fourth floor. She slid the key card into the slot and the door opened. A light came on as they stepped into the room.

Falkon looked around. It was a large room, decorated in subtle shades of blue and green. A tele-screen took up one wall. There were two large reclining sofas, a desk built into one wall, a fireplace.

There was a large bedroom and bathroom, and a small kitchen that offered snacks and drinks.

"Nice place," he muttered.

Ashlynne nodded. "We need some new clothes." She went to the tele-screen and flipped through the channels until she found an all-night shopping channel. She looked through their catalog, picked out several changes of clothes, underwear and shoes, then turned to Falkon. "Pick out whatever you want."

He opted for a pair of black pants, a gray long-sleeved turtleneck sweater that would hide the collar around his neck and the manacles on his wrists, and a pair of calf-high black boots.

"Is that all you want?" Ashlynne asked.

Falkon nodded. "I'll pay you back."

"There's no need." She confirmed their order and ended the transmission.

"Yes, there is."

She sighed. There was no point in arguing with him. "I'm hungry." She picked up the phone and dialed the main desk. "Do you want anything?"

"Sure. The thickest steak they've got and all the trimmings."

He went to look out the window while she ordered. The city was brightly lit, a maze of streets lined with tall buildings, their mirrored windows reflecting the light. A pair of mono-rails snaked overhead. Despite the late hour, the streets were crowded. Like most big cities, the stores and entertainment centers here were open twenty-four hours a day.

Tomorrow he would be free. The first order of business would be to find a way to get rid of the shackles that branded him a prisoner, then he would need to find a transport that would take him to Romariz. And Drade.

Drade. For the first time, be began to think he might actually have a chance at the revenge he craved so desperately.

There was a knock at the door and when he

opened it, an android handed him several packages. Falkon signed for the delivery, then carried the boxes into the bedroom and dropped them on the floor. One way or another, he would pay her back.

A few minutes later, a bell rang in the kitchen, signaling the arrival of their meal.

Ashlynnc looked at Falkon expectantly, but he made no move toward the kitchen. With a sigh of resignation, she went into the kitchen and opened the servet door. Picking up the tray, she wondered why she had even considered the possibility that he would wait on her. Months of slavery in the bowels of the mine had not made a slave of him. She doubted if anything could.

She carried the tray into the living room and sat down. Uncovering the tray, she placed the dishes on the table.

Sitting down beside her, Falkon hit the control on the arm of the sofa, and the tele-screen came to life. He selected an all-news station, and there was Drade, bigger than life. Jayson looked impressive as hell in his uniform, his medals all shiny, his dark brown hair cropped short.

Falkon leaned forward, everything else forgotten, as he listened to what his old enemy was saying.

"Following the unprovoked attack on Tierde, Romariz was quick to offer support. Clean-up has begun." Drade smiled into the camera. He'd always had more than his share of charm, and he poured it on now. "A new shipment of prisoners from Daccar has been assembled, and the mine will be fully functional again within the next week, assuring that there will be no shortage of the black crystals."

"Thank you, Commander Drade. In other news . . ."

Falkon shook his head. Quick to offer support, indeed. He wouldn't be surprised to learn that Romariz had been behind the attack in the first place. Troops from Romariz had probably been hovering nearby, waiting to step in as soon as the Hodorian Army had completed its attack. Romariz would assume control, not only of the mine, but of the star base, offering its protection from further attack. Tierde was a small, peaceful planet with a small population. Its people would have no recourse but to accept. After all, they had signed a peace treaty with Romariz; and once Romariz was in power, there would be no way to get rid of them short of all-out war. Falkon swore softly. To his knowledge, the only planets in the quadrant that were still free of Romarian rule were Daccar, Polixe, and Cherlin Four.

"Falkon? Is something wrong with your dinner?"

"What?" He glanced at Ashlynne.

"Is something wrong? You're not eating."

"No, everything's fine." He stared at the food on his plate, determined to enjoy the meal. "Just fine."

"What are you going to do when you leave here?"

"Settle an old score." He pushed the plate away, his appetite gone.

"You mentioned that once before, but you never told me with whom."

"Drade."

"The man on the news?"

Falkon nodded. "He's the bastard who killed my family."

"And you won't rest until he's dead, will you?" She looked at him thoughtfully a moment. "I'll never see you again, will I?"

"No." He smiled at her as he ran the backs of his fingers along her cheek. "That should make you happy, Princess."

"Yes, it should." But it didn't. She thought of the time they had spent together. He had saved her life, comforted her when she was sad, dried her tears, treated her as an equal instead of a useless decoration, made her feel, made her think, shown her that she had more courage than she had ever imagined. Kissed her . . .

With a clarity that was sudden and startling, she realized she was in love with him.

Falkon frowned as he watched the play of emotions move across Ashlynne's face. Her gaze met his, open and honest, hitting him with the force of a laser blast, and he knew in that moment that he didn't want to let her go, that he didn't want to see her married to another man. He wanted her for himself, had wanted her from the moment he had first looked up and seen her staring down at him, her eyes wide with horror and pity.

He stood up slowly, walked around the table, and reached for her. She went to him willingly, everything she was thinking, everything she was feeling, shining in the emerald depths of her eyes.

"This will never work." His hand cupped her cheek.

"I know." Her arms slid around his waist.

"I'm a wanted man." His fingertips slid down her neck, resting in the hollow of her throat. He could feel her heart beating there, its rhythm increasing at his touch.

"I'm engaged to Niklaus." She stood on tiptoe, pressing her body against the hard length of his.

"I won't rest until my family is avenged." His hands slid over her shoulders, down her back, his fingers running lightly up and down her spine.

"I know." Her hands slid under his shirt, moving restlessly up and down his back. She loved the way his skin felt beneath her palms, the sudden intake of his breath when she touched him.

"Ashlynne." Her name was a low groan on his lips as he lowered his head, his mouth covering hers in a desperate, hungry kiss that stole the breath from her lungs and the strength from her legs.

She leaned into him, wanting to be close, closer, wanting all of him, his hands and his lips, his heart and his soul.

His mouth was like fire, his tongue a living flame, and she reveled in it, craved it, devoured it as if it were the elixir of life itself.

He was murmuring her name, raining kisses on her lips, her cheeks, her eyelids, the tip of her nose, filling her with a wild abandon, a primal pulsing need that would no longer be denied.

She wanted to laugh with the wonder of it, cry from the overwhelming sense of joy that filled her heart and soul with both pleasure and pain.

Sweeping her into his arms, he carried her down the hallway and into one of the bedrooms. He sat down on the edge of the bed, then fell back on the mattress, carrying her with him, so that her body covered his. His hands tunneled into her hair, cradling her head.

And then he kissed her again and yet again, and the fire between them burned hotter and brighter.

She lifted his shirt, drawing it over his head and tossing it aside, so that she could run her fingers over his chest, press kisses to his throat, his shoulders, feel his skin grow hot beneath her touch. She kissed the number four branded on his arm, a fierce ache growing inside her for the pain he had suffered. His desire for her was evident, and she thrilled to the knowledge and the power it awakened within her.

He unfastened her dress, drew it down over her hips, his gaze hot as he tossed it aside and removed her undergarments.

"Beautiful," he murmured as he bared her body to his gaze. "So beautiful."

She moaned as he kissed her breasts, then drew her down on top of him and kissed her again, and again.

"Ashlynne . . ." His voice was ragged with want and desire and need.

"Don't stop."

"Are you sure?" He gazed up at her, his eyes dark with passion. "I don't want to hurt you."

His knuckles brushed her cheek. "I don't want to do something you'll regret later."

"I'm sure." She cupped his face in her hands and kissed him gently. "I've never been more sure of anything in my life."

Murmuring her name, he rolled onto his side, carrying her with him.

She sighed as their bodies came together, warm flesh to warm flesh. "I love you," she murmured. "Do you know how much I love you?"

"Ashlynne . . . I don't deserve you. You're fine and beautiful and I have nothing to offer you. No home, nothing."

"You'll be my home," she whispered fervently. "And I'll be yours."

And with those simple words, she stole his heart and his soul.

He made love to her gently, tenderly, aware that this time, the first time, would be something she would always remember. He worshiped her with his hands and his lips, adored her with every touch, every caress, whispered that she was beautiful, that he needed her, wanted her, with every fiber of his being, every breath in his body.

And when he took her, when his body at last merged with hers and they hovered on the edge of the world, he said the words he had never thought to say again, saw the tears well in her eyes as he whispered, "I love you."

Chapter Nineteen

Ashlynne sighed as Falkon hugged her close. Never, she thought, never had she imagined love would be like this. Never had she dreamed it would be as wonderful, as thrilling, as soul-shatteringly beautiful.

She ran her fingertips over his chest, lifted her hand to his mouth, felt his lips move against her palm.

"Are you all right?" he asked. "I didn't hurt you?"

"No." She felt herself smiling and couldn't stop. "You didn't hurt me."

He turned on his side. "What are you thinking?"

She ran her hand over the collar at his throat, her smile widening. "I'm thinking you're still my slave, Number Four."

"Am I?" His voice was a growl.

"Yes, and as such, you must do my bidding."

"Ah," he said. "As always, your wish is my command, princess, only tell me what you want."

He watched her cheeks turn pink as she whispered, "Then I wish for you to make love to me again."

"So soon?" He lifted one brow, unable to resist teasing her, yet pleased beyond words that she wanted him again, as he wanted her.

"The thought doesn't please you?"

"I shall always do my best to please you, my lady," he replied fervently. "Only tell me what you wish me to do."

She sighed, as if she were giving it some thought. "Kiss me, then," she said.

"Where?"

"Here." She touched her lips with her finger. "And here." She touched her cheek. "And here." She touched her left breast, moaning softly as his lips moved from her mouth to her cheek to her breast.

"Anything else?"

"Surely a good servant need not be commanded in all things," she whispered breathlessly.

"Then I may do this?" His hand stroked her leg from knee to thigh. "And this?" He drew his hand slowly upward, over her belly until it covered her breast.

And then he rose over her, his eyes hot with desire as he made love to her again.

She had thought the first time the most wonderful, the most magical experience of her life.

But with every kiss, with every caress, he showed her that she still had a lot to learn.

Ashlynne rolled onto her stomach, her elbows propped on his chest. "We really have to find a way to get rid of that collar," she said. "I'm sorry, you know, for all the times I hurt you."

"It's all right. I probably had it coming."

"Oh, you did," she said, grinning. "But I'm still sorry." She ran her fingertips over the collar. "How will we ever get it off?"

"I'll find a way. I'm sure there's someone on Trellis who'll remove it, for the right price."

"We'll have it done, no matter what the cost."

"I don't have any credits, remember?"

"I do, remember?"

He shook his head. "No. I'll find a way."

"I think you forget yourself, Number Four," she said.

"Is that right?"

"Indeed," she said imperiously.

He laughed softly. "Very well, my lady, I am at your command."

"Good. I find that dreadful collar offends me deeply, and I wish you to be rid of it as soon as possible."

"For once, my lady, we are in complete agreement."

"Falkon, how did you ever put up with me?" With her finger, she traced the number four branded on his arm. "I treated you so horribly." Leaning down, she brushed her lips over the brand. "Did it hurt very badly?"

He grunted softly. "Bad enough."

"I wish there was some way I could undo all

241

the pain you've endured, all the misery I caused you."

"Come here, sweetheart," he said, tucking her beneath him, "and I'll show you how you can make it up to me."

She smiled up at him as she gathered him into her arms. "Your wish is my command."

Ashlynne woke in his arms, smiling. It had been a night she would never forget. They had made love and slept and loved again, and each time had been more wonderful than the last. Never had she felt so treasured, so beautiful or desirable. He made love to her with infinite tenderness, arousing her, filling her, completing her.

She glanced out the window. The sun was just rising. Turning her head, she looked at the man sleeping beside her. How handsome he was! And how much she loved him. When had it happened, she wondered, when had he become important to her? Maybe she had loved him all along, she mused, for he had been in her every thought since the day she first saw him lying in a pool of his own blood.

She felt her cheeks grow hot when she realized he was awake and watching her.

"Morning, princess," he drawled.

"Hi."

"You all right?"

"I'm better than all right," she replied, and felt her cheeks grow even hotter.

He grinned, looking inordinately pleased with himself.

"You don't have to look so smug about it," she muttered.

"No? Tell me I'm not the reason you're blushing."

"You're not. I just feel good this morning."

"Uh huh. And I guess I had nothing to do with that, either."

"Oh, all right, you had everything to do with it. Are you happy now?"

"Yes, ma'am," he replied.

He was laughing now, and she was laughing with him. Happiness bubbled up inside her, warm and effervescent. What more could she ask of life, she thought, than to wake up in his arms every morning for the rest of her life?

"What are we going to do now?" She hadn't meant to ask, was afraid to hear the answer.

Falkon took a deep breath, let it out in a long sigh. Until this very moment, he had intended to go after Drade, to exact vengeance for the deaths of his wife and child, even if he lost his own life in the process. But now . . . he looked at Ashlynne and knew he couldn't leave her, knew that without her, life would not be worth living.

"Falkon?"

He heard the tremor in her voice, knew she was waiting for his answer. "If I asked you to go away with me, would you go?"

"Yes." She answered without hesitation.

"And if I asked you to marry me, would you still say yes?"

"Oh, yes!"

He laughed softly. "I'll hold you to it, you know."

"I hope so."

"Very well, princess. Tomorrow we'll leave this rock and go to Cherlin Four. I have a friend there. We can stay with him until we decide what to do."

Cherlin Four. She had never been there, of course, but she had heard of the people. She had seen pictures of them once. They were a tall race, covered with very fine hair from head to foot, save for their faces. Oddly, the men were unable to grow beards. "Can we get married there?"

"Sure." He grinned at her. "Now that that's settled, I could use a shower."

She nodded, feeling somewhat disappointed. She had been hoping he would make love to her again.

He stood up, turned, and lifted her into his arms.

"What are you doing?"

"I told you. I need a shower."

"But—"

"So do you." He carried her into the bathroom, turned on the shower, and stepped inside.

"Falkon!"

"Yes, princess?" He gazed down at her, his eyes filled with silent laughter.

"Nothing."

He put her on her feet and reached for the soap. Her eyes widened as he began to wash her. It was the most erotic sensation she had ever known, feeling his rough soapy hands move over her skin. She felt herself blush from head to toe, but made no move to stop him. And when he was through, she took the soap from his hands and washed him in return. And then they made love, there in the shower, standing up with the hot water running over them.

She was washing him for the second time when she heard a loud knock on the door. "Who could that be?"

Falkon shook his head. "I don't know."

"I'll go see." Stepping out of the shower, she put on a fluffy white robe, wrapped her hair in a towel, and went to the door. "Who is it?"

"Niklaus."

Niklaus! She stared at the door. It couldn't be!

"Ashlynne, open the door."

"I . . . I just got out of the shower." She glanced over her shoulder. Falkon was standing in the doorway, water dripping from his hair. "Give me a minute to get dressed," she called, and turned away without waiting for his answer. "What arc we going to do?"

"Get dressed," he said, reaching for his trousers. "Hurry."

She did as he asked, and when they were both dressed, he handed her the controller, then held out his arms. "Do it."

She shook her head.

"Do it, Ashlynne."

At his urging, she depressed the control to lock his wrists together. He followed her into the living room and sat on the floor, his knees drawn up to his chest. "Activate the controls on my ankles," he said, "then open the door."

Again, she did as bidden; then, slipping the controller into the pocket of her pants, she opened the door. Three men stood in the hall-way. She recognized Niklaus at once.

"So," he said, "we meet at last."

"Yes." Ashlynne glanced at the other two men, then looked at Niklaus.

"Brill, Tallman, wait outside," he said, and, stepping into the room, he closed the door. He studied her for a moment, his gaze moving over her as if she were an animal or a piece of furniture he was thinking of buying. "You're even prettier than your photo," he mused aloud.

"Thank you."

He looked around the room, his gaze settling on Falkon. "I was told you weren't alone."

"Oh? By whom?"

"The guard at the port of entry. I would have been here last night, but I was away, and only learned of your arrival this morning."

"I was coming to see you."

"Yes, I'm sure you were, but I couldn't have you traveling the streets alone."

"I'm not alone."

"So I see." Niklaus went to stand in front of Falkon. "I've heard about you," he said.

Falkon bit back the sharp retort that rose in his throat and forced himself to look properly humble and subdued, as befitting one who was supposed to be a slave.

"Commander Casman told me about your escape." Niklaus looked over his shoulder at Ashlynne. "You must have been quite frightened."

She hesitated a moment before answering. "Yes. Yes, I was."

"I was told this man took you against your will, yet here he is, shackled hand and foot. Would you care to explain how that came about?"

Ashlynne glanced at Falkon, her mind whirling. "He took me prisoner and stole a cruiser. When he learned that you and I were engaged, he decided to come here and . . . and hold me for ransom. He said you would pay whatever he asked to get me back."

"Go on."

"After we landed, I managed to get the controller away from him."

"Why didn't you call me when you arrived?"

"It was late, and I was tired. I wanted to be rested before we met. I bought some new clothes so you wouldn't be ashamed of me."

Hassrick's gaze moved over her once again. The blue velvet pants and matching soft silk top were obviously new, as were the matching soft leather boots.

"I see. And what were you going to do with him?"

Ashlynne paused. She wanted desperately to look at Falkon, but she didn't dare. "Keep him, of course. He is, after all, my slave, and quite a good worker."

"I was told you appeared quite fond of him. Casman said you were quite adamant that he shouldn't be hurt."

"Number Four is my property," she replied. "And all that I have left of value, now that my home is gone."

A shadow passed over Hassrick's face. Was it regret?

"Number Four is a valuable asset, you know," she went on, "for all that he can be troublesome at times."

Hassrick grunted softly. "Yes, I'm sure that's

true. Several people have been inquiring as to his whereabouts."

"Oh?"

"Yes. Well," Hassrick said briskly, "let us be on our way, shall we? Where's the controller?"

"I have it."

Hassrick smiled as he held out his hand. "I'll take it."

"I'm quite able to manage, thank you."

"I'm sure you are, my dear, but there's no need for you to be bothered with him any longer."

"What do you mean?"

"I mean I'm in charge now."

"What are you going to do with him?"

"I've not yet decided. For now, we shall take him with us." He waggled his fingers. "The controller, Ashlynne."

She could think of no reason to refuse.

Hassrick took the controller from her hand, stared at it a moment. "I've heard of these, of course, but never had the opportunity to use one."

Falkon went suddenly tense as Hassrick ran his thumb back and forth over the controller.

"Let's see," Hassrick mused, "this activates the manacles on his wrists, and this the shackles on his feet. And this . . . What does this do?" he asked.

Ashlynne felt suddenly sick to her stomach as his thumb hovered over the top of the controller. She screamed, "Nicholas, don't!" as his thumb depressed the top of the controller, but it was too late.

With a strangled cry, Falkon went rigid as the pain reflex was activated.

She watched in horror as he writhed on the floor, unable to escape the pain, his body convulsing, his face a mask of anguish. She clenched her hands into tight fists, her own body trembling, as the punishment went on and on. She looked at Niklaus, stunned to see that he was actually enjoying Falkon's pain.

Niklaus looked at her and smiled. "It's always wise to remind subordinates who is in charge, don't you agree?"

Knowing it wouldn't do to appear overly concerned and knowing, somehow, that Falkon would suffer for it if she did, Ashlynne nodded. "Yes, of course."

She looked back at Falkon. His face was damp with sweat, every muscle in his body was trembling violently. He lay on the floor, panting, his body gradually relaxing as the pain decreased and finally ended.

She watched him gather his strength, watched him rise to his feet on legs that still trembled, his face expressionless, his eyes dark with unspoken fury.

"Well," Niklaus said, slipping the controller into his pocket. "Shall we go?"

Chapter Twenty

Falkon sat on the floor in the back of the shuttle, vainly trying to control his anger. To be a prisoner again, when freedom had been within his grasp, was almost beyond bearing. He felt his rage build as he recalled the sheer enjoyment evident on Hassrick's face when he activated the controller. The man had done it for no other reason than to watch him squirm, Falkon thought bitterly, and then frowned, wondering if the man suspected something was going on between him and Ashlynne. It occurred to him that Hassrick might have activated the controller simply to watch Ashlynne's reaction. It seemed unlikely, and yet . . . He swore under his breath, knowing there would be hell to pay, and he would be the one to pay it, if Hassrick discovered what had happened the night before.

There was no point in dwelling on what might happen, he thought, and turned his attention to the view outside the window. They had left the city behind and were passing through a wide expanse of countryside. Arkata was a fertile land, lush with green grass and a wide variety of trees, shrubs and flowers. Long-haired cattle grazed on the hillsides and rested in shady glens.

After an hour or so, they passed through a small city and then they were in open country again.

From time to time, Falkon heard Hassrick pointing out sights of interest to Ashlynne.

He shifted on the floor, unable to get comfortable with his hands and feet shackled.

They rounded a sharp curve in the road. Ahead, lay a huge walled jinan. An intricate letter *H* was woven into the double wrought-iron gates that swung open at their approach.

Falkon swore under his breath. The Hassrick holding was bigger than many of the cities he had been in.

The road was paved with crushed white stones that glistened in the sunlight. Tall trees lined the driveway. Acres of verdant grassland surrounded the house, which resembled a gothic castle. Several smaller buildings were located on either side of the house.

As soon as the shuttle craft pulled up in front of the house, the front door opened and a man who was obviously a servant hurried down the stairs. He opened the door for Hassrick, bowed low and then stepped aside as his master stepped out of the vehicle.

Turning, Hassrick offered Ashlynne his hand.

Hassrick's two companions got out of the craft. One of them opened the door for Falkon and motioned for him to get out.

"Can't," he said.

"Lord Hassrick?"

"What is it, Brill?" Hassrick glanced over his shoulder. Seeing the problem, he pulled the controller from his pocket and unlocked the shackles on Falkon's ankles.

Falkon slid out of the craft and the two men immediately moved up beside him, Brill on his left, the other man on his right.

"Well," Hassrick said, taking Ashlynne firmly by the arm, "what do you think?"

"It's . . . it's quite lovely."

"Yes. I think you'll be happy here. Brill, take the prisoner to the detention area and lock him up."

"Yes, sir."

Ashlynne's heart constricted as she watched the two men lead Falkon away. It wouldn't do to make a fuss, yet she had a sinking feeling in her stomach that she would never see him again. She couldn't lose him now, she thought desperately, not when they'd been through so much. Not when she loved him.

"What are you going to do with Number Four?" she asked as Niklaus led her up the stairs.

"He's a slave," Hassrick replied. "We'll put him to work, of course."

Falkon paced the floor, cursing his luck with every step. Freedom had been within his grasp, and now it was gone. He paused to stare out the small barred window. He was in a cell again, albeit a much nicer one than the one on Tierde, but a cell nonetheless. He had been surprised to find slaves on the Hassrick estate, but they were there, imprisoned in a long row of small huts located at the bottom of a hill, out of sight of the house.

Several guards patrolled the grounds, along with some of the biggest, meanest looking dogs Falkon had ever seen. Even if he could find a way out of the cell, even if he could get past the guards and the dogs, there was no way over the wall, which was a good fifteen feet high and probably laser shielded.

Damn! He had to find a way out of here. But how?

Ashlynne paced the floor of her room, too nervous to sit still, too worried about Falkon and their future to concentrate on anything else. Niklaus had shown her to her room when they first arrived, saying he would show her the rest of the house later, suggesting that she might like to take a nap after the long journey. But she was too worried about Falkon to rest. In an effort to relax, she had taken a hot bath, then changed into one of her new gowns, a silky soft dress of pale lavender that managed to be modest and provocative at the same time. She had bought it with Falkon in mind, would not have worn it now except that it was the only thing she had that was suitable to wear to dinner.

Going to the window, she stared out over the grounds, wondering where the detention area was. Falkon was down there somewhere, locked in a cell. He would hate being a prisoner again, hate being confined in a small space.

She turned and looked around the room. She was a prisoner, too, she thought, even though her prison was quite the biggest, most comfortable room she had ever seen. The carpet on the floor was white, at least two inches thick. The walls were a pale, pale blue. There was a small sofa, an enormous bed covered with a silky blue comforter. Large windows overlooked the yard. There was a white brick fireplace in one corner. A tele-screen filled one wall. The adjoining bathroom was equally plush. But it was still a prison, and she was promised to a man she didn't like, a man she didn't trust, though she wasn't sure why. He treated her well enough, seemed concerned for her welfare, endeavored to make her comfortable, and yet there was something about him that made her cringe. She remembered the look on his face when he had activated the controller. He had done it on purpose, she thought, done it simply for the pleasure of watching Falkon writhe in agony.

Falkon. She glanced at the bed, and wished, shamelessly, that he was there, that they could make love again. Would they ever make love again?

A knock at the door drew her attention. "Lady Ashlynne?"

"Yes?"

"Sir Hassrick requests that you join him in the library in thirty minutes. He would like you to meet his parents."

"Very well."

"I shall come for you then."

"Thank you."

She had thought it strange that she hadn't met his parents earlier, but Niklaus had told her they were away for the day. She was not looking forward to meeting them, or to discussing the wedding. How could she marry Niklaus when it was Falkon she loved? And what would happen if she refused, if she told Niklaus she loved Falkon?

She was certain Niklaus would not want her if he knew she was no longer a virgin. She knew, just as certainly, that Falkon's life would be forfeit if Niklaus learned what they had done.

Briefly, she contemplated telling Niklaus part of the truth, that she was sorry, but that she was in love with someone else and could not honor their engagement. Niklaus was a proud man. It was unlikely that he would still want to marry her if she loved another. But would he let her take Falkon? He had no right to refuse her. Falkon was her property, after all. But could she take that chance? What if she told Niklaus she wanted to break their engagement and he agreed, and then refused to let her take Falkon when she left? She couldn't leave him there.

With a sigh, she sat down on the bed and put on the soft slippers that matched her gown.

A moment later, one of the servants arrived to escort her to the library.

Niklaus's father was a tall, imposing man, with iron-gray hair, a clipped mustache, and cold blue eyes. He wore a pair of black trousers and a dark green shirt. He rose as Ashlynne entered the room. His wife was rather plain, with short, curly black hair and dark brown eyes. She wore a brilliant pink jumpsuit. A jeweled bracelet sparkled on her left wrist. His parents both radiated the calm assurance that seemed to be an innate characteristic of all people who were born to wealth and privilege.

"Mother, Father, this is Ashlynne. Ashlynne, this is my father, Rugen, and my mother, Zahara."

Rugen came forward, smiling. "At last," he said, "you're here. Welcome, daughter."

For all his kind words, she did not feel welcome.

Zahara smiled and held out her hand, and Ashlynne crossed the room to take her future mother-in-law's hand in hers.

"We were so sorry to hear about your parents," Zahara said. "You must consider this your home now, dear."

"Thank you."

Zahara beamed at her, then patted the seat beside her. "Sit down, dear. We have much to discuss."

"Ah, yes," Rugen said. Moving to a cupboard set into the wall, he withdrew a crystal decanter and filled four glasses. "The wedding." He handed each of the others a glass. "Let us toast the bride and groom."

Ashlynne forced a smile. She was never going to be happy here, she thought. Never. There was no love in this house, no warmth or caring between Rugen and Zahara.

"So, my dear," Zahara said, "have you thought of a date?"

"No, not yet," Ashlynne replied. "So much has happened."

"Yes, dear, of course, but life goes on."

Ashlynne nodded.

"We were thinking of next month," Rugen remarked.

"Next month?" Ashlynne exclaimed. "So soon?"

"Well, there's no reason to wait, is there?" Niklaus asked.

A reason, she needed a reason. And then it came to her. "You seem to forget, I've not had time to mourn my family properly."

Niklaus and his father exchanged glances that Ashlynne could not interpret.

"I'm afraid I'm really not in the proper frame of mind to plan our wedding, Niklaus," she said quietly. "You do understand, don't you? Besides, I should like some time for us to get acquainted. We are, after all, strangers to each other."

"Yes, of course. You must think me quite insensitive to your loss. It's only that I've waited for you for so long." He smiled at her. "Take as much time as necessary."

"Thank you."

"How much time will you need?" Zahara asked.

"Six months should be sufficient."

"Six months!" Rugen said.

"That's rather a long time, don't you think?" Zahara said.

"A year is the normal length of time on Tierde," Ashlynne said.

"I should think three months would be sufficient," Rugen said.

Niklaus looked at Ashlynne. "Will three months be long enough? We can plan the wedding in that time. It will give you something else to think about."

"Yes," Zahara said. She patted Ashlynne on the arm. "Don't you agree, dear? Keeping busy is the best thing."

"Yes, I guess so," Ashlynne said. Three months. Surely, in three months, she would be able to find a way to get herself and Falkon out of there.

Chapter Twenty-one

Dinner was a formal affair, the four of them sitting at a large table spread with expensive china and crystal and gold flatware.

They spoke of the wedding, discussing the menu, the guest list, the food for the reception following the ceremony.

After dinner, Niklaus took her on a tour of the house. One room was filled with expensive paintings and ancient tapestries, another held a collection of blue-green Venusian glass. There were more bedrooms than she could count, each one lavishly appointed, all with fireplaces and tele-screens, one with a waterfall.

He switched on the outdoor lights and they walked around the grounds. She saw rabbits scurrying here and there, peacocks, a trio of deer. The stable held a dozen hot-blooded horses. Long haired cattle and curly-haired sheep grazed on the verdant hillsides.

"It's amazing," she said. "Simply amazing."

Niklaus smiled, his face fairly glowing with pride.

"I should like to see Number Four while we're here," she said.

"You worry overmuch for his welfare, my dear."

"Perhaps, but I should like to see him just the same. The man saved my life at great risk to his own. The least I can do is make sure he is comfortable."

"Yes, I suppose so," Niklaus agreed.

They walked down the narrow path that led to the detention area. It had become a common practice for the wealthy to keep slaves. Ashlynne had never given it much thought, until she met Falkon. It had been a fact of life on Tierde, as it was in other places. The Confederation had abolished the death sentence; incorrigible prisoners were sent to the prison planet Jaol with no hope of pardon, while criminals who were considered nonviolent were sold to those who could afford them. The credits earned from the sale of slaves paid the wages of the prison guards. She wondered how Falkon had escaped being sent to Jaol. He was a hired mercenary; certainly he would be considered dangerous.

Hassrick's family kept six slaves. She tried not to notice the faces of the imprisoned men as she walked down the line of barred huts, but it was impossible. They all looked at her with eyes empty of hope.

Niklaus paused at the last hut.

Drawing a deep, steadying breath, Ashlynne peered inside. "Number Four?"

She heard him swear, and then he walked out of the shadows. He stopped several feet from the door. His face was set in hard, implacable lines, his blue-gray eyes were cold when he looked at her.

She wanted to smile at him, to tell him she loved him, but she couldn't, not with Niklaus standing there beside her, listening to every word.

"Are you well, Number Four?" she asked, unable to keep the tremor from her voice. Why was he looking at her like that? Surely he knew locking him up had not been her idea. "Is there anything you need?"

He shook his head, his gaze moving past her, his hands clenching when he saw Niklaus.

Ashlynne glanced over her shoulder. "He's very good with horses," she said. "Perhaps you can find a use for him in your stable."

Niklaus shrugged. "Perhaps." He frowned as he pulled his portacom from his pocket. "Excuse me, my dear, I need to take care of something over at the barn. I don't know how long I'll be. Can you find your way back to the house?"

"Yes, of course."

With a curt nod, he turned and headed across the yard toward the stable.

Ashlynne turned back to Falkon. "Are you all right?" she asked anxiously.

He approached the door then, his expression softening. "Yeah, I'm fine." He grinned ruefully. "This reminds me of the time you and your friend paid me a midnight visit."

Ashlynne nodded, pain twisting through her heart as she thought of Magny.

"Why did you and your friend come down to the mine that night? What were you looking for?"

"You, of course. Magny thought you were very handsome. She talked about you all the time."

"Yeah?" He reached through the bars and stroked her cheek. "And what did you think?"

She covered his hand with her own and drew it down over her breast. "I thought you were a scoundrel."

"Ah, that cuts me to the quick."

"A very handsome scoundrel."

He laughed softly. "Is that why you were always following me around?"

"I was not!" she exclaimed, and then shrugged. It was true and there was no sense lying about it. She looked past him into the hut. It was small, but clean, a vast improvement over his cell at the mine. There was a narrow bed against one wall, a single chair, a square table. "We have to get out of here."

"I'm open to any suggestions you've got." He glanced at the door between them. It was solid and could only be opened by entering the right code into the keypad. His free hand slid up to curl around the bars.

"Maybe I can find the code."

"Maybe."

"They must have them written down somewhere."

"Yeah, unless the same code opens every door."

"Well, they still might have it written down," she insisted.

He shrugged. "Maybe. So, how are things with Hassrick?"

"He wanted to get married right away, but I told him I needed some time to mourn my parents. Why do you think he's in such a hurry?"

Falkon grunted softly. The answer was obvious to him. She was beautiful, desirable. What man wouldn't want her?

"Ashlynne, why are you still here?"

Falkon withdrew his hand and took a step backward.

Ashlynne turned at the sound of Niklaus's voice. "I was just leaving."

Later that evening, Niklaus escorted Ashlynne into the solarium. It was, Niklaus informed her, tradition for the family to meet there each evening before bedtime.

Zahara took Ashlynne aside. She switched on the tele-screen and a variety of wedding gowns appeared, along with veils and shoes.

"That one is quite lovely," Zahara remarked, pointing at a bright yellow gown of crushed velvet. "Although the color might not be right for you. Perhaps it comes in green. Or would you prefer a more old-fashioned look?"

"I prefer white," Ashlynne replied. She had dreamed of being married in a long white gown and veil ever since she was a little girl and had seen an old photograph of her great-grandmother's wedding. These days, vivid colors had replaced the once-traditional white, but she didn't care about style or fashion. She wanted a satin gown and a gossamer veil and a bouquet of snow roses . . . She blinked back her tears. She had wanted Magny to be there with her, had wanted to walk down the aisle on her father's arm. What difference did it make what she wore, when she couldn't marry the man she loved, when her best friend and her parents couldn't be there to share the day with her?

"White? No, I don't think so." Zahara shook her head. "It simply won't do. What will people say?"

"You're right, of course," Ashlynne agreed. What difference did it make what she wore?

"Yes, I think the spring green," Zahara said, nodding. "It will look wonderful with your hair and eyes."

Several minutes passed by while Zahara clicked through a number of different styles. Ashlynne watched the screen, paying little attention to the discussion between Niklaus and his father until Rugen mentioned Tierde, and the mine.

"Niklaus, what about the mine?" Ashlynne asked. "I heard the Romarians had taken it over."

"Yes, temporarily," Niklaus said.

"Temporarily? I don't understand."

"The mine belonged to your family," Niklaus said. "The Confederation cannot claim control so long as there is an heir."

She stared at Niklaus, finally comprehending what he was saying. Of course, the mine belonged to her now. Why hadn't she thought of that before? Not only the mine, but her parents' considerable fortune, as well.

"After the wedding, we shall return to Tierde," Niklaus remarked. "Until then, Commander Drade and his troopers are overseeing production."

Drade! The man Falkon blamed for the death of his wife and child.

Chapter Twenty-two

Falkon paced his cell, unable to sleep. Time and again he went to the small barred window and peered into the darkness. He could see the second story of the house, barely visible beyond the rise. Lights shone in several of the windows. He wondered if Ashlynne was still awake, how she had passed the evening, if she had been alone with Hassrick.

Jealousy burned bright within him at the thought of Hassrick touching Ashlynne, holding her in his arms, kissing her . . . damn!

His hands curled around the bars. He had to get out of here!

He stood at the window, watching the lights in the house go out one by one.

Turning away from the door, he stretched out

on the narrow cot, his arms folded behind his head, but sleep would not come.

"Falkon?"

He was at the window in two long strides. "Ashlynne, what are you doing down here?"

"I wanted to see you."

He reached through the bars, his fingers stroking her cheek. "Are you all right?"

"Yes, I'm fine."

"Come here."

She moved closer to the window. Standing on tiptoe, she leaned forward, her eyelids fluttering down as he kissed her.

She was sweet, so sweet. He cursed the door standing between them, wishing he could take her in his arms. He had never thought to fall in love again, had forgotten how overpowering it could be.

Ashlynne sighed as he took his lips from hers. Just one kiss, and her whole body was trembling, quivering with desire. "I wish—"

"What do you wish, princess?"

"I wish you'd stop calling me that."

He grinned at her. "Tell me."

"I wish we could make love."

He couldn't see her face clearly in the darkness, but he had a feeling she was blushing. "I know." He reached through the bars again, his hand cupping her face.

"I love you," she murmured. "I love you so much."

"Ashlynne . . ."

"Tell me," she said.

"I love you, too."

She covered his hand with hers and rubbed her cheek against his palm.

"You said Hassrick wants to get married right away. Have you set a date?"

"In three months."

Falkon grunted softly. Three months. If he couldn't find a way out of here by then, he never would.

"Niklaus said we're going to Tierde after the wedding."

"Oh?"

Ashlynne nodded. "He's going to take over running the mine." She hesitated a moment. "He said it belongs to me now."

"I thought the Romarians had confiscated it."

"So did I, but the mine didn't belong to the Confederation. It belonged to my father. Falkon . . ."

"What?"

"Never mind." There was no point in telling him that Drade was on Tierde. Not now. There was nothing he could do about it, nothing to be gained in the telling.

"What is it?"

"Nothing. Just that Niklaus has assigned you to work in the stable. You start tomorrow."

He grunted softly. Shoveling manure was a hell of a lot better than digging crystals out of a dark mine deep in the bowels of Tierde.

She squeezed his hand. "I'd better go before I'm missed." She leaned forward for his kiss, whispered, "Goodnight, I love you," then turned and ran up the path to the house.

Falkon turned around, his back against the door as he glanced at his surroundings. "Goodnight, indeed," he muttered.

He was roused first thing in the morning. A servant brought him breakfast. It was hot. It was good. It was filling. He reminded himself again that things could be worse, that he could be back in the mine, but he had a hard time convincing himself. A prison was a prison, whether it was a cold dark cell or a furnished room. And he was damned tired of being locked up.

Twenty minutes later, the door to his hut opened. A man stood just outside the door. He was close to seven feet tall, with short black hair, narrow brown eyes, and the biggest hands Falkon had ever seen. A deep scar scored his right cheek. He wore brown leather pants and a garish green shirt. He carried a stun gun in a thick leather holster. But it was the controller that caught and held Falkon's attention.

"I am Moldaur, in charge of this section of the estate. You are to report to the barn immediately. Bryson will give you your orders for the day. Is that clear?"

"Oh, yeah."

"Insolence is not tolerated here," Moldaur warned. "Do what you are told, and you will be well treated. Any trouble you cause will reflect on me. I do not like slaves who cause me trouble." He tapped the controller with his knuckles. "Do so, and you will regret it."

269

"I've heard the drill before," Falkon muttered.

"You will return here for the midday meal, and again at the end of the day. Do not be late."

"Is that all?"

Moldaur let out a sigh. "Remember what I said."

The Hassrick family had a good eye for horseflesh. Five blooded mares and two stallions occupied the barn. Horses were rare, and a luxury few could afford.

He spent the morning mucking the stalls. It was a chore most found odious; Falkon enjoyed it. He liked the way the barn smelled, the air filled with the scent of sweet hay and horseflesh and the not-totally-unpleasant odor of manure.

At noon, he returned to his cell for the midday meal. A tray awaited him. As soon as he stepped into the cell, the door closed and locked behind him; thirty minutes later, the door opened.

He returned to the barn, felt a peculiar catch in his throat when he saw Ashlynne standing inside the doorway. She was wearing a pair of sleek red pants, soft knee-high black boots, and a long-sleeved white sweater. He stared at her, trying to recall if he had seen her in pants before, trying to ignore the heat pooling in his groin. She had her back to him, petting one of the mares.

"Good afternoon, my lady," he said quietly.

She turned to face him. "Hello, Number Four," she said, her voice carefully devoid of emotion. "Would you saddle this horse for me, please? I should like to ride."

"As you wish, my lady." His gaze caressed her.

"And saddle one for yourself."

Bryson appeared. "Excuse me, Lady Ashlynne, but he has work to do."

Ashlynne spoke without looking at him. "Excuse me, Mr. Bryson, but Number Four belongs to me. He may work here when I have no need of him, but he is mine to command, and he will do as I tell him. Is that understood?"

Bryson cleared his throat. "Lord Hassrick . . ."

Drawing herself up to her full height, Ashlynne looked at Bryson. "Lord Hassrick does not own Number Four. I do. And I wish to have him accompany me."

A faint flush crept up the man's neck. "Yes, my lady." He inclined his head in a respectful gesture and left the barn.

"Well done, my lady," Falkon said with a roguish grin.

"Thank you, Number Four," she replied, happiness bubbling up inside her at seeing him again, being close to him again.

She watched while he saddled the mare she had chosen, then saddled another mount for himself.

Moments later, they rode out of the barn. Falkon rode behind her, as was proper for a servant.

Ashlynne kept her mare to a sedate pace until they were out of sight of the barn, and then she drummed her heels into the mare's sides.

The horse snorted, bucked, and then shot forward, running like the wind.

Ashlynne glanced over her shoulder. Falkon was coming up fast behind her.

"Can't catch me!" she hollered. She leaned forward, one hand lightly patting the mare's neck. "Let's go, girl!"

They let the horses run until they slowed of their own accord. Ashlynne drew rein beneath a lacy blue willow tree and slid from the saddle. Laughing, breathless, she turned to watch Falkon dismount. He was grinning at her.

"We won!" she exclaimed.

"Hah. We let you win."

"You did not."

"Sure we did. Come on, we need to cool the horses out."

Side by side, they walked across the verdant grass, leading their mounts.

"I've seen whole countries smaller than this place," Falkon remarked.

Ashlynne nodded. She had known Niklaus was rich, but this was far beyond anything she had imagined.

"Does he know where you are?"

"No. He went to a meeting with his father. His mother was entertaining friends. I pleaded a headache and said I needed some fresh air."

Reaching over, Falkon took the reins from her hand and tethered both horses to a tree, and then he drew her into his arms and kissed her.

With a sigh, she leaned into him, every other thought burned away by the touch of his lips on hers, the sheer delight of being in his embrace. She wrapped her arms around his waist and held him tight, felt his body's response to her nearness. His lips were warm, his tongue a sweet invasion that quickened her desire and sent heat curling through her belly.

She moaned softly as his hands slid up and down her back, delved under her sweater to caress her skin.

"Ashlynne?"

"Yes," she whispered. "Oh, yes."

He lowered her to the ground, stretched out beside her, and drew her into his arms. For a long while, he did nothing but hold her, and then he kissed her again, gently at first, as if she were a fragile flower that might wither beneath his heat. But she didn't want gentleness, not now, not when it seemed like days and days since she had been in his arms.

"Tell me," she said. "Tell me you love me. That you've missed me as much as I've missed you."

"You know I do," he replied, his voice husky with desire.

"Tell me."

"I love you, princess, more than my life."

She smiled at him. "I used to hate it when you called me that, you know."

"I know. Why do you think I did it?"

She punched him on the arm, then rolled on top of him.

"Now what?" he asked, grinning.

"Now this." She ran her tongue over his lips. "And this," she murmured, and kissed him, hungrily, deeply. Desire ran hot and swift through her veins and she pressed herself against him, wanting him, wanting all of him.

Sitting up, she tugged at his shirt, drawing it over his head, tossing it aside.

He looked up at her, one brow raised. "Now you," he said.

She felt a blush rise in her cheeks as she removed her sweater, sighed with pleasure as his hands moved over her skin. Rough, callused hands. Strong hands. Gentle hands.

The rest of their clothing disappeared as if by magic and then, with a low, sexy growl, he tucked her beneath him. His weight was a welcome burden and she gave herself to him completely, heart and soul, mind and body. She was his, would always be his.

She closed her eyes, caught up in the wonder of his touch, the magic of his love. Magny had told her that love between a man and a woman was the most wonderful thing in the world, but she had never believed it, until now, had never known that love could be so beautiful, fill her with such a sweet ache.

Fulfillment washed over her in waves and she cried his name. Tears welled in her eyes as the love in her heart overflowed and spilled down her cheeks.

Ashlynne traced lazy circles on his belly. His skin was warm, his stomach hard and ridged with muscle. She ran her finger over a jagged scar on his chest. There was another on his left arm, another on his thigh. She knew the one on his right shoulder was from where the laser had struck him when he fought the Hodorians. Remembering that brought her parents to mind.

"Hey," he asked, frowning. "Are you all right?"

She nodded, even as her eyes filled with tears. He raised himself up on one elbow and

gazed down at her. "What's wrong, princess?"
She laid her hand over the scar on his right
arm, and he knew what she was thinking, what
she was remembering. Muttering an oath, he
sat up and drew her into his arms. She clung to
him, her body racked with sobs.

Knowing there were no words he could say
that would ease her pain, he held her tight, one
hand lightly stroking her hair, until her sobs
subsided.

"I'm sorry," she said, sniffling. "I didn't mean
to cry all over you."

"I don't mind." He kissed the tip of her nose.
"I needed a bath anyway."

She laughed through her tears, loving him all
the more. What a comfort he was! It was hard
to imagine a time when he hadn't been there
for her.

He brushed a wisp of hair from her cheek,
wiped the tears from her eyes with his fingertips. "We should probably be going back."

"I don't want to."

"I know, but sometimes even a princess has
to do things she doesn't want to."

He stood up and offered her his hand and
when she took it, he pulled her to her feet,
then folded her into his arms and kissed her.
And then he gave her a swat on her bare
behind.

"You'd best get dressed right quick," he said,
his voice gruff, "or we'll never leave."

Niklaus was pacing back and forth in front of
the barn when they got back.

"Where the devil have you been?" he

demanded as he lifted Ashlynne from the back of her horse. "I was just about to send Brill to find you."

"I'm sorry if I worried you," she said, though she doubted he had been worried at all. "I didn't mean to be gone so long." She smiled up at him. "It's just so beautiful here, I forgot the time."

He grunted softly, somewhat mollified by her praise. "Why did you take him? Slaves aren't permitted the use of the horses."

Ashlynne glanced at Falkon, who was unsaddling her mare. "He's been a loyal servant," she said. "At home, he always rode with me, in case something happened." It was a bald-faced lie, but it was the only excuse she could think of.

"I see. And what did you think might happen to you here?"

She shrugged. "I don't know. My father always insisted I ride with someone in case I was thrown, or my horse stepped in a hole."

"Next time you want to ride, I'll go with you," Niklaus said, taking her by the arm. He looked at Falkon. "Be sure you cool the horses out properly and give them a good rubdown."

Falkon nodded. Jaw clenched, he watched Hassrick lead Ashlynne away.

Chapter Twenty-three

Falkon paced the floor of his hut, his mood bleak. Six and a half weeks had passed since they'd arrived in Arkata. He had spent the days working in the barn, mucking stalls, grooming the horses, cleaning tack. When he wasn't in the barn, he was sent to work in the fields with the other slaves. Keeping the grounds looking the way the Hassricks wanted required constant care. It was work that could have been done by androids, but androids were more expensive than slaves. Falkon didn't think the cost had anything to do with the reason Hassrick kept slaves. The man could afford a hundred androids, a thousand. It was the feeling of power, of control, that Hassrick enjoyed, the sense of ownership, of being better than those around him.

He ran his hand over the collar around his neck. Of all the slaves on the Hassrick estate, he was the only one forced to wear the thick collar and shackles.

Of course, the Hassrick slaves were well taken care of. They might not live in luxury, but the huts were kept clean, the food was plentiful if unimaginative. They were allowed to bath regularly. It was far better than working in the mines, but that didn't make it any easier to bear. Bars were bars and prison was prison.

He had spoken to the other slaves, questioning them about the estate. They had assured him there was no way out save through the front gate, which could only be opened from inside the house, or with a key code. Not only were the walls too slick and too high to be scaled, but they were electrified. The prisoners all had horror stories of slaves who had been killed trying to go over the wall, or who had been mauled and killed by the dogs that prowled the outer perimeter, or who had been shot by the guards while trying to escape.

He listened and nodded, but he hadn't given up, not yet.

Ashlynne came to see him whenever she could sneak away from the house. She had told him that plans for the wedding were moving forward. Her dress had arrived, Zahara's secretary was busily writing out invitations, the cook was planning the menu. She had told him that the house servants were working day and night, readying rooms for guests who would be arriving early or staying late. Her future mother-in-law had decided she hated the furnishings in the main salon and the room was being completely redecorated. She hadn't found the code for the keypad, and didn't dare ask about it, for fear of arousing suspicion.

Going to the door, he watched the sun come up. Another day of enforced labor, of doing another man's bidding.

Ashlynne came down to the barn just before midday.

"I wish to go riding, Number Four," she said. "Go saddle my horse."

"Yes, my lady."

A short time later, they were riding toward the far end of the estate. As soon as they were out of sight, Ashlynne reined her horse to a stop. Falkon rode up beside her. Leaning forward, he kissed her.

"I was hoping you'd come today," he said.

"I had a feeling you needed to get away for a little while."

"You got that right. Sometimes it's all I can do to keep from laying into Bryson."

"Falkon, you mustn't!"

"Dammit, Ashlynne, I'm going slowly insane."

"I know." She stroked his cheek. "I know. Please, just be patient."

"I'm trying." He glanced over his shoulder. "Come on, I want to get as far away from the house as possible."

They rode for almost an hour. Falkon glanced at Ashlynne. She seemed distracted, and he wondered what was bothering her. It wasn't like her to be so quiet for so long.

He reined his horse to a halt in a small glen.

Dismounting, he tethered both horses to a tree, then lifted Ashlynne from the saddle.

"What's wrong?" he asked.

She looked up at him, her eyes troubled. "Nothing."

"Ashlynne, don't lie to me."

"Kiss me, Falkon." She wrapped her arms around him and drew his head down. "Kiss me, kiss me."

She was hiding something from him, and he wanted to know what it was, but somehow, with her mouth urgent on his and her hands moving over him, it didn't seem to matter.

"Falkon, oh, Falkon." She clung to him, murmuring his name over and over again, and he surrendered to her touch, letting her do what she would, not resisting when she pulled him down to the ground. She kissed him again, and then dissolved into tears.

"Ashlynne, what's wrong?"

"I . . ." She took a deep breath. "I'm pregnant."

Of all the things he had expected her to say, that was the furthest from his mind. Pregnant!

She was looking up at him, waiting for him to say something, anything. Pregnant . . . He thought of Maiya. He hadn't been there when their daughter was born. He'd been off fighting a war on Calaas Ten. By the time he'd returned home, his daughter had been almost two months old. He hadn't been there when she died, either, he thought bitterly. He had been off fighting another war. He lifted his hand to the collar at his throat.

"Falkon?"

He ran his knuckles along her cheek. Where

would he be when this child was born? "Are you sure?"

She pulled away from him and sat up. "I'm sure. You don't want it, do you?"

The pain in her voice was like a knife slicing into his heart. "Ashlynne . . ." He drew her back into his arms. "It's not that. It's just . . ." He shook his head.

"Just what? What are we going to do?"

"Beats the hell out of me." He lifted her into his lap and wrapped his arms around her.

"I guess it isn't very good timing, is it?" she asked.

"Not very." He grinned at her. "But I'll tell you one thing. You're not marrying anybody else."

She laughed, and then grew sober once again. "I'll tell Niklaus tonight that I've changed my mind, that I've decided to go back to Tierde."

"And you think he's gonna let you go, just like that?"

"Why not? Surely he won't want to marry me if I tell him I don't love him."

"I think you're overlooking something."

"What?"

"The mine."

"What about it?"

"I don't know, but I've got a feeling . . ." He shook his head. He couldn't put it into words, but deep in his gut he had a feeling that Hassrick had been involved in the attack on the mine. But why?

"I'll tell him tonight."

* * *

Ashlynne stared at Niklaus. "What do you mean, it doesn't matter?"

"People rarely marry for love these days, my dear. You know that. It was your father's wish that we wed, and we shall be married, as planned."

"But I don't want to marry you. I never did."

"But you will."

"No."

"You're acting like a child, Ashlynne. We will be married, as planned. End of discussion." Pivoting on his heel, he walked toward the door.

"I'm pregnant." The words were out before she could call them back.

He stopped in mid-stride and turned, very slowly, to face her. "What did you say?"

"I'm pregnant."

"You're lying."

Ashlynne shook her head. "No. It's true."

"Who's the father?" he asked, and in the same breath, answered his own question. "Number Four. It's him, isn't it?" he demanded with a sneer. "That's why you were so worried about him."

She didn't deny it, didn't care what Niklaus thought of her. He would have to let her go now.

"You will marry me, Ashlynne, as planned."

She stared at him in disbelief. "You can't be serious."

"But I am."

"What will you tell your parents about the baby?"

"I shall say it's mine." His smile was cold. "You're very beautiful, after all. No one will be surprised to learn that we consummated the marriage before the vows were said."

"I won't be a party to such a despicable lie."

"The choice is yours, of course. You may leave, if you wish."

It was too easy. She stood there, waiting, her stomach in knots.

"It might interest you to know that there are several people attempting to discover the whereabouts of your Number Four. The Romarians are searching for him. One of their commanders, Drade, I believe his name is, seems very anxious to find him." Niklaus drew the controller from his pocket and ran his thumb over the activation panel. "It seems Commander Casman also wants him. Dead or alive."

She looked at Niklaus, and felt suddenly sick. "You wouldn't."

"It's up to you, my dear."

"Why are you doing this?"

"You needn't worry your pretty little head about that. Shall I tell my parents the wedding is off?"

She stared at the controller nestled in his hand, the memory of the last time Niklaus had activated it vivid in her mind. "No."

Niklaus smiled at her as he slid the controller into the pocket of his trousers. It was a decidedly triumphant smile.

"Now, I think it's time you went up to bed, my dear. Mother is planning a party for tomorrow night. You'll want to look your best."

The party was nothing short of a nightmare. Ashlynne stood beside Niklaus, a fake smile on her face as she greeted their guests, but all she could think of was Falkon. She had gone to the barn that afternoon, but he hadn't been there. She had gone to his hut, her stomach churning with fear when she saw that it was empty. She had questioned Bryson, but he claimed he didn't know Falkon's whereabouts. The giant, Moldaur, also claimed ignorance. At last, in desperation, she had gone to Niklaus, who had assured her that Falkon was in no danger, so long as she did as she was told. She'd had no choice but to believe him.

She sat across from Niklaus at dinner, smiling and making polite conversation with the people seated on either side of her, and all the while she was heartsick. Where was Falkon?

There was dancing after dinner. Niklaus claimed the first dance, his father the second. Knowing Falkon's fate depended on her, Ashlynne played her part well. She laughed and smiled and pretended to be the happiest woman in the galaxy, and all the while her stomach was churning and her heart was sick with worry.

When Niklaus claimed her for another dance, she pleaded a headache and asked to go outside. As soon as they were alone, she turned on him. "Where is he? I won't go on with this charade for another minute until I know he's all right."

Niklaus made a tsking sound. "You really care for him, don't you? How unfortunate. What would your father think, I wonder, if he knew?"

"I want to see Falkon. Now."

"Ah, so he has a name, does he?"

"Now, Niklaus."

"Very well." He went to speak to his mother, then motioned for Ashlynne to follow him.

Heart pounding, she followed Niklaus down three flights of narrow, winding stairs. The air grew colder as they descended. At each landing, lights came on automatically, illuminating their way.

She was shivering when Niklaus paused before a stout wooden door. He punched the code into the keypad and the door swung open. A light came on inside the room as they crossed the threshold.

Ashlynne glanced around, her apprehension growing. The floor was made of stone, the walls were made of rock, cold and gray and damp. "What is this place?"

"It was a prison, in days long past."

"A prison?"

"Yes. My great great grandfather built the house on top of it. This way, my dear."

He led her down a narrow corridor and made a sharp right turn.

Ashlynne sucked in a deep breath. A large room opened off the corridor. Small, iron-barred cells lined both sides of the room. All were empty save one.

"Falkon." She breathed his name as he rose from the floor, blinking against the light.

"You see," Niklaus said. "He is unharmed, for the moment."

"What do you mean, for the moment?" she asked, though she knew the answer.

"I mean his continued good health depends entirely on you." Niklaus withdrew the controller from his pocket and activated it with a flick of his thumb.

Ashlynne cried out as Falkon dropped to the cold stone floor, his body convulsing violently. And when the tremors had almost ceased, Niklaus hit the controller again.

"Stop it!" She whirled around to face Niklaus. "Stop it! I'll do anything you want! Anything, I swear it. Only please stop."

Niklaus nodded, his expression smug. "Yes, I thought you would see things my way."

Ashlynne ran toward the cell. "Falkon. Falkon." Reaching through the bars, she clutched his shoulder. She could feel the tremors coursing through him. She gasped as a sharp pain exploded in her hand and sizzled up her arm. With an effort, Falkon rolled away from her, breaking her grip on his shoulder.

Tears welled in her eyes and ran down her cheeks, the pain in her own hand forgotten as she watched him writhing on the ground. How did he endure it? Her hand and arm still tingled from where she had touched him. She couldn't imagine how painful it must be for him.

A low moan escaped his lips as the controller's effects ended. White-faced and trembling, he grabbed hold of the bars and pulled himself to his feet.

Ashlynne stood up, her eyes filled with sympathy. And love. "I'm sorry," she whispered. "So sorry."

"Not . . . your fault." He took a deep breath. "Are you all right?"

She nodded.

Niklaus came up behind her. "It's time to go."

"No!"

"We have guests, my dear, remember?"

"Please let me stay. Just a few more minutes."

"No."

She turned to face him. "Please, Niklaus. Give us a few minutes alone." He was going to refuse. She saw it in his eyes. "I'll beg if I have to." Dropping to her knees, she clasped his hand in both of hers. "Please?"

He jerked his hand from hers, his expression one of disgust. "Very well. Five minutes should be time enough to say goodbye. I'll wait by the door."

"Thank you."

Niklaus didn't reply as he turned and walked away.

"Dammit, Ashlynne, don't you ever go down on your knees to that bastard again."

"It was worth it." She reached for him through the bars, her arms wrapping around his waist. "I told him I didn't want to marry him. I even told him about the baby, but he said it doesn't matter, we're getting married as planned."

"And if you refuse?"

She looked up at him, the answer there in her eyes.

"Yeah," he muttered. "That's what I thought."

"I can't let him kill you."

"He will anyway. You must know that."

"No!"

With a sigh, he lowered his head and kissed her. His lips moved over hers. Sweet, so sweet.

She looked up at him when he drew away, her eyes searching his. "Falkon . . ."

"Do what he wants, Ashlynne. Don't defy him. It will only cause you pain and unhappiness."

"What are you saying?"

"I want you to forget about me when you walk out that door. You have the baby to think of now. Nothing else matters."

"You can't mean that!"

"I've brought you nothing but trouble, princess. You'll be better off without me."

"That's not true!"

He placed his hand over her belly. "Take care of yourself. And the little one. Don't give Hassrick any reason to hurt either of you."

He backed away from her, and she reached for him, tears streaming down her cheeks. "Falkon!"

"Ready, my dear?"

She froze at the sound of Niklaus's voice behind her. Heart aching, she looked at Falkon. "I love you." She mouthed the words, blinking back her tears as Niklaus took her by the arm and led her away.

Falkon stared after Ashlynne, knowing he would never see her again. Hassrick had informed him that the two of them would be returning to Tierde immediately after the wedding. Hassrick would take over the running of the mine. Falkon's fate would be decided by Drade.

He laughed softly. His fate had been decided long ago.

Chapter Twenty-four

Ashlynne moved through the next few days like a sleepwalker. She was nauseous in the morning, tired all the time. Every time she thought of Falkon, locked up in a cold, dark cell, she wanted to cry. And she did cry. Constantly. She wept for him, for herself, for her unborn child, for the loss of her parents, who would never see their grandchild. Hassrick had little patience with her tears. Sometimes, when he looked at her, she was certain he hated her.

She counted the days until the wedding, trying desperately to think of a way to make him change his mind. Unable to sleep, she prowled the house in the dark of night. One night she had gone down to the dungeon in hopes of seeing Falkon, but the door had been locked. She had spent an hour punching random numbers into the keypad, hoping she might hit the right sequence, but to no avail. Defeated, she had returned to her room and cried herself to sleep.

Her initial dislike for Niklaus was quickly turning to hate. She had no choice but to accede to anything he desired, knowing that, if she refused, Falkon would be made to suffer for her disobedience.

There were parties and gatherings almost every night in the month before the wedding. Ashlynne would have much preferred to stay in her room. She was nauseous almost constantly and wanted nothing more than to stay in bed and be left alone. Niklaus was coldly unsympathetic. He didn't care that food and wine made her sick to her stomach or that dancing made her dizzy. Putting up a good appearance was everything to Niklaus. She was his fiancée, and she had to play the part, had to pretend she was happy and eager to wed him. She must smile and laugh as if her whole world wasn't falling apart. Dance with Niklaus's friends. Listen politely to conversation that bored her to tears. Be agreeable to his mother, respectful to his father.

The days passed quickly, too quickly. And soon the day of the wedding was upon her.

Ashlynne looked at herself in the mirror and grimaced. The dress Zahara had chosen was green. Puke-green, she thought, with a shoulder-length veil and soft-soled slippers.

A short time later, she stood beside Niklaus, fighting the urge to vomit as she spoke the words that made her his wife. It was like a nightmare, only worse. There would be no waking up from this one. Tomorrow and for all tomorrows she would still belong to Niklaus.

It would have been the happiest day of her life if the man standing beside her had been Falkon.

Falkon. Pain twisted through her heart whenever she thought of him. She had begged Niklaus to let her see him again, but he had adamantly refused. The last time she had asked, he had threatened to activate the controller if she bothered him about "that man" again.

And now she was Mrs. Niklaus Hassrick. She stood in his arms, stiff and unyielding, as he lifted her veil and claimed his first kiss as her lord and husband.

"Smile." He hissed the word at her as they left the church.

She did as he told her, smiling and laughing like a robot as she accepted the congratulations of the wedding guests.

Later, she sat beside him at the lavish twelve-course dinner that followed the ceremony, danced the first dance with him, the second with her new father-in-law. She accepted more congratulations and good wishes, and all the while she was dying inside.

It was near dawn when the party ended. Exhausted and sick at heart, Ashlynne followed Niklaus up the stairs to his chambers, which occupied the third floor of the house.

She stood in the middle of the sitting room. It was a masculine room, decorated in shades of dark brown and rust. There was a tele-screen on one wall, a shelf filled with old books and an antique clock. There was a large basket of fruit and a bottle of champagne on the marble-topped table beside the sofa.

"Sit down, my dear," Niklaus said. He removed his jacket and tossed it over the back of a chair.

She sat on the edge of the luxurious leather couch, unable to still the trembling in her hands.

Niklaus sat down across from her. Opening the wine, he poured a glass and handed it to her.

She didn't want it, but she drank it anyway, hoping it would calm her nerves.

"Relax, my dear." He leaned back, his legs stretched before him, one arm flung over the back of the chair. "You needn't worry. I've no intention of bedding you."

Her surprise must have shown on her face, for he laughed softly. "I'm afraid I've no taste for another man's leavings."

"Then why did you marry me?"

"All in good time, my dear. You look tired. Why don't you go to bed?"

She didn't question him, didn't care, at that moment, why he had been so determined to marry her. All she wanted was to be alone. She put her glass on the table and stood up, then hesitated. "Where should I sleep?"

"Never let it be said that my manners are lacking where my new bride is concerned. Please, take my bed. I'll use the couch."

With a nod, she left the room.

Falkon paced the dark cell. Today was Ashlynne's wedding day. Hassrick had visited him earlier to make sure he knew.

He stared into the darkness, wondering if Hassrick intended to leave him down here in isolation until he went slowly insane. Weeks and weeks of darkness, relieved only when one of the servants brought his meals. Oppressive darkness, so heavy he felt as though it were smothering him. Nothing to see. Nothing to do. He had lost track of time, didn't know if it was day or night. Only the arrival of food broke the endless monotony, and even then he was left to eat in darkness.

It was her wedding day. Was she alone with her new husband now? Sharing his bed? The thought burned through him, eating at his soul like acid. She was his. His, dammit! She carried his child. What right did Hassrick have to marry her?

He drove his fist into the wall again and again, a wordless cry of jealousy and rage rising in his throat, emptying into the darkness.

The sound of his own scream jolted him back to sanity. Pain exploded through his hand, up his arm. He cradled his wounded hand, feeling the warmth of his blood fill his palm. Stupid, he thought. Stupid, stupid, stupid!

Filled with bitter despair, he sank down on the floor and closed his eyes. Ashlynne, forever lost to him.

Her hands were still trembling as she removed her wedding gown. In spite of Niklaus's declaration that he didn't want her, she had locked the door.

Naked, she stood in front of the mirror, one hand splayed across her belly. Falkon's child was in there. Falkon. She closed her eyes, wondering if she would ever see him again. Niklaus intended to use Falkon to keep her in line. She stared at her reflection, her eyes widening as a new thought occurred to her. She would do what Niklaus asked, but with one proviso. She would insist on seeing Falkon. She would tell Niklaus that she had to see Falkon so that she would know he was still alive. She would insist on seeing him once a week, just to make sure.

The thought of seeing Falkon again made her smile. She had thought of him all day, wished it had been he standing beside her when she spoke her vows.

Slipping on the pale blue nightgown Zahara had chosen for her bridal night, Ashlynne crawled under the covers and closed her eyes, and in her mind Falkon was there beside her, his arms warm around her, his eyes dark with desire. . . .

She woke to find her bags packed and breakfast waiting.

"You'll have to hurry," Hassrick said. "Our flight leaves in an hour."

She blinked up at him. He hadn't made any mention of a honeymoon, nor did she want one. "Where are we going?"

"Tierde."

"Today?"

He nodded. "I'll wait for you downstairs."

"Wait." She sat up, holding the covers over her breasts. "What about Number Four?"

"What about him?"

"Is he going with us?"

"No."

"I won't go without him."

"You are my wife now," he reminded her. "And you will do as I say."

"He belongs to me, and I won't go without him."

He regarded her thoughtfully for several moments, and then nodded. "Perhaps it would be wise to bring him along. Hurry now."

Falkon blinked against the morning light. For the first time in weeks, he was outside again. He drew in a deep breath, filling his lungs with the scent of fresh air, of earth and grass. He didn't know what Hassrick had planned for him, and at the moment, he didn't care as long as it got him out of that dark hole.

A shuttle waited in front of the house. Hassrick's bodyguards stood nearby.

One of them opened the back door and motioned Falkon inside.

He glanced over his shoulder at Hassrick. "Where are we going?"

"Get in."

"Where's Ashlynne?" he asked, then reeled back as Hassrick struck him across the face, the heavy ring on his left hand slicing into his cheek.

"You will not speak my wife's name again," Hassrick said. "Now, do as you were told."

Anger boiled up inside Falkon. There was little he could do with his hands shackled, yet he had an overpowering urge to try, and only the sight of Ashlynne coming down the stairs kept him from attacking. By Jupiter's rings, she looked like an angel. She wore a dress of some clingy pink material that outlined every curve. Her hair was coiled atop her head and held in place by a jeweled clip; one long curl fell over her shoulder.

She stopped near Hassrick. "What's going on?" she asked, nodding in Falkon's direction. "What happened to him?"

"Just a little discipline," Hassrick retorted. "Get in. We're late."

One of the bodyguards shoved Falkon into the backseat and sat down beside him. The second bodyguard took the other side. Hassrick activated the shackles on his feet.

Moments later, they were speeding through the city toward the space dock.

Ashlynne settled herself in her seat as the cruiser lifted off. Pulling a palm-sized portareader from her pocket, she selected a book and pretended to read, but the words on the screen were a blur. She was going home, only her home was gone, her parents were gone, and she was as much a prisoner as Falkon. She had dared not protest when Hassrick locked him in the cargo hold. She could still see the angry cut on his cheek, the blood dripping from the wound, the barely restrained anger in his eyes. She had to be careful, for both of them.

The Hassrick cruiser was sleek and fast. Hassrick rode up front, with the pilot, leaving her blessedly alone.

Now that it was too late, it occurred to her that she might have made a serious mistake in insisting Falkon go with them to Tierde. In her anxiety to have Falkon with her, she had forgotten that Drade was waiting on Tierde.

They arrived at Enjine Base Nine late that night. Hassrick had called ahead and made arrangements for a room. Ashlynne bit back her protest when Falkon was taken to the detention level, telling herself it would be for only one night.

Their room was small, just a bedroom with bathing facilities adjoining, nothing like Commander Casman's lavish quarters. She undressed in the bathroom, then slipped under the covers of one of the twin beds.

She could hear Hassrick's voice coming from the bathroom, though she couldn't distinguish the words. She wondered who he was talking to so late, but she didn't really care. Tomorrow they would be back at the mine. She didn't want to see it again, didn't want to be reminded of what had happened there, of all she had lost.

With a sigh, she burrowed under the covers and closed her eyes, wondering if the nightmare would ever end.

Chapter Twenty-five

The mine looked much as she remembered save for the addition of a gate on this side of the bridge. The buildings that had been destroyed had been replaced. There was a new domicile for the mine manager, new cells for the slaves. For there were slaves. Almost a dozen of them.

The slaves emerged from the bowels of the mine just as they arrived, eleven men fitted with the heavy collars that marked them as slaves, their faces and bodies covered with layers of fine black baneite dust.

The prisoners came out of the mine one by one and made their way to the cells, looking neither right nor left. It bothered her, their complete lack of interest in what was going on around them.

A guard trailed behind them, closing the cell doors, which locked automatically.

She slid a glance at Falkon, who was standing beside her, his hands securely shackled. She could feel the tension radiating from him as he contemplated returning to the mine. She had pleaded with Niklaus to let Falkon work up at the house, but he had adamantly refused.

"We have servants," he had replied coldly. "We don't need a dirty slave."

She heard Falkon swear softly, turned to follow his gaze.

A tall man with cropped brown hair and light brown eyes was striding toward them. He moved with the pride and arrogance that seemed to be characteristic of all military men, whatever their race or allegiance.

She recognized him immediately as the man she had seen interviewed on the tele-screen. Drade. The man behind the attack on Falkon's home.

A smile broke over Drade's face when he saw Falkon. "Niklaus!" he exclaimed. "You'll get a fat reward for bringing this one in."

Niklaus grinned as he shook the other man's hand. "I'm counting on it."

Drade laughed good-naturedly. "You should have it by the end of the week. Not that you need it."

"Excuse me," Ashlynne said, "but Number Four belongs to me."

Niklaus turned to glare at her.

Drade lifted one brow. "And who is this lovely creature?"

"My wife. Ashlynne, this is Commander Drade. He's been looking after the mine."

"Ah, Lady Hassrick, it is indeed a pleasure to meet you."

"Number Four belongs to my family."

Drade smiled expansively. "Be that as it may, he's an escaped slave."

"How can that be," she asked quietly, "seeing as how he is here?"

Drade looked at Hassrick and grinned. "A good point."

"He was never an escaped slave," Ashlynne said. "When we were attacked, he escorted me to safety. I would not be here today if it weren't for his loyalty and devotion. I will not have him executed."

Niklaus took Drade aside. Ashlynne could not hear their words, but she had the feeling that Niklaus was telling Drade that it was necessary to keep Falkon alive.

"If you insist." Drade slapped Niklaus on the back. "But I'm afraid that means you can't claim the reward."

Niklaus's smile seemed to fade a little around the edge as he muttered, "As you said, I don't need it."

"Indeed."

A look that could only be called conspiratorial passed between the two men.

"Well," Niklaus said, "we'll leave him in your capable hands."

"Don't worry about Number Four," Drade replied. "I'll take good care of him."

Was it her imagination, or was there a very real threat in those words? But she had no time to wonder. Taking her by the arm, Niklaus led her to a waiting shuttle and hurried her inside.

She looked out the window, her gaze lingering on Falkon, wondering if she would ever see him again.

Ashlynne stared at the house, unable to believe her eyes. "How?" she asked. "When?"

"Men working around the clock," Hassrick replied.

She shook her head. A new house stood where hers had been. A bigger house, three stories high, surrounded by a high wall. The windows were of Hodorian stained glass, very rare, very expensive. The grounds were landscaped with exotic plants and flowering shrubs. She saw a new barn in the distance.

"Well, shall we go in?"

Ashlynne nodded, amazed that he had built a house so quickly. He had hired a staff, too, a cook, a maid, a housekeeper, someone to tend the grounds, a groom to look after the three horses that had been sent ahead. She smiled faintly as he introduced her to the staff. The cook was a grim-faced man named Ogger; the housekeeper looked as if she had just graduated from school. She was young and pretty, with long red hair and slanted brown eyes. Ashlynne wondered, fleetingly, if Hana was there to do more than tidy up the place.

Niklaus followed her as she went from room to room. It was a large, spacious house, beautifully furnished, but she knew it would never be home. She remembered her parents' house, the cozy fireplace, the sense of security she had known there. Her bedroom had been filled with the treasures of her youth. She felt old now, lost and alone.

Her rooms were located on the south end of the second floor. His were at the other end of the house.

"I'll see you at dinner," Niklaus said. "Drade will be joining us."

With a nod, she closed the door to her room. The tears came then, hot swift tears that did nothing to ease the ache in her heart.

Falkon stood at the door of his cell, staring out into the compound. The new cells were no better than the old ones. They were just as small, just as dark. The only improvement was that he now had a hard narrow cot to sleep on instead of a hard dirt floor. Of all the rotten luck, he thought bitterly. Not only was he back at the mine, but Drade was in charge, at least temporarily.

Drade, who strutted around like some little tin god. Drade, who was sure to make his life a living hell. A living hell that started at dawn the following morning.

Breakfast was the same as always: a hunk of dark bread, a bowl of gruel, and a cup of the hot bitter brew so dear to the heart of the Romarians.

He was given a quarter of an hour to eat and relieve himself, and then the manacles on his wrists were activated and he was ordered out of his cell. When all the slaves were assembled, they were herded into the mine.

He kept his face carefully blank as he passed

Drade and ducked into the shaft's opening. Once inside, his hands were released.

The underground cavern was enormous, lit here and there by small lamps that offered only enough light to work by. The black crystals, so precious to the Confederation, did not come easy. The ground was broken with a pulse axe, and then the crystals were dug out of the earth by hand. It was dirty, back-breaking work. The crystals were large and heavy, yet for all that, they were amazingly fragile.

The slaves toiled in the mine from dawn till noon, at which time they were given a break for the midday meal, and then it was back to work until dark. Seven days a week. A world without sun, without warmth. Without her.

During the next two days, he watched the comings and goings of the guards. There were fewer now than there had been before. As far as he could tell, there were only four guards on the premises; two who watched over the prisoners while they toiled in the mine, and two who patrolled the compound at night.

He had been in the mine just over a week when one of the slaves went berserk. With an inhuman shriek, he hurled himself at one of the guards. The results were immediate, and fatal.

The slave dropped to the ground, writhing in agony. A shrill scream erupted from his throat as pain shot through every nerve while the collar around his throat slowly strangled the life from his body.

The guard pointed at Falkon. "You. Haul his carcass out of here."

Wordlessly, Falkon grasped the dead man by

303

the ankles and dragged him out of the mine. Emerging from the bowels of the cavern, he paused a moment, basking in the warmth of the sun on his face.

"What's going on?"

Squinting against the sunlight, Falkon saw Drade striding toward him.

"I asked you a question, Number Four."

"See for yourself."

Drade grimaced as he glanced at the dead man. "What happened?"

Falkon shrugged. "He attacked a guard."

Drade grunted, then gestured toward the bridge. "Get going. We'll dump him in the ocean."

Resisting the urge to refuse, Falkon slung the dead man's body over his shoulder and headed for the gate. Drade punched in the code and the heavy iron gate swung open.

It was a quarter of a mile to the ocean. Falkon was sweating profusely by the time they reached the water. A natural dock formed by a long finger of land extended about twenty yards into the surf. Falkon carried the body to the end of the jetty and dumped it into the water. He stood there a moment, feeling the spray on his face, wondering what his chances were of overcoming Drade and making a break for the jungle.

He cursed as Drade activated the manacles on his hands. The man was a lot of things, but he wasn't stupid.

Turning, Falkon walked back to the beach. "Why?" he asked. "Why did Hodore attack the mine? Why did they destroy Myrafloures?"

"Let's go, slave."

"Answer me, dammit."

Drade laughed softly. "I don't owe you any explanations."

"You owe me plenty."

Drade ran his finger over the controller. "Amazing, what this can do, don't you think?"

Falkon's hands curled into fists. His gaze bored into the other man's. "Go ahead, use it." Heart pounding, he waited, wondering what foolishness had prompted him to say such a thing. Drade had always been a bully, always enjoyed inflicting pain. At the academy, he had delighted in tormenting the incoming cadets.

He took a deep breath as Drade's thumb hovered over the controller, looked up as the sound of hoofbeats reached his ears. Ashlynne! Mounted on a snow-white stallion, her hair flowing wild around her shoulders, she looked like an avenging angel.

She reined her horse to a halt a short distance from where they stood. "What's going on?"

She directed her question to Drade, but her gaze rested on Falkon.

He bit back a grin at the sound of her lady-of-the-manor tone.

"Just disposing of a dead slave," Drade replied easily. He smiled at her, his gaze moving over her in a long, slow look that bordered on insolence.

"What killed him?"

"He attacked one of my men."

"I see."

Drade shrugged. "It happens sometimes. They all go a little mad after a while.

Fortunately, there's always a ready supply of rebels like this one to take their places."

"Number Four is not to be hurt," Ashlynne said. "He belongs to me, not to you. Nor to Niklaus. You would do well to remember that."

"Yes, my lady. Your husband made that quite clear. Of course, if he attacks one of my men, he'll have to suffer the consequences."

"He's not to be hurt," she said again. "If anything happens to him, I will hold you personally responsible."

It was an empty threat, and they both knew it. Niklaus was in charge. She had no power at all.

"Yes, my lady," Drade replied. "I'm sure Number Four appreciates your concern, but we've got to be getting back now."

Ashlynne gazed at Falkon, drinking in the sight of him, longing to go to him, to wipe the bitterness from his eyes, the perspiration from his brow.

"Are you well, Number Four?" she asked.

He looked up at her, his expression closed, his jaw rigid.

"Number Four?"

"I'm fine."

"Are they treating you well?"

"Oh, yeah," he replied, his words edged with bitterness. "Food fit for a king. A feather bed. A hot bath and a massage every night." He regretted his words as soon as he spoke them. Pain flickered in the depths of her eyes.

Drade laughed. "Let's go."

Falkon looked at Ashlynne and shook his head, silently asking her forgiveness.

Drade poked Falkon with the riding crop he

always carried. "Move it, slave. Being out in this hot sun is making me thirsty." He touched his forefinger to the brim of his cap. "Pleasure seeing you again, Lady Hassrick."

Ashlynne nodded, her heart aching as she watched Falkon turn and walk back toward the mine.

"I'll be leaving first thing tomorrow morning," Hassrick said. He sat back in his chair, a look of utter contentment on his face as the housekeeper filled his wineglass. "Thank you, Hana."

Hana smiled at him, then turned and walked toward the door, her hips swaying provocatively.

"You're leaving?" Ashlynne said.

He nodded, his gaze following Hana.

"How long will you be gone?" She tried to keep the excitement out of her voice.

"No more than a week. I have business on Hodore."

"Hodore!" she exclaimed. "What kind of business could you possibly have there?"

"Nothing you need concern yourself with. I'll require your signature on a few documents before I go."

"What documents?"

He looked at her, a lazy smile playing over his lips. "I think it would be in your best interest to assign ownership of the mine to me."

She stared at him. "Why would I do that?"

"Perhaps I phrased it wrong. It would be in Number Four's best interest if you did as I asked."

The unspoken threat made her stomach clench. "And if I refuse?"

"I'm afraid your slave might meet with an unfortunate accident."

"And what's to keep him from having an 'accident' once I sign?"

Niklaus regarded her through narrowed eyes. "I get the feeling you don't trust me, my dear."

She looked at him, her hands tightly clenched in her lap, but said nothing.

Niklaus blew out a sigh. "Very well. When I return, I'll have some papers for you to sign."

"What kind of papers?"

"It doesn't matter. You will sign them."

She nodded. "Of course."

"I see we understand each other."

She nodded again, then excused herself and went to her room. Going to her computer, she typed in her password, then wrote a short letter of instruction, which she sent to her father's older brother, Samuel. Much to her father's chagrin, Samuel had entered the ministry and was a priest of the old religion on Cannus Twelve. Aside from Falkon, he was the only man she trusted.

When Ashlynne woke the next morning, the maid, Kerolena, informed her that Niklaus had left for Hodore. Her first thought was that she was free. Sitting up, she raised her arms over her head and stretched. Free!

She bounded out of bed, not wanting to waste a minute of the precious few days she would be alone.

"What will you be wanting for breakfast?" Kerolena asked.

"I don't care. Anything!"

With a nod, Kerolena left the room.

Ashlynne took a long, hot shower, dressed quickly in a pair of dun-colored riding pants and a lavender silk shirt. She slipped on a pair of thick socks, pulled on her boots, and hurried downstairs for breakfast. She hardly tasted what was placed before her, and when she was finished, she left the house and went to the barn. A short time later, she was riding toward the mine.

He didn't think, didn't feel. Ignoring the dull, nagging pain in his back and shoulders, he dug in the hard, dark earth. It was about eleven, as far as he could tell. He'd been at work for five hours and had another hour or so to go before he'd get a break. And then another six hours after that.

He glanced at the men laboring beside him. The one on his left was from Daccar. From whispered conversations over the last week and a half, Falkon had learned that there was increasing unrest on Daccar, that the people were starting to put their petty wars behind them, finally realizing that if they didn't stand together, Romariz would destroy them. There were rumors that Drade was away from the mine, and that Hassrick had made some sort of alliance with Brezor, the ambassador of Cenia. Falkon had been unable to hide his skepticism when he heard the news. Cenia was a distant planet of strange yellow-skinned people, though it wasn't the color of their skin that set them apart, but the fact that they followed a religion that had been outlawed in every other known galaxy, a religion that practiced human sacrifice.

But that was not his problem, not now.

"Number Four."

Stifling a groan, he rose to his feet and glanced over his shoulder.

"You're wanted outside."

Outside. The slaves were never summoned outside before dark.

The manacles on his wrists snapped together as he made his way along the narrow shaft that led up, up, to the mouth of the cavern.

He emerged, squinting against the sunlight.

"Here he is, Lady Hassrick."

Ashlynne? Here?

"Thank you."

He blinked against the sunlight, wondering what she was doing there, in the middle of the day, alone.

"I'm taking him with me."

"I have no clearance for that."

"I do."

The guard shook his head. "I can't release him without written authorization from Lord Hassrick or Commander Drade."

"Of course you can't." She smiled as she reached into her pocket and withdrew a sheet of paper. "And here it is."

The guard took the paper and read it quickly. "Very well, my lady. When will you be bringing him back?"

"In a few days. I have some work for him to do up at the house."

"Yes, ma'am. Here." He handed her a controller. "You'll be needing this.

"Thank you." She dropped the controller into her pocket. "Come along, Number Four."

Wordlessly, he fell into step behind her horse, admiring the way the sun danced in her hair, wondering what miracle she had wrought to get him out of the mine.

As soon as they were out of sight of the compound, Ashlynne reined her horse to a halt. Taking the controller from her pocket, she released his hands, then took her foot from the stirrup. "Well, come on," she said, "unless you want to walk."

He swung up behind her and she urged the horse into a lope, riding down the beach until she came to a small sheltered cove.

When she reined the horse to a halt, Falkon slid over the horse's rump, then stood looking up at her.

"Aren't you going to help me down?"

He looked at her, then shook his head. "I'm filthy." He was beyond filthy, he thought, covered with the dirt and sweat of the last week.

"I don't care."

She held out her arms and he lifted her from the back of the horse, letting her body slide slowly down his own as he lowered her to the ground.

She wrapped her arms around his neck. "I missed you," she whispered.

There weren't words enough to say what he

was feeling. Instead, he drew her close and kissed her, hard and quick, and then again, slow and gentle, his mouth moving lightly over hers, his tongue teasing her lips.

"Falkon . . ." She moaned his name, her hands moving restlessly up and down his bare back, reveling in the feel of his sun-warmed skin, the way his muscles quivered at her touch.

It had been too long, too long. Desperate for his touch, she pulled him down on the shimmering golden sand, her hands feverish as she tugged at his breeches.

He removed his boots, then settled back on the sand, grinning roguishly. "Gonna have your way with me, are you?"

"Just as soon as I can," she retorted as she flung his breeches aside.

He watched through heated eyes as she quickly shed her own clothes, and then he gathered her into his arms and kissed her, his clever hands moving over her, caressing, teasing, arousing her until she writhed beneath him, lost in the wonder of his touch. Her hands roamed over his back, his shoulders, delved into the silky soft hair at his nape. She was dying, she thought, being devoured by the heat of his mouth moving over her flesh, a hungry flame that left tiny fires of need burning in its wake.

She was ready, more than ready, when he rose over her, his body merging with hers, filling her, completing her, as their hearts and spirits blended, soaring toward that one moment when two were truly one.

* * *

Falkon brushed a kiss over her cheek. "How did you manage this?"

They were lying in each other's arms, sated. Content.

"Niklaus has gone to Hodore."

"Why?"

"I'm not sure. What difference does it make?"

Hassrick had gone to Hodore. Perhaps the rumors he'd heard had some foundation in truth, after all. And Drade was gone, too. Coincidence?

"We have a whole week to be together."

"And how are you going to explain this to him when he gets back?"

"I don't know. I'll worry about it when the time comes."

He lifted himself up on one elbow, his hand splayed across her belly. "Are you all right?"

"Fine. Well, mostly fine. I still get a little nauseous sometimes."

"You're beautiful. Do you know that?"

"You are."

He laughed derisively. "Yeah."

She lifted one hand, her fingers running over the thick lynaziam collar at his neck. "Is it terribly uncomfortable?" She ran her fingertips over the manacles on his wrists.

"Uncomfortable?" He snorted softly. "You could call it that, I guess."

"I wish I could remove it."

"Yeah, me, too." He hated the collar, hated the way it felt almost as much as what it stood for.

"Someday," she murmured.

313

"Yeah," he said bleakly. "Someday." He looked down at her, frankly admiring the soft curves of her body, the sweep of her lashes, the way her hair looked spread over the sand, silver over gold. The warm satin smoothness of her hip and thigh pressed intimately against his own. Her breasts were full, her belly slightly rounded with new life. A child. His child. His woman . . . He had a sudden, unwelcome image of Ashlynne in Hassrick's bed, writhing in pleasure in Hassrick's embrace.

"What is it?" Ashlynne asked, alarmed by the sudden darkness in his eyes. "What's wrong?"

"Nothing."

"Tell me."

"I was just thinking of you. With him."

She frowned. "What do you mean?"

"You know what I mean."

"Oh." She caressed his cheek. "We don't sleep together."

He looked at her in disbelief. "Never?"

"Never. He said he didn't want another man's leavings."

Falkon stared down at her. "Yet he still married you, knowing about the baby," he mused. Why? That was the question. And the mine was the answer. Ashlynne owned the mine. If she had died in the attack, the mine and its profits would have been taken over by the Confederation and Hassrick would have lost his chance to be in control.

"Falkon?"

"Are you sure he didn't say why he was going to Hodore?"

"He just said business. Oh, he did say he would have some papers for me to sign when he got back."

"What else did he say?"

"He wanted me to sign the mine over to him."

"Did you?"

"No."

He drew her close, in sudden fear for her life. If Hassrick could convince Ashlynne to give him the mine, he would have no further need of his wife. Especially a wife carrying another man's child.

"Don't sign anything that gives him control of the mine, Ashlynne," he said urgently. "Promise me."

"I won't."

"Do you know if Drade went with him?"

"He didn't say. Why?"

"I think the two of them must be plotting something."

"What?"

"I don't know. But Drade craves power. He always has. That's why he allied himself with the Romarians. Because they're the most powerful influence in the galaxy. I think he was behind the attack on the mine."

"That doesn't make sense. Why would the Romarians want to attack the mine?"

"I don't think the Romarians had anything to do with it. I think it was a plan hatched by Drade and Hassrick."

"But why?"

He shook his head. He had given it a lot of thought in the last few weeks. "You were supposed to be visiting Hassrick the week the mine was attacked. I think someone screwed up and attacked early."

Ashlynne stared up at Falkon, remembering how surprised Hassrick had been to hear from her. No wonder. He had been certain she was dead, killed in the explosion that had destroyed the jinan. But that would mean . . . She shook her head. "No, it can't be true." Yet even as she said the words, she knew, deep inside, that it was.

"Be careful, Ashlynne."

"I don't want to think about that now." She gazed up at him, her heart swelling with such love she thought it might burst within her breast. No matter that she was married to Niklaus, Falkon was the husband of her heart, the other half of her soul. She saw him, and her spirit soared. The sound of his voice thrilled her. The touch of his hand made her quiver with longing. He was in her every thought, as much a part of her as her hands and feet, as the child growing within her. How had she ever lived without him?

She held him close, giving thanks to whatever fate it was that had brought him to Tierde, and was immediately overcome with a wave of guilt and remorse. How could she be so selfish? He had lost his wife and child, spent months in captivity. He was still a prisoner. She would have spared him all that, if she could, and yet if his life had been different, they never would have met.

She clung to him, afraid, so afraid, of losing him.

"Ashlynne, what is it?"

She buried her face in his shoulder, refusing to meet his eyes.

"Ashlynne?"

She shook her head, unable to speak past the lump in her throat, not wanting him to see the tears burning her eyes.

"What is it, princess?"

"I love you," she whispered. "I love you so much, I'm . . . I'm afraid." She choked back a sob. Everything she had ever loved had been taken from her—her parents, her best friend, her home. She couldn't bear to lose him, too.

Falkon slid one hand under her chin and tilted her head up so he could see her face. The love shining through her tears reached deep into his heart. "Ashlynne. Sweetheart."

Cupping her face in his hands, he kissed her gently, tenderly. He didn't have to ask what she was afraid of, didn't have to wonder what she'd been thinking. He knew her thoughts as well as he knew his own.

Hoping to distract her, he stood up. "Come on," he said, taking her by the hand and lifting her to her feet. "Let's go for a swim."

She glanced at the ocean, at the white-tipped waves tumbling over the shore, then looked at Falkon. "You really could use a bath," she remarked. "And so could I." Bits of the fine black dust that covered him clung to her skin.

"Second best idea you've had all day," he said with a grin.

"Can't catch me," she cried, and letting go of his hand, she sprinted toward the water.

He caught her where the surf met the sand

and they landed in the water together. She squealed as a wave broke over them.

On hands and knees, they faced each other, then Falkon picked up a handful of sand and rubbed it over her left arm.

"What are you doing?" she asked.

"Washing you."

"With sand?"

He nodded, picked up another handful of sand, and rubbed it over her right arm. It felt surprisingly refreshing.

"My turn," she said. They spent the next ten minutes washing each other and then went for a swim.

They left the water hand in hand. Back on the beach, he drew her into his arms for a quick kiss, and the fire between them sparked to life once more.

Sinking down on the sand, he made love to her again, felt her tears drip like warm rain on his face.

Wrapping her in his arms, he held her tight, one hand stroking her hair. He shouldn't have come here with her. When Hassrick found out, there would be hell to pay for both of them. For himself, he didn't give a damn, but he didn't want Ashlynne hurt. She'd already suffered enough.

"Tell me," she whispered.

"I love you."

"Again."

"I love you, more than my life."

"Falkon, let's leave here, now, today! Let's run away!"

"How far do you think we'd get on that horse?"

"We'll take the shuttle."

"And then what?" He kept his voice light, but his mind was already turning, planning. Enjine Base Nine was out of the question; they couldn't go there. But the shuttle would get them as far as Nardin. From there, they could get transport to Cherlin Four.

"Falkon?"

"Are you sure you want to do this?"

"I'm sure."

He kissed her soundly, then stood up and pulled her to her feet. "Let's do it."

Exhilarated by the promise of freedom, they dressed quickly. Falkon helped her mount, then swung up behind her.

It was, he thought, shaping up to be one of the best days of his life.

Chapter Twenty-six

When they were within sight of the house, Falkon dismounted and Ashlynne activated the shackles on his wrists. Trailing a respectful distance behind her horse, he followed her through the massive side gate and around the back of the house to the stable.

A man came forward to help her dismount. His gaze moved over Falkon, his expression blatantly disapproving as he took the stallion's reins and led it into the barn.

"Come along, Number Four," Ashlynne said.

He fell into step behind her. The new house was even more impressive than the old one, he mused, and wondered if, one day, she would be sorry she had left it all behind for a man who had nothing.

When they reached the front of the house,

she turned to face him. "Wait here. I'm going inside to tell Kerolena that I've decided to go shopping in the city."

Falkon nodded.

"I won't be long."

Ten minutes later, she was back, followed by a tall, sour-faced man. Falkon recognized him as one of Hassrick's bodyguards, but he had eyes only for Ashlynne. She had changed her riding clothes for a green dress that made her eyes glow like emeralds, and a pair of low-heeled white boots. She had a large bag slung over one shoulder.

"Let's go, Number Four."

He obeyed without question.

The sour-faced man opened the door of the shuttle and handed Ashlynne inside.

"Thank you, Brill," she said coolly. "Get in, Number Four."

Falkon ducked inside and sat in the rear seat. A moment later, the shackles on his ankles snapped together.

Brill slid into the driver's seat.

It took the better part of two hours to reach Partha. It was a large city laid out in concentric circles. The shopping area was in the center. It was a beautiful city. The buildings, made of white sandstone and glass, reflected the sun's light, so that the whole city seemed to sparkle. The streets were wide, lined with trees, trees that had almost become extinct only a few decades ago. Fortunately, the people of Partha had realized their value before it was too late.

Brill parked the shuttle on the landing strip, exited the vehicle and opened the door for

Ashlynne. She released the shackles on Falkon's hands and feet and stepped out of the craft.

Falkon followed her. He stood to one side, his head bowed, his hands clasped, trying to look properly submissive.

"Oh, Brill, I think I left my bag on the floor." She smiled at him. "Would you get it for me, please?"

With a grunt, Brill leaned into the vehicle.

As soon as his back was turned, Ashlynne pulled the stun gun from her pocket and fired it at his back. He dropped to the ground like a rock.

"Where'd you get that from?"

She shrugged. "It's the one I took from Casman's quarters."

"You've had it all this time?"

She shook her head. "No. Niklaus took it from me. I found it in his room." She glanced around, afraid someone might take notice of what was going on, but luckily, the area was deserted, at least for the moment. "What are we going to do about him?" she asked, nodding at Brill.

Falkon found a length of rope in the back of the shuttle. He quickly lashed Brill's hands and feet together; then, slinging the big man over his shoulder, he carried him to a large recycling receptacle and dumped him inside. The man landed with a resounding thud.

"Hurry," Ashlynne called, and climbed back into the shuttle.

Falkon scrambled into the driver's seat, hit the controls, and the shuttle shot forward. It was a remarkably speedy craft, easy to handle. He looked over at Ashlynne and grinned. "Nice work, sweetheart."

She grinned back at him. "Thank you. Where are we going?"

"To Nardin. We can get a transport to Cherlin Four from there."

"Cherlin Four? What's there?"

"Darf."

"What's a darf?"

"He's a who, not a what, and he owes me a favor."

It was remarkably easy to find transport. There was a cruiser preparing to leave for Cherlin Four when they arrived. Ashlynne signed for the necessary credits, and ten minutes later, they were on their way.

Ashlynne took hold of Falkon's hand as the ship lifted off. She had packed one of Niklaus's shirts in her bag and Falkon had slipped it on before they entered the space port. The shirt was dark blue, with a high neck and long sleeves, effectively covering the collar and cuffs that marked him as a slave.

She hadn't said anything to him before, but she didn't care for space travel. The wild flight from Enjine Base Nine had been her first experience. She had hoped it would be her last.

Falkon looked over at her and smiled. "You all right?"

She nodded. "How long will it take us to get there?"

"We should arrive tomorrow afternoon." He squeezed her hand. "You'll like Darf."

"Where did you meet him?"

Falkon chuckled. "I met Darf about four years ago in a run-down cantina on Cherlin

Four. A couple of drunken Hodorians were giving him a hard time. They had him shoved up against a wall. One of them had a knife. They were laughing at him, said they were going to shave his whole body so they could see what was under all that hair."

"What happened?"

He shrugged. "I was a little drunk myself and looking for a fight, so . . ."

"So you went to his rescue?"

"Yeah. Those Hodorians are big, but soft. When they were gone, Darf and I celebrated our victory. By the time the bottle was empty, we were good friends."

"Is he married?"

"Yeah. You'll like Chaney."

Ashlynne nodded uncertainly. In her sheltered life, she had rarely met people from exotic planets. She had seen pictures of other races: the hairy people of Cherlin Four, the yellow-skinned people of Cenia, the giants of Andoria.

Falkon squeezed her hand reassuringly.

"Relax, sweetheart. People are pretty much the same all over, no matter what they look like."

The flight to Cherlin Four was uneventful. Ashlynne stared at the tele-screen located on the back of the seat in front of her, but her mind was elsewhere. Brill had probably made his way back to the house by now. No doubt he had contacted Niklaus. One thing she was sure of—Niklaus wouldn't let her go without a fight. He wanted the mine. That was why he had married her. Not because he had promised her father, not because he wanted her, but because of the mine. But it would never be his. She had seen to that.

It was late afternoon when they arrived on Cherlin Four.

Ashlynne couldn't help staring as they made their way through the space port. Cherlin Four had been designated by the Confederation as the neutral planet for this quadrant, and people of every race and culture intermingled. Giants and dwarfs moved side by side. She had never realized people came in so many sizes and colors.

Outside, they found a shuttle for hire. Falkon gave the driver directions, then climbed into the backseat beside Ashlynne.

Moments later, they were underway.

Falkon frowned as the driver kept glancing at him. "Something wrong?"

"Those shackles you wear."

Falkon cursed softly as he tugged the sleeve of his shirt down over the cuff on his left wrist.

"Get them off you, I can."

"Really?" Ashlynne leaned forward. "How?"

"Expensive, it is."

"It doesn't matter. Can you do it now?"

"Now, yes."

The shuttle made a sudden turn, snaking back the way they had come. A quarter of an hour later, the driver stopped in front of a rather disreputable-looking building.

Ashlynne looked at Falkon. "I don't like this," she whispered.

"Give me the gun."

She slid it to him while the driver exited the shuttle.

"Coming, are you?" the driver asked.

"What is this place?" Ashlynne asked.

"Live here, I do." The driver opened the shuttle door. "Coming, are you?"

"Let's go," Falkon said. He got out of the vehicle, turned, and offered Ashlynne his hand.

The driver led the way. Ashlynne stayed close to Falkon, her heart pounding with trepidation.

The house was just what Ashlynne expected: small, dark, and dirty. A large spotted hound growled at them from a corner.

The driver waved at a dingy couch. "Down, sit," he said. "Back soon will I be." And so saying, he left the room.

Ashlynne glanced at the couch, and remained standing. So did Falkon.

"We shouldn't have come in here," Ashlynne whispered. She sent a wary glance at the dog. The animal stood in the corner, hackles raised, teeth bared.

The driver emerged a few minutes later carrying a long, silver metal tube. "Pay first you must," he said.

"How much?" Falkon asked.

"To my account, one thousand credits." The driver punched his account number into a grimy-looking comport, and Ashlynne made the necessary transfer of funds.

Falkon lifted his arms. "Get busy."

The driver nodded, and then, in a quick move, he drew a knife and pressed the point into Falkon's belly.

Falkon had been expecting something like that and he was ready for it. Palming the stun gun, he fired it at point blank range. The knife and the silver tube clattered to the floor; the driver dropped down beside them, paralyzed from head to foot.

Falkon picked up the silver tube and turned it over in his hands. There was a single switch at one end.

"How does it work?" Ashlynne asked.

"I'm not sure." Sitting down on the edge of the couch, he pressed the tube against the shackle on his right foot and depressed the switch. The shackle on his ankle opened and fell to the floor.

In moments, he was free.

He lifted a hand to his throat, turned his head from side to side, sighed with pleasure at being able to move without the edge of the collar pressing into his skin.

Ashlynne glanced down at the driver. "Let's get out of here."

With a nod, Falkon grabbed her hand and they left the house.

Ashlynne glanced up and down the deserted street. "Now what?"

Falkon opened the door of the shuttle. "Get in."

She didn't argue. "I'll say one thing," she murmured as she closed the door. "Being with you is never boring."

Ashlynne peered out the window while Falkon parked the shuttle. The house, which was round, was located in the middle of a patch of stubby yellow-green grass. Several shaggy sheep grazed in the shade of an enormous tree, the likes of which Ashlynne had never seen. The leaves, a peculiar burnt orange in color, were huge and diamond-shaped.

She followed Falkon up the narrow pathway that led to the front door.

He took her hand in his. "Relax."

"What if they don't like me?"

"They'll love you."

He rapped sharply on the door. It swung open a few moments later to reveal a tall male covered from head to foot with pale beige hair. He was, Ashlynne thought, rather homely, with his wiry hair and pale yellow eyes.

"Falkon! Bless the stars, what are you doing here?" The Cherlin threw his arms around Falkon. "Damn, I'm glad to see you."

"Easy, Darf," Falkon said, laughing. "You're gonna smother me!"

Darf backed off. "I forget how weak you humans are," he said, a grin spreading over his face. His gaze rested on Ashlynne. "Now, who's this pretty little thing?"

Falkon slid his arm around Ashlynne's shoulders. "Ashlynne, this is Darf. Darf, Lady Ashlynne of Myrafloures."

Darf stared at Falkon, his expression one of surprise, and then respect as he bowed to Ashlynne. "Pleased to make your acquaintance, my lady," he said. "Welcome to our home."

"Thank you."

"Darf," called a female voice, "who's at the door?"

Darf clapped Falkon on the arm. "What are you waiting for? Come on in."

They followed their host inside, where they were met by a female with curly brown hair. Her eyes were also yellow, though of a brighter, more golden hue than her husband's.

"Falkon!" she squealed, and hurled herself into his arms.

The female was as pretty as the male was homely, Ashlynne thought, only then noticing that neither of the Cherlin wore clothing. Covered as they were with hair, she supposed there was no need.

The living room was large and airy. There were fur rugs on the floor, modernistic paintings on the walls, a shelf of vidbooks and movies, another shelf filled with a variety of exotic animals and fish carved from ebony wood.

Falkon introduced her to Darf's wife, Chaney, who also bowed to Ashlynne, then fluttered around, inviting them to sit, asking if they wanted something to eat or drink.

Ashlynne declined, but Falkon accepted a drink.

"Now," Darf said, when they were all settled, "tell us everything. Last we heard, you had been sent to the mines of Tierde. We feared you had been killed in the attack."

"Obviously not," Falkon replied.

"Obviously."

Chaney leaned forward, her eyes alight. "Tell us, Falkon, how did you get away?"

"It's a long story."

"We have time," Chaney said.

"Yes," Darf said, "start at the beginning." He glanced at Ashlynne, a speculative gleam in his eyes. "And don't leave anything out."

"Well," Chaney exclaimed an hour later, "that's some story." She looked at Ashlynne and smiled. "We are expecting our first child, as well."

"Is that right?" Falkon said. "Congratulations, you two. I know you've been trying for quite a while." He grinned at Darf. "I was beginning to wonder about your . . . ah . . ." He glanced at Ashlynne and Chaney. "Virility."

Darf punched Falkon's shoulder. "Very funny."

"When is your baby due?" Chaney asked.

"I'm not sure," Ashlynne replied. "In about six months, I think. Yours?"

"Any day now."

Ashlynne nodded. "You don't look it," she said, then blushed.

Chaney laughed good-naturedly as she ran a hand over her hairy belly. "I can hide quite a bit under all this."

Darf ruffled his wife's hair. "So, Falkon, how long are you two going to stay?"

"I'm not sure. Have you heard anything of Daccar?"

Darf grunted. "Your home is at peace for the first time in thirty years."

Falkon looked stunned. "I don't believe it."

Darf nodded. "There was a battle with the Romarians shortly after you were captured. Your people allied with the barbarians of Swernolt and emerged victorious. Daccar, Swernolt and Romariz signed a treaty."

Falkon swore under his breath. A treaty with Romariz. It was unthinkable. All these months, he had thought of nothing but vengeance. "Have you heard anything of an alliance between Romariz and Cenia?"

Darf shook his head. "No, but I heard through a reliable source that Drade has been

The Captive

seen on Hodore in the company of the Cenian ambassador."

"Drade." Falkon's hands clenched as he imagined them around his enemy's throat. He should have kept that damnable collar. He'd like to see Drade squirming on the ground, just once, his body writhing in agony. Just once before he killed him.

"Falkon?" He turned his head to see Ashlynne staring at him, her brow furrowed with concern. "Are you all right?"

"Sure."

"Maybe you should let it go," Darf said quietly. "There's nothing to be gained from revenge."

"Isn't there?" Falkon met his friend's gaze.

"Would you risk your future, or Ashlynne's future, to avenge the past? Vengeance will serve no purpose. It will not bring Maiya or your daughter back to you, nor ease the pain of their loss."

Falkon looked at Ashlynne and knew his friend spoke the truth. What was past was past, and could not be resurrected. And Ashlynne . . . As much as he yearned to avenge Maiya's death, he would not put Ashlynne's life, or the life of their unborn child, in danger.

"You speak wisely, as always," Falkon said. Not long ago, he had wished for a chance to spend the rest of his life with Ashlynne. Now that he had that chance, he would be a fool to throw it away. Sliding his arm around her waist, he drew her close. "To hell with Drade," he said, and felt a sense of peace wash over him as Ashlynne looked into his eyes and smiled.

Chapter Twenty-seven

"What do you mean, she's gone?" Niklaus glared at Brill through the tele-screen.

Brill shook his head. "I mean she's gone. She hit me with a stun gun, and he tied me up. They took the shuttle and left."

"Did you try to find them?"

"Yes, sir. I have people looking for them now."

"Double your search. I want her waiting for me when I get back."

"Yes, sir."

Niklaus closed the transmission, then turned to his companion. "I want you to send some men to Daccar."

Drade nodded. "I'll take care of it."

"Do you have any idea where he'd go?"

"I doubt if he'll go home," Drade replied. "It's

a possibility, of course. But I think he's smarter than that."

"Well, he can't just disappear."

"No. He has a few close friends. I'll send my men to check them out."

"We've got to find her," Niklaus said. "Brezor won't be put off much longer."

"I have an idea," Drade remarked, "though you may not like it."

"Let's hear it."

"If we can't locate Lady Ashlynne in time, we could find someone to take her place. Brezor has never seen her. The imposter can sign the necessary papers, and when she's served her purpose—" Drade shrugged. "She'll disappear."

Niklaus tapped his knuckles on the arm of his chair. It might work. At the moment, it was the best option they had. Time was running out. The Cenian ambassador was not a patient man. He had arranged for the Cenians, disguised as Hodorians, to attack Tierde in return for a partnership in the mine in order to assure that he would have a steady supply of the black baneite crystals. A partnership in the mine, and the ambassador's silence. Niklaus needed both.

"Find me a suitable woman," Niklaus said. "And then find my wife. When you do, bring her to Arkata. Make sure no one sees you."

With a nod, Drade left the room.

Niklaus went to the window and gazed out into the darkness of the Hodorian night. Where was she? And what was he going to do with her when she was found? He shied away from the obvious answer but, in the end, he knew he would have no choice. Once she signed the mine over to him, he would have no further use for her. She would be just another loose end.

He blew out a sigh, wondering how things had gone so wrong so quickly. It had all started out innocently enough—a casual conversation with the Cenian ambassador, who was eager to be part of the Confederation, eager to fuel his ships at Tierde, rather than make the long journey to Ohnmahr. Brezor had mentioned that if Hassrick would put in a good word with Marcus and the other members of the Mining Confederation, he would make it worth his while.

It had been a way out, and Hassrick had jumped at it. Unbeknownst to his father, he had made several bad investments, had borrowed credits and cash he could not afford to repay. Because of that, his family was on the brink of losing everything they had worked for, everything they owned. All Hassrick had to do was convince Marcus to admit Cenia to the Confederation. Hassrick had agreed, confident of his ability to convince his future father-in-law to see things his way. Brezor had cleared Hassrick's debts and made a large deposit to Hassrick's private account. It had all seemed so easy, until Marcus refused to admit the Cenians to the Confederation.

In desperation, he had gone to Drade. It had been Drade who suggested the attack on Tierde. Invite Ashlynne to Arkata. Attack the mine. Marry the girl, and the mine would be his. The Cenian ambassador could have access to Tierde and the baneite crystals and all would be well. Hassrick had been appalled by the idea, but, in the end, he had agreed. But the attack hadn't gone as planned, either. Due to an error in timing, the attack had taken place a week early. He had thought all was lost, and then, as if by miracle, Ashlynne had showed up. But even that had gone wrong. He had never been eager to marry her, but on meeting her, he had been smitten by her beauty, by her apparent innocence, only to discover that she was soiled goods, no better than a Hodorian streetwalker. Worse, she had stubbornly refused to give him thc mine.

Nothing had gone as planned.

Only now, when it was too late, did he begin to wonder if perhaps Drade had had an agenda of his own.

Chapter Twenty-eight

Ashlynne turned on her side and ran her foot up and down Falkon's leg. She had been a little embarrassed when it came time to go to bed and Darf had asked if they wanted to share a room. She'd felt her cheeks grow hot when Falkon grinned at his friend and replied, "What do you think?" She couldn't help wondering what Darf and Chaney thought, but she didn't really care. She wanted nothing more than to be with Falkon, to hold him in her arms. She ran her fingertips over his cheek, along his jaw, and down his neck.

"I guess you're glad to be rid of that awful collar," she mused aloud.

He grunted softly. "You have no idea."

"Have you always been a warrior?"

"I guess so." He grinned into the darkness. A warrior. He liked the sound of that. He wasn't sure if he was a warrior, but he had always been a fighter.

"Haven't you ever wanted to do anything else?"

"I don't think I know *how* to do anything else."

"How long are we going to stay here?"

"I don't know. Why? Do you want to leave?"

"No. I just . . . What are we going to do about Niklaus, about—"

"About what?"

"About us?"

Falkon grinned at her. "Is that a marriage proposal?"

She made a face at him. "Of course not," she said tartly.

"Another hope crushed," he muttered. "Though I can't blame you. I'm no prize, that's for damn sure."

"Stop that. I think you're wonderful."

"You just like me."

"Yes," she said solemnly. "I do. Tell me everything will work out. Tell me we'll always be together, no matter what."

"Ah, sweetheart, I wish I could promise you that."

"Tell me," she said, blinking back her tears, "even if it's a lie."

"We'll always be together." Lifting one hand, he wiped her tears away. "Don't cry, sweetheart."

"I love you," she whispered. "I love you so much."

"I know," he said. "I know." He kissed her lightly. "I love you, too, princess."

She grinned at him through her tears. "Don't call me that."

He drew her closer. "I don't know what's going to happen in the future, Ashlynne, but if it's up to me, I'll never let you go."

"Never?"

"Never."

It was a promise and a wish wrapped in a single word.

They spent a pleasant week with Darf and Chaney, and yet Ashlynne could feel the underlying restlessness that plagued Falkon. Often, late at night, she woke to find him pacing the floor, or standing at the window, staring out into the darkness. She told herself there was nothing to worry about, that it would just take some time for him to adjust to being free, but she knew, deep down inside, that he was worried. And so was she. Niklaus would look for them, of that she was certain. He wanted the mine, and he wouldn't rest until it was his. Until they resolved things with Niklaus, they couldn't return to Tierde. Nor could they go to Daccar. Without being told, she knew that Niklaus would have people there, waiting, just in case Falkon decided to return to his home. Her biggest fear was that Falkon would decide to go back to Tierde, to confront Niklaus face-to-face.

"Ashlynne?"

"Did you say something? I'm sorry, I guess my mind was elsewhere."

Chaney smiled. "It wasn't important. Are you feeling all right?"

"Yes, fine."

"Something is bothering you. Do you want to talk about it?"

"No. Yes." Ashlynne sighed. "It's Falkon."

"He's not happy here?"

"No, it's not that. He's just . . . restless."

Chaney nodded. "Yes, I've sensed that. He's free from the mine, from the restraints, but he still feels trapped. Helpless."

"Yes, exactly. He hasn't said so, but I think he wants to go home."

"That's not hard to understand. Don't we all long for home, wherever it might be?"

"Yes, I suppose so. My mother . . ." Ashlynne hesitated as the pain of her mother's loss stabbed through her again. "My mother was from Earth. She always hoped to go back for a visit, but there was never time. And now . . ."

Chaney's eyes filled with sympathy and understanding. "I'm sorry," she said softly. "You and Falkon have been through so much. You're lucky, to have found each other."

"Yes. I love him more than he'll ever know."

"That's easy to see."

"Is it?

"Oh, yes. I can see it in your eyes whenever you look at him, the way you need to touch him."

Ashlynne felt her cheeks grow warm. "I wasn't aware that it was so obvious."

"I recognize it only because I have felt it myself."

Ashlynne glanced at the clock. "How much longer do you think they'll be gone?"

"Not long."

Ashlynne nodded. Falkon and Darf had gone into the city to see if they could learn anything more about the attack on the mine. She had wanted to go along, but Falkon had insisted she stay home with Chaney. She had never liked waiting. She hadn't realized quite how much until now. Where was he?

Falkon lifted his glass and sipped his drink. If the informer they'd found was to be believed, Hodore was innocent of the attack on the mine.

"What about the two Hodorians I saw?" Falkon asked.

The informer, whose name was Kye, glanced around. He was a little man, with pale skin and enormous golden eyes. Leaning forward, he drew his cloak more closely about him.

"Imposters," Kye whispered. "Cenians disguised as Hodorian soldiers."

Falkon grunted softly as he remembered the day after the attack. They had stopped at a pool to drink and Ashlynne had washed her hands. She'd had some sort of greenish powder under her fingernails. She hadn't known what it was and he'd been too worried about getting away to give it much thought at the time.

"Do you know who organized the attack?" Darf asked.

Kye nodded, his gaze darting into the far corners of the room. "I have a name."

Falkon leaned across the table. "What is it?"

"It will cost extra."

"We've already given you five hundred credits," Darf exclaimed. "What more do you want?"

"Five hundred more."

"Done," Falkon said. "Give me the name."

"Drade."

Falkon swore softly. Drade, always Drade.

Kye shifted nervously in his seat, his restless gaze moving around the room.

"Can you tell me anything else?" Falkon asked.

Kye shook his head. "I've said enough." He pushed back his chair, preparing to leave.

"Not so fast." Falkon's hand snaked out, closing around the little man's forearm. "Has the name Hassrick come up in any of this?"

"Hassrick? Niklaus or Rugen?"

"Either one."

Kye settled into his chair once more. "I have heard that the young Hassrick needs money very badly to repay a debt. I have heard that his family stands on the brink of ruin."

"Go on."

"No, no, I can tell you no more."

"Listen, you slimy little weasel, I've given you a thousand credits," Falkon said, tightening his hold on Kye's wrist. "You'll tell me everything you know, or I'll break your arm, and then your neck."

"They are in it together," Kye said. "Hassrick, Drade, and the Cenian ambassador."

"The Cenian ambassador," Darf said. "What's he got to do with this?"

Kye shook his head. "I know not. I only know

the three of them were seen together on Hodore, both before and after the attack."

"It just gets better all the time," Falkon muttered.

Kye stared at Falkon. "You have something Hassrick wants very badly. Be careful."

"Why are you telling me this?"

"You fought on Riga Twelve."

Falkon nodded.

"I was there."

"During the fight?"

"Yes. You saved my life."

Darf slammed his fist on the table. "He saved your life, yet you charged him a thousand credits for information? What kind of low life scum are you?"

"I have a family to feed," Kye said. "And I know that Falkon's woman can well afford the cost."

"It's all right, Darf," Falkon said. He released his hold on Kye's arm. "Go on, get out of here."

The little man needed no urging. Huddling deeper into his cloak, the cowl pulled close around his face, he moved slowly toward the door, looking neither right nor left.

"Well," Darf said. "That was interesting."

"Yeah. It all makes sense now."

"It does? How about explaining it to me?"

"Hassrick needed money. Cenia has been trying to find a way into the Confederation so they don't have to go all the way to Ohnmahr for fuel. Not only is it a long journey, but the crystals of Ohrnahr lack the strength and longevity of those mined on Tierde."

"Where does Drade fit in?"

"I'm not sure, but I think he must be the middleman. Cenia probably promised him a place of power in exchange for his help. Ashlynne's father refused to consider accepting Cenia into the Confederation, so Hassrick decided to get rid of Myrafloures. Ashlynne was supposed to be on Trellis when the mine was attacked, but somebody got the dates wrong."

Falkon grunted softly as the pieces seemed to fall into place. "No wonder Hassrick was so eager for the marriage to take place. With Ashlynne still alive, Romariz couldn't take over the mine, and he still had a chance to fulfil his bargain with the Cenians."

"Falkon . . ."

"What?"

Darf lowered his voice. "I think we're being watched."

"Where?"

"The three men at the end of the bar. They've been watching us for quite some time."

Falkon leaned back in his chair and stretched his arms out to the side, as if he were working the kinks out of his back. From the corner of his eye, he could see three men in long dark coats standing at the far end of the bar near the door. "Got 'em."

"Do you recognize any of them?"

"The one on the right. His name's Roge. He works for Drade. I want him alive."

Darf muttered an oath. "Why is it this happens every time you show up?"

"You're just lucky, I guess," Falkon replied with a devil-may-care grin. "Think how dull your life would be without me."

"Nothing wrong with dull," Darf retorted. "I like dull."

Falkon stood up and moved toward the door. "You coming?"

Darf sucked in a deep breath and exhaled in a long sigh. "What do you think?" He stood up, muttering, "Chaney's gonna be madder than a Hordorian hellcat."

Moving casually, Falkon walked toward the door. Darf paid the bill, then followed Falkon outside.

"Have you got a weapon?" Darf asked.

"Stunner. You?"

"I'm always armed when I go anywhere with you," Darf replied dryly.

Falkon grinned. He could feel the adrenaline flowing.

"They're coming," Darf whispered.

"I hear 'em."

"You got a plan?"

Falkon shook his head and continued walking. "Where does this street go?"

"Branches off a few yards down. If you go left, it leads into the business district. The other way leads into a dead end."

"Okay, the dead end it is."

"Let's hope it isn't," Darf muttered bleakly.

The alley was long and dark. A high wooden fence blocked the far end. Falkon went halfway down and moved to the left; Darf moved to the right.

The three men paused at the head of the alley. They conferred a minute, then two of them entered the alley. The third waited on the street.

Falkon stood with his back to the wall, listening. The two men walked quietly, pausing every few seconds. There was the sound of a scuffle, followed by a grunt. The second man passed in front of him, and there was no time to wonder if Darf had won or lost. He fired the stunner. In the flare of light that followed, he saw Darf standing over the other man, his golden eyes gleaming. He glanced at the alley entrance and saw that the third man was gone.

"That was too easy," Darf said. "I don't like it."

"Yeah." Falkon looked at the man he'd stunned. It wasn't Roge. Neither was the man sprawled at Darf's feet. "Did you kill him?"

Darf shook his head. "No," he answered with some regret. "Do you want me to?"

"No. Let's go home."

"The women? Are we going to tell them about this?"

"No, I don't think so."

Chapter Twenty-nine

Darf's dwelling was dark when they arrived, and Falkon knew, deep in his gut, that the house was empty.

Darf paused and sniffed the air. "Someone's been here."

"Yeah," Falkon muttered, and knew that the men in the bar hadn't been sent to spy on them or to kill them, but to delay them. "Drade."

Darf turned to face him, his pale yellow eyes glowing in the dark. "Drade?"

Falkon nodded. "They've taken the women."

With an oath, Darf turned and ran toward the house. Flinging open the door, he darted inside. "Chaney? Chaney!"

A cold dark anger settled over Falkon as he followed Darf into the house. He stood inside the door, waiting, listening to Darf's footsteps as he went from room to room calling his wife's name.

"They're gone." Darf's voice. Flat. Empty. "What do we do now?"

"We go to Trellis."

Darf didn't ask why. Going to a small closet, he withdrew a pair of weapons and tossed one to Falkon. "Let's go."

Ashlynne sat close to Chaney, taking comfort from the other woman's nearness. She lifted a hand to her neck, her fingers exploring the thick lynaziam collar. How had Falkon endured it for so long? She felt as if she was choking. Every time she moved her head, she felt the edge cutting into her skin. The shackles on her hands and feet were equally heavy and uncomfortable.

She kept her gaze lowered, refusing to look at the man sitting across from her. She recognized him all right. Drade.

She lifted a hand to the collar again, remembering all too well the sight of Falkon writhing on the ground, his body twitching uncontrollably as waves of pain speared through him.

"You'll get used to it."

Ashlynne looked up to find Drade grinning at her.

"So, you're Falkon's new woman," Drade mused. "He always did have good taste."

Ashlynne glared at him. She was scared clear through. She and Chaney had been watching a movie when four men had burst into the house. In less than five minutes, she and Chaney had been fitted with collars and shackles and hustled into a shuttle. A short time later they were in a cruiser headed for Arkata.

Her fingers traced the edge of the collar. "Why are you doing this?"

"Just following orders."

"Whose orders?"

"Whose do you think?"

She shook her head, wincing as the collar scraped her skin. "He wouldn't."

Drade grunted softly. "You should have signed the papers when he asked you to. All he wanted was the mine. He would have let you go. Now . . ."

Drade shook his head, and with that single, simple gesture, Ashlynne knew that her worst fears were about to become reality. Niklaus was going to get rid of her. He might not kill her, but he was going to put her out of his life. After she gave him the mine. She touched the collar at her throat again, and knew that she would do whatever he wanted.

A bubble of hysterical laughter rose in her throat. Maybe they would send her back to Tierde to take Falkon's place in the mine. "Falkon . . ." His name rose to her lips.

A victorious smile spread over Drade's face. "Falkon. We'll have him, too."

"You hate him, don't you? Why?"

"Why?" Drade's eyes glittered with loathing. "Ask him. Ask him about the woman he stole from me, about the battle honors that should have been mine."

"You were in love with his wife?" Ashlynne asked, stunned.

"She should have been my wife," Drade said,

his voice cold and bitter. "He knew I was in love with her, knew I wanted to marry her. Did he care? No! He was always jealous of me. She should have been my wife," he said again. "And now she's dead because of him."

"But you had her killed. Falkon said—"

"Are you mad?" Drade stared at her. "I loved her."

"But . . ." Ashlynne shook her head. "He blames you."

"I would never have done anything to hurt Maiya. I was on my way to Daccar when I heard of the attack. I had hoped to get there in time to get her away, but I was too late."

"I'm sorry."

Drade stood up. "So am I," he said coldly, and left the cabin.

"His hatred is eating him alive," Chaney remarked.

Ashlynne nodded. It was eating at Falkon, too, she thought, and wondered what he would think when he learned he had been hating Drade for something he hadn't done.

They reached Arkata the following day. Still encumbered by the lynaziam collar and shackles, Ashlynne stood in front of Niklaus, humiliation burning in her cheeks. Again, she thought of Falkon, of the days and nights he had lived in bondage, his every waking moment controlled by the heavy collar at his neck.

She took a deep breath and squared her shoulders, hoping Niklaus couldn't see how very frightened she was. "Where's Chaney? What have you done with her?"

Niklaus looked up from the papers spread before him. "Your furry friend is being looked after."

"The way you looked after Falkon?"

Niklaus looked faintly amused as he replied, "Indeed, I believe she's in the same cell."

"You can't leave her in that dungeon!" Ashlynne exclaimed. "She's going to have a baby."

Niklaus shrugged. "That's what females do. I should think you would be more concerned about your own future." He tapped his finger on a stack of papers. "There are a few things I need to have you sign."

"What things?"

"I think you know."

"You want the mine."

"Yes." He sat back in his chair. "You've caused me a great deal of unnecessary trouble."

Ashlynne glared at him. If he was waiting for an apology, it would be a long time coming.

Hassrick stood up, his hands resting on the top of the desk. "Don't make this more difficult than it has to be," he said. "I don't want to hurt you, or your friend, but there's a great deal at stake here."

She stared at the man who was her husband, and knew he would stop at nothing to get what he wanted. His next words confirmed it.

"Drade has found me a woman who looks much like you. If necessary, we'll bring her here and have her take your place. In that case, we'll have no further use for you."

"You wouldn't," she gasped. But he would. And she knew it. She folded her arms over her belly. If she died, her baby would die with her. Die before it ever had a chance to live.

"It's up to you."

"And if I do as you ask, what then?"

"Why, I'll let you and your friend go, of course."

He was lying. She could see it in his eyes, hear it in his voice. "How do I know you'll let us go?"

"I guess you'll just have to trust me, won't you?" He reached into the top drawer of his desk and withdrew a controller, which he placed on the desk. "I grow weary of this, Ashlynne." He picked up a pen and offered it to her. "Sign the papers."

"No."

He reached for the controller. Before she could tell him she had changed her mind, pain exploded through her, stealing the strength from her legs, the breath from her lungs. She gasped as she hit the floor, her body twisting, turning in a vain effort to escape the agony that engulfed her.

When would it end? Would it ever end?

It was frightening, to have no control over her body's movements, humiliating to lie there, twitching uncontrollably while Niklaus stared at her in mild amusement.

Gradually, the spasms lessened, leaving her lying there, gasping for breath.

"Are you ready to sign now?" Niklaus asked.

Taking hold of a corner of the desk, she pulled herself to her feet. "Yes."

"I knew I could count on you to be sensible."

She lifted her arms. "You'll have to free my hands."

"Of course." Picking up the controller, he released the shackles on her hands, then offered her the pen again. "I'll need your signature here," he said, pointing at the bottom of one of the papers. "And here."

She signed where he indicated. When she was finished, she dropped the pen on the desk.

Niklaus nodded. "Thank you, my dear," he said, and activated the shackles on her hands.

"There's something you should know," Ashlynne said.

"Is there?"

She nodded. "I sent a letter to my uncle on Cannus Twelve the night before you left for Hodore."

Niklaus laughed softly. "Did you?" He picked up the papers, folded them in half, and put them in the top drawer of his desk. "Thinking of running away and taking holy vows, were you?"

"No. I told him I was afraid you were going to force me to sign the mine over to you, and that if he heard that I had done so, it would only be because I was in fear for my life. I told him I suspected you were going to kill me. As you know, documents signed under duress are invalid. I told him if he didn't hear from me as usual, it would mean I was dead."

It was part truth and part lie. She stood there, her hands clenched, hoping Niklaus would believe her.

Niklaus stared at her, his eyes narrowed, his expression ominous. "It seems I underestimated you." Rounding the desk, he went to the door and opened it. "Drade, my wife would like to go visit her friend."

"Well, there's the house," Darf said. "Now what? We don't even know if they're in there."

"I know." They were hunkered down near the front gate of the Hassrick estate. It was after midnight, and there were no lights showing in the house.

"Well, do you know how we're going to get them out?"

Falkon shook his head. "No, but it shouldn't be too hard for us to get in."

"I was afraid you'd say something like that," Darf muttered sourly. "There's just one thing wrong with that plan. Once we get in, we might not be able to get out."

"I'm open to suggestions."

"I suggest you raise your hands, very slowly."

Darf sighed.

Falkon swore.

"Up," Brill said. "Now."

Slowly, Falkon stood up. He was about to turn around when pain splintered through his skull, and the world went dark.

He heard voices. Opening his eyes, he blinked against the light.

"So," a familiar voice said, "all the players are here."

"Drade."

Falkon sat up, one hand reaching for the back of his head, only to find that his hands were bound. He stared at the shackles on his wrists. He didn't have to touch the collar at his throat to know it was there.

He stared up at his old enemy. "Where's Ashlynne?"

"In the dungeon, I believe, with your Cherlin friends."

"Is she all right?"

Drade nodded. "For now."

"I want to see her."

Drade chuckled. It was a dry, mirthless sound. "I'm afraid it doesn't matter what you want. She's being sent to the mine in a few days, along with the other two."

The mine! Falkon shook his head in disbelief. "You can't mean that."

"It was her husband's decision." He stressed the word husband. "Not mine."

"She's pregnant."

Drade shrugged.

"Chaney," Falkon said. "What of Chaney?"

"She's in labor."

"Is Hassrick sending the baby to the mine, too?"

"Hardly."

Falkon glanced around, recognizing the hut where he had been imprisoned before.

Drade stood near the door, a controller in one hand. "Don't you want to know what he's going to do with you?"

Falkon grunted softly. "From the look on your face, I'd say you can't wait to tell me."

Drade smiled. "You're being sent to Cenia. Can you guess why?"

Falkon stared at Drade. It took every bit of self-control he possessed to keep the horror growing within him from showing on his face. It was late summer on Cenia, the time when the Cenians sacrificed an enemy warrior and a young virgin to their blood-thirsty gods as an offering to insure success in battle and fertility in their women.

"Exactly so," Drade said. "Hassrick has offered you to Brczor. He thought it quite fitting that you be sacrificed with a virgin, since you had stolen one from him."

"Don't let him send Ashlynne to the mine."

"It's out of my hands."

"She'll die there."

A shadow that might have been regret passed through Drade's eyes. "I believe that is his intent."

"Dammit, Drade, don't do this to her. She's got nothing to do with what's between the two of us."

"I told you, it was her husband's idea. He was not happy to find his bride pregnant by another man."

"Then change his mind. You've manipulated enough people in your life. It should be easy for you."

"It seems a fair trade to me. The death of the woman you love for the death of the one I loved."

Falkon sprang to his feet. He lunged forward, his bound hands reaching for Drade's throat, his only thought to choke the life from the bastard who had killed his wife and daughter.

Too late, he remembered the collar at his throat, the controller in Drade's hand. With a strangled cry, he dropped to the floor of the hut as shards of pain lanced through him.

He lay there, gasping and covered with perspiration when it was over.

"You always were the impetuous one," Drade remarked.

"You killed her," Falkon said when he could speak. "Why?"

Drade stared down at him. "What are you talking about?"

"You ordered the attack on my home. Why? You knew I was gone."

Drade shook his head. "You damn fool. I tried to talk General Ralf out of it, I told him you hadn't returned to Daccar, but he knew we'd been friends and he didn't believe me. I got to your place as soon as I could, but I was too late. An hour too late," he murmured, his voice laced with bitter regret. "Just one hour too late."

Falkon sat up, his back braced against the wall. Lifting his hands, he wiped the sweat from his face. "I don't believe you."

"Believe what you like," Drade snapped. "But if you had stayed home, where you belonged, she would be alive today."

The truth of Drade's words penetrated every fiber of his being, more agonizing that the excruciating effects of the collar.

"I got there too late," Drade said heavily. "And so did you." He stared past Falkon, his thoughts turned inward. "I loved her," he said quietly. "She should have been mine. They both should have been mine."

Falkon stared at Drade, feeling Drade's pain

as if it were his own. "Don't take your hatred for me out on Ashlynne. I'm begging you. Let her go."

"She's Hassrick's wife, and he wants to be rid of her. There's nothing I can do."

"Push, Chaney," Ashlynne said. "Push hard." Chaney writhed on the narrow cot, her hands grasping the bars behind her head, as she sought to expel the child from her womb.

"Relax, my love," Darf said. "Do not fight the pain." He stood in the cell across the way, his hands clenched around the bars, his face a mask of concern. Chaney had been in labor for the last seven hours, an unusually long period of time for a Cherlin female.

"Chaney, listen to Darf," Ashlynne said. She wiped the perspiration from Chaney's face. "Try to relax between contractions."

Chaney nodded. She turned her head to the side and focused on her husband's face.

"I love you," Darf said. "Try not to think about the pain. Think about our child. Think of how much I love you."

She nodded, gasping as another pain splintered through her.

"I see the head," Ashlynne exclaimed. "Push!"

Chaney screamed, pushed, and the head and shoulders emerged.

A moment later, Ashlynne cradled a tiny furry body in her hands. She looked over at Darf, smiled at Chaney.

"It's a girl." She spoke through a mist of tears. Never, she thought, never had she seen anything as miraculous as the infant mewling softly in her arms.

"Is she all right?"

Ashlynne pulled the blanket from her cot and wrapped it around the baby, then laid the child in Chaney's arms. "See for yourself. She's perfect."

In the way of mothers everywhere, Chaney counted each finger and toe, ran her hand over the tiny furred head and body.

Ashlynne pressed one hand over her womb as she watched her friend. In a few months, she, too, would be giving birth. Where would she be when the time came? Where would Falkon be? Would they ever be together again?

Chapter Thirty

Falkon paced the narrow cell, his agitation growing. He had to get out of here, had to get Ashlynne out of here, but how?

He paused at the door, staring out into the darkness, Drade's words echoing in his mind. *I loved her. She should have been mine. They both should have been mine.* All these years, he had hated the man for something he hadn't done.

Looking back, his mind unclouded by hate and thoughts of vengeance, he was forced to confront a bitter truth. Maiya had been in love with Drade, but Falkon had wanted her, and when Drade was sent out on a special training mission, Falkon had pursued her relentlessly. He knew now that Drade would have made Maiya a far better husband than he had. Drade had spoken of his plans for the future. He had intended to marry Maiya, to give up his career in the Army. It was only after Falkon married Maiya that Drade had gone over to the Romarians.

He rested his forehead against the rough wooden door. All these years he had blamed Drade for Maiya's death when the guilt had been his.

"I'm sorry, Maiya," he murmured. "Forgive me."

He looked up at the sound of footsteps, saw Drade coming toward him. "What do you want?"

Drade shook his head. "I don't want anything from you."

"Just come to gloat?"

Drade shrugged.

"How's Ashlynne?"

"She's well."

"And the Cherlin?"

"The female gave birth last night. They leave for Tierde in the morning."

"Drade, don't do this. I'm begging you."

"I begged you once," Drade retorted, his voice bitter. "I begged you not to marry Maiya. It was you who refused to listen then."

"I loved her, too."

"No! No. You only wanted to prove you could take her from me."

"That's not true." But even as he denied it, he knew that, even though he had loved Maiya, he had relished the thought of taking her from Drade. Though they had been friends, they had always been rivals, competing for the highest scores in the academy, for the highest honors in battle, always going head-to-head to see who could be the best, the fastest.

"What's behind all this?" Falkon asked. "You owe me that much."

"Hassrick was in financial trouble. Brezor offered him a way out."

"Where do you fit in?"

Drade shrugged. "I was with Hassrick when he made the deal with Brezor. When Marcus refused to admit the Cenians to the Confederation, I suggested the attack on the mine. If Marcus was killed, I knew Hassrick would gain control of the mine through Ashlynne. If the attack failed, then I knew Romariz would step in and take over. Either way, I would have access to the mine."

"What did you have to gain from all this?"

"Don't you know?"

Falkon thought about it, and he did know. "I heard that Hodore had secretly allied with Romariz, but that was just to cover up the truth, wasn't it? They've allied with Cenia. And when they have access to the mine, they'll have the fuel they need to attack Romariz." He shook his head. "You're running true to form, aren't you? First you sold out to Romariz, and now to Cenia."

"Think whatever you want."

"Hodore and Cenia aren't strong enough to go up against Romariz. Who else is involved?"

"Riga Twelve. Polixe. Hodore. Trellis, of course. I have convinced them to put their petty squabbles aside for the greater good of all."

Falkon frowned thoughtfully. "What of Andoria and Swernolt?"

"They refuse to join us without Daccar."

All the minor powers of the galaxy, Falkon mused. Combined, they had enough men and firepower to bring Romariz to its knees. "What of Daccar?" he asked.

Drade glanced away. "They have not yet agreed, but they will."

"Why, Drade?" he asked. "What's in it for you?"

Drade shook his head, refusing to answer.

But Falkon knew, just as he knew he had done Drade a terrible wrong. "Revenge," he said. "For Maiya."

"Yes!" Hatred flared in the depths of Drade's eyes. "I helped the Romarians get where they are, and I will bring them down." Drade shook his head. "She was married to you, but you were never there. I was the one she turned to when she was lonely, the one she turned to when she needed help."

Falkon took a deep breath. "I loved her. I couldn't help it. But I was wrong to take her from you. I know that now, and I'm—" His hands tightened around the bars. "I'm sorry."

Drade didn't say anything, only stood there, staring back at him, making Falkon wonder if he, too, was remembering the past, when the two of them had been almost inseparable, when they were both young and eager for war.

And then Drade nodded. "She was too good for either of us."

It had taken five years, Falkon mused, but they had finally found something they could agree on.

"You've lost whatever you hoped to gain,"

Falkon said. "Our people will never unite with Cenia. The counsel will not listen to your advice, or follow you into battle. You know that, don't you? You are a traitor in their eyes, stripped of your rank. They will never forgive you for what you've done."

"And you are their hero."

Falkon slammed his fist against one of the bars. "Some hero!"

A slow smile spread over Drade's face and then, to Falkon's amazement, he laughed.

He was still laughing when he turned and walked away.

Chapter Thirty-one

Be careful what you ask for, daughter, lest you get it.

Her mother's words rang in Ashlynne's mind as she was pushed into a small gray cell. She had longed to go home again, but not like this. Her hair had been cut short, and she had been issued a pair of black breeches, a coarse shirt, and a pair of thick-soled boots.

She lifted a hand to her hair, her eyes burning with tears. Of all the things she had endured, standing with her hands and feet bound while a slave with dirty hands and fetid breath cut her hair was the worst. She had closed her eyes, remembering the touch of Falkon's hand moving in her hair, the way her hair had looked brushing against his chest when they made love, shining silver against dark bronze, and cried harder.

They were going to be slaves in the mine. She stood at the door, staring out into the darkness, remembering the look on Darf's face when Drade came to take the baby, the long anguished wail that had risen in Chaney's throat as her child was wrested from her arms. Darf and Chaney were also here, locked in adjoining cells. And Falkon . . . where was Falkon?

She stood at the door for what seemed like hours, her hands and feet feeling heavy from the unfamiliar weight of the shackles she wore. She was aware of the collar at her throat every time she swallowed. It made her feel as if she was going to choke to death. How had Falkon endured it for so long? *Falkon, where are you?* He wouldn't be able to save her now. She placed her hand over her belly, a terrible pain engulfing her as she glanced over her shoulder at the grim surroundings. She would give birth to her child in this awful place, and then they would take it from her, as they had taken Chaney's child, and she would never see it again.

Sinking down on the hard, narrow cot that was her bed, she closed her eyes and prayed that she would die in childbirth.

It was still dark outside when she was roused from a troubled sleep. A man thrust a bowl and a cup into her hand.

She looked at it in horror. She couldn't eat

the food, knew she would be violently ill if she tried.

"You'd best eat it," the guard said gruffly. "You won't get nothing else until midday."

She stared at the dull brownish meal made of ground Horth grubs and triticale and shook her head. "I can't."

"Suit yourself," he said, and turned away, muttering under his breath about the sheer lunacy of having women working in the mine.

She put the bowl on the floor, sipped the lukewarm bitter tea.

A quarter of an hour later, the door to her cell swung open and she was ordered outside. She saw Darf and Chaney a short distance ahead, but when she started to go to them, a guard stopped her.

"Keep your place in line," he growled.

She stared at the entrance to the mine, and then the line began to move. She followed the man in front of her, ducking her head as she entered the mine's black maw. A guard thrust a pulse axe into her hands, showed her how to use it, and told her to get to work. The axe was bulky and heavy. She was paired with a man who had a drill, and for the next six hours, they worked side by side, loosening the dirt while a third slave carefully pried the black crystals from Tierde's tenacious earth.

By midday, the palms of her hands were blistered, her shoulders ached, her back ached, her head ached, and she was thirsty, so thirsty. And hungry.

A slave came by a short time later, passing out bowls of gruel and cups of tea. Closing her eyes, Ashlynne tried not to think of what was in the bowl as she forced herself to eat, but all she could see were dozens of fat brown grubs. It was all she could do to make herself swallow the thick, lumpy gruel. She ate it quickly, washed it down with the tea, only to have it all come up again.

Fifteen minutes later, they were ordered back to work.

The man working at her side patted her shoulder in an awkward gesture of support.

"Welcome to hell," he whispered, and thrust the drill into the hard, unyielding ground.

Chapter Thirty-two

Drade leaned back in his chair, a glass of Romarian wine in one hand. Soon it would all be over, the planning, the scheming, the lies. He had them all where he wanted them. The Romarians had grown overconfident and lazy. They looked out over the galaxy and thought they were in control, but he was the one in control.

Riga Twelve, Hodore, Cherlin Four, Cenia, Tierde, and Trellis, of course, had all agreed to put aside their differences. All he needed now was Daccar, and when he had Daccar, he would have Swernolt and Andoria as well. United, they would attack Romariz, defeat Ralf, and bring peace to the galaxy. And he would be the hero, the one who had done the impossible, the one to bring Romariz to its knees. At last, after five years of plotting and scheming, he would have his revenge.

And Falkon would have his. Drade blew out a sigh. He had hated Falkon, blaming him for Maiya's death, and yet, with one simple apology, Falkon had erased five years of bitter hatred.

He finished his wine and threw the glass into the hearth. It was time for the last act to begin.

Falkon stood up as Drade unlocked the door to his cell. "What the hell do you want?"

Drade lifted one hand. A long silver tube dangled from a thick chain. "Do you want to be rid of that collar, or are you going to stand there and glower at me all night?"

"If this is a joke, I don't find it very funny."

"Still as wary as a Hodorian merchant, I see."

"Wary of enemies bearing gifts."

Shaking his head, Drade crossed the floor.

Moments later, Falkon was free of the hated collar and shackles. "Why?"

"I thought about what you said. Daccar won't follow me, but our people will follow you." Drade grinned. "No one fights like the rebels of Daccar." He held out his hand. "Will you help me bring the Romarians down?"

With a nod, Falkon clasped his old friend's hand. "Let's do it."

"I think not."

Falkon glanced over Drade's shoulder to see Hassrick standing in the open doorway, a blaster in his hand.

Drade didn't turn around. "I need his help, Niklaus."

"No. He has no part in this. And neither do you, any longer."

"What do you mean?" Drade asked.

"I mean you have outlived your usefulness. Give me your weapon."

Drade withdrew his gun and dropped it on the floor. He shifted to the right a little, his gaze locking with Falkon's. Slowly, Drade lowered his gaze.

Following Drade's gaze, Falkon saw the small stunner shoved into the waistband of Drade's trousers. He nodded slightly, and waited.

"Now." Drade mouthed the word.

What happened next happened very fast.

Falkon grabbed the gun as Drade fell to the floor. Dropping to one knee, Falkon squeezed the trigger. Hassrick stared at Falkon as ribbons of bright light engulfed him, paralyzing him instantly. He pitched forward, the gun skittering from a hand gone numb.

Drade stood up, grinning. "Just like that night on Andoria." He picked up Hassrick's weapon and tossed it to Falkon, then holstered his own.

Falkon nodded as he shoved the gun into his waistband, then tossed the stunner back to Drade.

"Aren't you going to finish him off?"

Falkon looked down at Hassrick. It was tempting, but it was too much like cold-blooded murder, and that had never been his style. "No," he replied, certain he would regret it later. "Let's get out of here."

They took Hassrick's atmospheric transport. It was a small, comfortable craft, prized for its ability to maneuver quickly and efficiently.

"You should have killed him, you know," Drade remarked, "or let me do it."

"Yeah. What did he do with Chaney's baby?"

"He gave it to one of the servants to dispose of."

"What happened to it?"

Drade snorted softly. "She kept it."

"The baby's all right, then?"

"Far as I know."

When they arrived at the port of departure, Drade pulled out his Imperial pass, explaining that he was returning an escaped slave to the mines of Tierde.

Falkon, once again wearing the heavy collar and shackles, stood with his head down. *Hurry, hurry*. He wanted to shout the words. Every minute they delayed meant another minute Ashlynne spent in the mine . . . *I'm coming, sweetheart, I'm coming*.

At last, they had the proper clearance. A few minutes later they boarded a League cruiser bearing the Romarian crest.

Once inside, Drade removed the collar and cuffs and headed for the cockpit. "You ever fly one of these?"

Falkon dropped into the copilot's seat. "No." His gaze moved over the instrument panel. "Doesn't look too different from our own."

"It's not. Ready?"

Falkon settled back in his seat. "Let's do it."

Daccar glowed like a rare earth sapphire in the vast cosmos. Falkon felt a sense of exhileration as they drew closer. This had once been home, he thought, and in the back of his mind, he heard Ashlynne's voice. *I'll be your home*, she had said, *and you'll be mine*. Ashlynne. He closed his eyes and pictured her locked in a dreary cell, her life controlled by the collar at her throat, her nails broken, her skin covered with black crystal dust, her hands callused. *I'm coming. Hold on, sweetheart, just hold on*.

How? The word pounded in Ashlynne's mind. How had Falkon stood this day after day, week after week? Feeling like she was a hundred years old, Ashlynne lowered herself to the narrow cot that served as her bed and closed her eyes. She couldn't endure another day, another hour. Every muscle in her body ached. And she was dirty, so horribly dirty. Even if she was permitted to soak in a tub for an hour, she doubted she would ever be able to scrub away the fine black dust that covered her from head to foot.

She lifted a hand to her hair, felt her tears start as she touched the ragged ends. It seemed foolish to cry for something so mundane as her hair when there were so many other worse things to cry over, but she couldn't help it.

"Oh, Falkon," she whispered, "I'm glad you can't see me now."

Oh, Falkon, her heart cried, *I wish you were here*.

Falkon stood at attention before General Addiz and the six members of the counsel, his voice low and flat as he made his report. Drade stood beside him, as he had so many times in the past. In their youth, they had boasted that the two of them could take on the galaxy. Now, at last, they had their chance.

The members of the counsel regarded Falkon for several moments when he finished speaking, their faces impassive. It was an old trick, one he had often employed himself. He remained at attention, his gaze focused on the mural behind the counsel table. It depicted a scene from a mythic battle between Dacca and the fierce two-headed dragon, Aka-r.

"We will consider your remarks," General Addiz said at length. His hard gray gaze settled on Drade. "Your life has been spared in return for the life of Commander Falkon. Had you not returned with him, your life would now be forfeit. The two of you will wait here until we have reached a decision."

Rising, the general left the chamber. The other members of the counsel rose majestically and followed the general from the room, quietly closing the door behind them.

"Well," Drade remarked dryly, "that was fun. How long do you think it will take them to make up their minds?"

"Not long," Falkon replied dryly, and jerked his head toward the door.

General Addiz entered the room alone. He took his place at the head of the counsel table. He did not sit down, but stood there, his hands braced on the tabletop.

Falkon took a deep breath. Any decision reached this quickly had been decided before the counsel members left the room.

"Commander Falkon, despite the recent

treaty we have decided to join our forces with the other allies in their fight against Romarian rule."

"Thank you, General."

"Our fleet will rendezvous with the others on Swernolt. I trust you will join us."

Falkon shook his head. "I'm afraid I can't, General. I have other business to take care of."

"I will take your reasons into account before I order you to report to your ship."

"I have to go to Tierde," Falkon said. "My woman, Lady Ashlynne of Myrafloures, was sent to the mine as a slave. I can't leave her there."

"Myrafloures? Isn't she the daughter of Lord Marcus?"

"Yes."

The General frowned. "Is she not the heir to the mine?"

"It's a long story, General."

"I'd like to hear, when you have the time." The General drummed his fingers on the table-top, his expression thoughtful. "Very well. Commander Falkon, the mine on Tierde is vital to the allies. You will go to Tierde and take control of the mine. I will prepare the necessary documents."

"Thank you, General."

Addiz nodded. "I will expect a report from you when you arrive."

"Yes, sir."

"I will have a ship at your disposal." The general focused his attention on Drade. "What are your plans?"

"I want to fight."

"Very well. You will be reinstated, albeit with a reduction in rank until you have again proven yourself worthy to be an officer."

Drade nodded. "I understand."

"You will leave for Swernolt tomorrow."

"Yes, sir. Thank you, sir."

The general's gaze rested briefly on each man. "Good day, gentlemen."

"Well," Drade said when they were again alone in the room, "looks like I'm back where I started."

"You'll earn your rank back by the time the fighting's over," Falkon predicted. He held out his hand. "Good luck to you."

Drade took Falkon's hand in his. "And to you."

Chapter Thirty-three

Niklaus Hassrick stood at the window, gazing out over the vast acreage that had been in his family for generations. Years to build, he mused, and only a few moments to tear it all down. Behind him, he could hear his mother weeping softly, hear his father's voice as he tried to comfort her. They had both aged in the last few days. Well, he thought bleakly, so had he.

Drade had returned to Daccar.

Upon learning that Niklaus couldn't make good on his promise to deliver the crystals or repay his debt, Brezor had sent his agent to inform Rugen that he had ten days to vacate the premises. It had all come out then, all the dirty little secrets Niklaus had tried to hide.

"Why, Niklaus?"

The sound of his mother's voice, asking the

same question yet again, was more than he could bear. Turning on his heel, he strode out of the room.

Drade was out of reach, but he knew where Falkon had gone. If he hurried, he could be there, waiting, when he arrived.

Chapter Thirty-four

Falkon stepped out of the shuttle he had picked up at Enjine Base Nine. On the far side of the bridge, he could see the mine compound—the huts, the overseer's residence, the mine's yawning maw. It was late afternoon. Ashlynne would be down there, sweating side by side with the other slaves. Did she hate him yet?

Muttering an oath, he started across the bridge. Every minute he wasted was another minute she spent in that hell.

He walked past the huts, remembering all the nights he had spent locked up. If it had been bad for him, how much worse had it been for Ashlynne? She had been raised in a life of luxury, pampered and spoiled all her life. She had never known want or hunger or fear, until he'd come into her life. Somehow, he would make it up to her. Somehow.

He was about to duck inside the mine when two guards materialized out of the darkness, weapons drawn. Falkon backed up, and the guards emerged from the mine, followed by Niklaus Hassrick.

"Damn," Falkon muttered. "I should have killed you when I had the chance."

One of the guards stepped forward and relieved him of his weapon.

"Welcome home," Hassrick said. He held out his hand. "Does this look familiar?"

Falkon shook his head as he stared at the collar in Hassrick's hand. "No. Never again."

"Hold him!"

Rage. It welled up within him, simmering, boiling, exploding in a primal cry of defiance. He would never wear that collar again. Never! He had spent enough time sweating in a dark hole, breathing in his own stink. And now they had Ashlynne down there. It sickened him, enraged him, to think of her in that hellhole.

He pivoted sharply, his anger feeding on itself as he drove his fist into the face of the guard on his left. It caught the guard on the point of his chin, and he dropped to the ground, out cold.

The guard on his right raised his weapon, but before he could fire, Falkon kicked it out of his hand, then drove his knee into the man's face. Blood spurted from the guard's nose, spraying Falkon's shirt and face.

He backed away, looked up to find Hassrick pointing a weapon at him.

Hassrick tossed the collar at Falkon's feet. "Put it on."

"No."

"She's wearing one, too, you know."

The threat was all too clear. Falkon clenched his hands at his sides. "You wouldn't."

"I would, and I did."

Falkon sucked in a deep breath. He seemed to see the world through a red haze, a world that was empty of everything but the man standing before him, a man who had caused Ashlynne pain.

With a wordless cry, Falkon lunged forward. He felt a burning pain across his left shoulder and knew Hassrick had fired at him, but it didn't matter. Nothing mattered but killing the man in front of him before he could hurt Ashlynne again.

He reeled backward as Hassrick fired again, his hand going to his side, feeling the heat of the blast on his skin. He dropped to his knees, breathing hard.

Hassrick was grinning as he took a step forward. "I'm going to enjoy this," he said, and lifted the weapon once again.

Summoning all his energy, Falkon rolled to the left and grabbed the gun lying beside one of the fallen guards. He quickly rolled to the left again and felt the heat of the blast explode past his head as Hassrick fired.

"Missed me," he muttered and squeezed the trigger. From the corner of his eye, he saw the two guards reaching for their guns and he fired again.

Falkon took a deep breath; then, using the weapon for a crutch, he stood up. He spared hardly a glance for the three dead men as he turned and walked toward the entrance to the mine.

Ashlynne kept her mind carefully blank as she hefted the pulse axe. It was easier to think of nothing than to dwell on memories of the past. Only a few days in the mine, yet it seemed as though she had been there for years. It was hard to remember her other life, hard to recall a time when her skin had been clean, when she'd had a soft bed to sleep on, nice clothes to wear, good food to eat. It seemed she had always lived in the dark, burrowing into the ground like a sightless mole.

Yes, it was better to keep her memories at bay, but sometimes, late at night, when her body craved sleep and sleep wouldn't come, she opened the door to her memories and thought about Falkon, remembering the first time she had seen him on the landing dock, fighting for his freedom. His presence in the jinan had turned her whole world upside down. He had teased and tormented her at every turn, sparked her anger, fascinated her with his defiance. She had lost so much. It wasn't fair that she should lose him, too.

She lifted her hand to wipe the sweat from her face and her fingers brushed against the collar at her throat. She knew now why Falkon had hated it so. It wasn't just that it was heavy and uncomfortable and capable of inflicting the worst pain she had ever known; it was what it stood for.

She looked down the line to where Chaney and Darf were toiling side by side. She knew they were even more miserable than she was, and yet she envied them because they were together, and she would never see Falkon again.

Falkon. Her heart ached for him, yearned for him. If not for the child she carried beneath her heart, she would have given up, but she had to go on, had to be strong, for the baby, even though it would be taken from her.

She felt the sting of tears in her eyes and dashed them away. If she let herself cry now, she would never stop. She'd cry and cry, until she flooded the tunnel with her tears.

She paused in mid-swing at the sound of a commotion near the entrance to the mine. There was the dull whoosh of a laser blast, the sound of a man's scream. She bit down on her lip, certain one of the slaves had been killed trying to escape. And then she heard something she'd never thought to hear again— Falkon's voice, calling her name.

"Here," she cried. "Down here."

A guard stepped out of the darkness. "Shut up, slave, and get back to work."

"Falkon!"

"Ashlynne!" He moved past the guard. Wrapping one arm around her, he pulled her up against him.

"What the hell do you think you're doing?" the guard demanded.

"I'm taking my woman out of here." Falkon

leveled his weapon at the guard's chest. "I'm taking everybody out of here."

"You can't do that."

"Watch me."

The guard looked back at the entrance to the mine, his expression uncertain.

"They're dead," Falkon said quietly. "You can join them or not, it's up to you." He glanced at Ashlynne. "Are you all right?"

"I am now."

Falkon looked at the guard. "There's been a mistake. This is Lady Ashlynne Myrafloures. This mine belongs to her."

The guard looked at Ashlynne and at the gun in Falkon's hand, and shrugged. "Whatever you say."

"Falkon, is that you?"

"Damn right, Darf," Falkon called as he took the guard's weapon. "Get your furry butt up here. Tell the others to come out, too."

Taking Ashlynne by the hand, he led her up out of the mine.

One by one, the slaves emerged from the mine and gathered around Falkon. The guard brought up the rear.

"What's going on?" Darf asked.

"We're taking over." Falkon's gaze ran over Darf. His friend had lost a good deal of weight since he'd been in the mine. He stood with his arms around Chaney. "Come on," he said, "let's get out of here."

Ashlynne blinked in the sun's bright light, gasped when she saw Hassrick sprawled in the dirt.

She looked up at Falkon, only then noticing the laser burns on his shoulder and side. "You're been hurt!"

"I'm all right." His hand stroked her hair, and she looked away.

"Hey," he said, "it'll grow back."

She wrapped her arms around him. "I was afraid I'd never see you again," she whispered, and buried her face against his chest, not wanting him to see her tears.

He held her close while she cried, his lips brushing the top of her head.

"What now?"

Falkon looked up to see Darf and Chaney standing beside him.

The other prisoners stood behind them in a loose semicircle. The guard stood a little apart, looking uneasy.

"Darf, get the release mechanism," Falkon said, unwilling to leave Ashlynne's side for even a few moments. He looked at the slaves. "You're all free to go."

A hum of excitement rose in the air as the prisoners realized they were truly free.

Darf took the release mechanism from the guard and after removing the restraints from Chaney and Ashlynne, he freed the other prisoners, and then himself.

Ashlynne breathed a sigh of relief as Darf removed the collar from her neck, unlocked the shackles on her hands and feet.

She thanked him, then smiled at Falkon as she massaged her neck. "I feel like I could fly."

He nodded, knowing just how she felt. "Come on, let's get out of here. Darf, Chaney,

I've got good news for you. I know where your baby is. And she's fine."

"Where is she?" Chaney asked anxiously.

"She's with one of Hassrick's servants on Trellis. Once we get things squared away here, we'll send for her."

Chaney collapsed against her husband, weeping softly.

Falkon looked at the slaves milling around the compound. "There's an ASTC across the bridge. You're welcome to it. You can clean up in the overseer's house. Help yourself to whatever you need and go."

"Go," one of men said. "Go where?"

"Go to Cherlin Four," Darf said. "You'll be welcome there."

Amid a flurry of thank yous, the freed men headed for the overseer's house at the far end of the compound.

Ashlynne tugged on Falkon's hand. "What about them?" she asked, pointing at the bodies.

"We'll send someone from the house down to bury the guards. Hassrick's parents will probably want his body. Come on, let's get out of here."

Though she had been a prisoner only a short time, it felt strange to be free again. Ashlynne held tight to Falkon's hand as they walked up the path that led to the jinan. Darf and Chaney followed behind them.

Hana was reclining on one of the sofas in the living room when they entered. She stood up, her surprise clear in her eyes when she saw Ashlynne.

"Is this how you spend your days, Hana?" Ashlynne asked.

The housekeeper shook her head, her gaze moving from Ashlynne to the others and back again. "Shall I ask Kerolena to draw you a bath?"

"Yes. We'll all be wanting one. I'm putting Darf and his wife in the corner room on the second floor. And we'll be wanting something to eat after we've bathed."

"And where will the other—" Hana glanced at Falkon, who stood with his arm around Ashlynne's shoulders. "Where will the other gentleman be staying?"

"In my room."

Hana's mouth dropped open. She closed it quickly, her hands fluttering like lost birds. "And will Lord Hassrick be joining you and your . . . your guests?"

An image of Hassrick, lying sprawled in the dirt, flashed before Ashlynne's eyes. "No. That will be all, Hana."

With a nod, the housekeeper hurried out of the room.

"Nice place," Falkon muttered, looking around.

"Very," Darf said.

Ashlynne tugged on Falkon's hand. "Let's go upstairs. Your wounds need tending."

He didn't argue.

Ashlynne showed Darf and Chaney to their room. "If you need anything, just ask."

"Our thanks, Lady Ashlynne," Darf said.

Chaney clasped Ashlynne's hand in hers. "How can we ever repay you?"

"I didn't do anything."

"You've taken us into your home."

"You made me welcome in yours." Ashlynne smiled up at Falkon. "Here's the one who deserves our thanks."

"They can thank me later," Falkon muttered. "Which room is yours?"

"We'll meet you downstairs in about an hour, then," Ashlynne said.

Darf looked at Falkon and grinned. "Better make it two," he said, and drawing Chaney into the room, he closed the door.

Falkon reclined in a tub made of blue marble, his eyes closed, while Ashlynne bathed him. He could have done it himself, but it was far more pleasant to lie there and feel her hands moving over him, her breath warm upon his face.

When she finished, she sat back, expecting him to get out. Instead, he reached for her and lifted her into the tub with him, clothes and all.

"Falkon! What are you doing?"

"I'm lonely."

He settled her on his lap, facing him, and began to undress her, tossing her wet clothes on the floor.

He lifted her hands, anger and regret stirring inside him when he saw the blisters on her palms. Gently, he kissed first one hand and then the other. And then he placed his hand on her belly, his fingers spread wide. "I should be taking care of you."

She put her hand over his. "I'm fine." She smiled. "We're fine."

He wrapped his arms around her and held

her tight, his face pressed in the warm valley between her breasts. She smelled of sweat and crystal dust, of woman. Of home. He clung to her, thinking how close he had come to losing her forever, thinking of the long hours she had spent in the mine, laboring as no woman should be made to do, especially one with child. He thought of her toiling from dawn till dark, then locked in a stone cell, sleeping on a hard cot, eating food not fit for a warf hog. He thought of all she had endured, the loss of her home and her parents, and regretted that he could kill Hassrick only once.

He washed her gently from head to foot, his hands lingering on her hair. It was so short now, yet soft and silky beneath his fingertips.

When he finished, he stepped out of the tub and wrapped a towel around his waist, then turned and lifted Ashlynne from the water. He held her close for a moment, his breath catching in his throat as he felt her body pressed against his, the slight swell of her belly, the warmth of her breasts. He wrapped her in a thick towel, then carried her into the bedroom and sat her on the bed. "I'll make it all up to you somehow," he promised.

She placed her hand over his mouth. "Hush. None of it was your fault. Come, sit down now and let me look after your wounds."

"They're only superficial," Falkon said. He sat down on the edge of the bed, touched by her concern.

"They still need looking after," Ashlynne declared, and thanked the gods that Niklaus's aim had not been true, and that Falkon's injuries were no worse than they were.

She summoned Kerolena and sent her for a medikit. Kerolena offered to tend his wounds, but Ashlynne insisted on doing it herself, even though it made her stomach queasy. There were tears in her eyes when she finished.

With a sigh, Falkon gathered her into his arms and held her close. "There's no need to cry, sweetheart. It's all over."

She snuggled against him, her hands restless as they moved over his back and shoulders. She was free and he was here, and nothing else mattered.

"Falkon . . ."

He knew what she wanted, as he had always known. The towel he'd wrapped around her fell away, baring her to his gaze, to his touch, as he lowered her to the bed, then stretched out beside her.

It had all been worth it, he mused, every humiliation, every hour spent in the mine, every stroke of the lash. And when he felt her arms around him, felt her breath against his cheek as she covered his face with kisses, he knew he would willingly endure it all again.

He smiled down at her, feeling the sting of tears in his eyes. "I love you, princess."

"We'll never be parted again," she whispered, and cupping his face in her hands, she kissed him with her whole heart and soul. And then she looked at him, her eyes twinkling merrily. "And I love you, my prince."

Epilogue

Ashlynne gazed down at her sleeping son, surely the most beautiful sight she had ever seen. His hair was midnight-black, his eyes were blue, though Chaney had told her they would probably change color later. Her son. What a miracle he was, and how she loved him! It was hard to believe he was already a year old.

She looked up at Falkon, who was standing on the other side of the baby's bed, her heart quickening when his gaze met hers. The last year and a half had been the happiest of her life. She had sent the servants away, and so far she hadn't hired any to take their place. It was her house now, and she wanted to be the one to take care of it. Though it was shamefully extravagant, they had bought new furniture, rugs and drapes, so that the house reflected their taste instead of Niklaus's. The house, which had once seemed so cold, was home now.

Falkon had suggested sending for Darf and Chaney's daughter, but the couple hadn't wanted to wait, and they had left for Trellis the day after they were freed from the mine. They had located their daughter and at Falkon's urging, Darf and Chaney had moved to Tierde. Chaney had been with Ashlynne when her son was born.

Falkon had taken over the running of the mine. He refused to use slaves; instead, he had hired a dozen men, torn down the huts, and built housing for the workers and their families.

Best of all, she'd had the old-fashioned wedding she had always dreamed of. Drade had been there, and Darf and Chaney.

There was peace in the galaxy at last. The Romarians had been defeated and a new Confederation of planets had been established.

Life, she thought, had never been better.

"Happy, princess?"

"You know I am." She frowned at him. "Are you ever going to stop calling me that?"

Falkon came around the bed to stand beside her. He grinned as he put his arm around her shoulders and drew her close to his side. "No. It suits you." He kissed her cheek. "Have I told you lately how much I love you?"

"Not since this morning."

"I love you." He drew her into his embrace and kissed her again.

"And I love you," she replied. "You've given me everything I've ever wanted."

"Have I?"

"Well, almost everything."

"Tell me what you want, sweetheart, and it's yours."

"A daughter. I want a daughter."

"It may take a little time, but I'll do my best."

Ashlynne smiled up at him as she took him by the hand and led him into their bedroom.

And nine months later, she had everything she had ever wanted.

The Captive

Ever After

I have no words
that will cover you
as they should
my eyes
have
what you need to see

if my lips move
to tell you of my love
they will only kiss
press
to feel you
if I whisper with this taste
will you know . . .

my hands have
what you need . . . to trace
my love
touching you with fingers
of slight movement
easy . . . slide

if I press them to your lips
stopping the words
my love . . . will flow
for words
will not cover you
as they should

you own my soul
it folds inside your arms
resting on moist lips of

Amanda Ashley

a morning kiss

will the sound of my heated blood
coursing through veins of
desire
drown the silence
that surrounds when you are
gone from my side . . .

be gentle with this one
of no words . . . to cover
for he loves thee
beyond
reality

CHRISTINE FEEHAN
DARK DESIRE

With a new letter to the reader from Christine Feehan!

They were masters of the darkness,
searching through eternity for a mistress of the light....

The stranger silently summons her from across the continents, across the seas. He whispers of eternal torment, of endless hunger...of dark, dangerous desires. And somehow American surgeon Shea O'Halloran can feel his anguish, sense his haunting aloneness, and she aches to heal him, to heal herself. Drawn to the far Carpathian mountains, Shea finds a ravaged, raging man, a being like no other. And her soul trembles. For in his burning eyes, his icy heart, she recognizes the beloved stranger who's already become part of her. This imperious Carpathian male compels Shea to his side. But is she to be his healer...or his prey? His victim...or his mate? Is he luring her into madness...or will his dark desire make her whole?

Paradise

MADELINE BAKER, NINA BANGS, ANN LAWRENCE, KATHLEEN NANCE

The lush, tropical beauty of Hawaii has inspired plenty of romance. But then, so have the croonings of a certain hip-shaking rock 'n' roll legend. In these tales of love by some of romance's brightest stars, four couples put on their blue suede shoes and learn they don't need a Hawaiian vacation to find paradise. Whether they're in Las Vegas, Nevada, or Paradise, Pennsylvania, passion will blossom where they least expect it —especially with a little helping hand from the King himself.

___4552-4 $6.99 US/$8.99 CAN

MADELINE BAKER

She is a runaway wife, with a hefty reward posted for her return. And he is the best darn tracker in the territory. For the half-breed bounty hunter, it is an easy choice. His was a hard life, with little to show for it except his horse, his Colt, and his scars. The pampered, brown-eyed beauty will go back to her rich husband in San Francisco, and he will be ten thousand dollars richer. But somewhere along the trail out of the Black Hills everything changes. Now, he will give his life to protect her, to hold her forever in his embrace. Now the moonlight poetry of their loving reflects the fiery vision of the Sun Dance: She must be his spirit's song.

___4476-5 $5.99 US/$6.99 CAN

TIGER EYE
MARJORIE M. LIU

He looks completely out of place in Dela Reese's Beijing hotel room—like the tragic hero of some epic tale, exotic and poignant. He is like nothing from her world, neither his variegated hair nor his feline yellow eyes. Yet Dela has danced through the echo of his soul, and she knows this warrior would obey.

Hari has been used and abused for millennia; he is jaded, dull, tired. But upon his release from the riddle box, Hari sees his new mistress is different. In Dela's eyes he sees a hidden power. This woman is the key. If only he dares protect, where before he has savaged; love, where before he's known hate. For Dela, he will dare all.

RECKLESS HEART

MADELINE BAKER

They play together as children—the Indian lad and little Hannah Kincaid. Then Shadow and his people go away, and when he returns, it is as a handsome young Cheyenne brave. Hannah, now a beautiful young woman, has never forgotten her childhood friend—but the man who sweeps her into his powerful arms is no longer a child. He awakens in her a wild, erotic passion she has never known. But war is about to erupt in the Dakota Territory, a war that will pit the settlers against the Indians. Both Hannah and Shadow know that the time is coming when they will have to choose between happiness and hatred, between passion and duty, in a conflict that will test to the limit the steadfastness of their love. . . .

___4527-3 $5.99 US/$6.99 CAN

Dorchester Publishing Co., Inc.
P.O. Box 6640
Wayne, PA 19087-8640

Please add $2.50 for shipping and handling for the first book and $.75 for each book thereafter. NY, NYC, and PA residents, please add appropriate sales tax. No cash, stamps, or C.O.D.s. All orders shipped within 6 weeks via postal service book rate. Canadian orders require $2.00 extra postage and must be paid in U.S. dollars through a U.S. banking facility.

Name_____
Address_____
City_____State_____Zip_____
I have enclosed $_____ in payment for the checked book(s).
Payment <u>must</u> accompany all orders. ❑ Please send a free catalog.
      CHECK OUT OUR WEBSITE! www.dorchesterpub.com